THE AUTOMOBILE ASSASSINATION

A 1940S MURDER MYSTERY

THE ERDINGTON MYSTERIES BOOK 2

M J PORTER

M J PUBLISHING

❀ Created with Vellum

This book is dedicated to my wonderful great-granny, Annie Holmes, who lived throughout much of the twentieth century and knew how to tell a good story (and how to cheat at cards when playing with her great-grandchildren, but that's another story).

PROLOGUE

He made his way through the deep darkness of night, the moon hidden behind thick clouds that promised rain in a few short hours. He dare not even risk using a flashlight, determined to rely on his memory of the oft-travelled road and nothing else.

Behind him, the distinctive whine of a motor engine could be heard, and he shook his head. Tonight was not a good night to be followed, but he knew someone was staying just out of sight. No doubt, they thought they were far enough back that he wouldn't hear the motor engine, but the wind stirred, blowing the sound towards him. It had been doing so as soon as he'd emerged from the centre of Birmingham to head towards Erdington.

The pick-up of his supplies had gone without a hitch. As so often, he'd ridden to the correct location, taken receipt of the items he needed, but after that, everything had become that little bit harder.

His legs ached, and he wished to stop for a breather, but there was no time. He had to finish his task before the sun rose, or there'd be trouble. And now was not the time to come to the attention of those who directed the operation. There was unease there. The business they were in was lucrative, but if the reports coming from Europe were believed, the war effort was finally going well and in favour of the Allies. That just might mean that there wouldn't be too much longer to profit from their current operations.

He thrust his hand over the billowing bag in the basket at the front of the bicycle. He didn't want to lose his supplies. They were easy enough to misplace when he wasn't cycling along country lanes. He'd spent many a worried hour tallying his stock to ensure it was correct. They were strict taskmasters, the people on whose behalf he worked.

As he worked to flip the bag closed, he felt himself lurch forward, his right foot hitting the floor, and then his left, juddering to a stop, the bicycle seat trying to hit him as he flew through the air, knocked by the force of the rear wheel.

He cursed under his breath, aware silence was necessary, as he tumbled to the ground. The flapping bag was coming open in the fall, the contents spilling around him as though a halo, bright even though there was little light by which to see. Lurching to his hands and knees, he scrabbled around for the tipped out contents, only for a bright yellow light to appear before him, from the way he'd been cycling, the light blinding him. It was whoever had been following him.

He bent low, a shriek pouring from his mouth, but he couldn't hear it, not above the sound of screeching brakes, the rumble of an engine and the cries of the other person who'd not seen him until it was too late and now tried to avoid running him over with the powerful motorbike. He tried to move out of the way, but the light still came at him, dazzling him, and he cried out once more.

There was a terrible crunch of metal hitting metal, of something falling, and then the engine died, taking the lights with it. He stumbled to his feet, the silence deafening.

"No, no, no," he mumbled, running now, fearful that others would see him, only to stop just as abruptly as his bicycle had. He peered down at his pile of spilt supplies, and he swallowed heavily. He knew what needed to be done.

CHAPTER 1

ERDINGTON, MONDAY SEPTEMBER 4TH 1944

Sam Mason rubbed his hand over tired eyes. He'd been hunched over his desk since early that morning. He couldn't deny that Sergeant Jones seemed to be onto something if he could just determine what was prickling at his consciousness.

The counterfeit scam had rumbled on for too long now, and only yesterday, Jones had been made to hand over the case to the more senior police officer. It hadn't gone down well with Jones. As much as Sam Mason disliked the other man, he wanted him to succeed in this endeavour. With all the talk in the station still about The Custard Corpses, as the newspapers had insisted on calling the Middlewick Murders, or rather, the solving of the Robert McFarlane case as he thought of it, Sam was keen to forget the whole thing.

If he could just work out who was doing what and how they were doing it, Jones would be able to take the acclaim for solving the pesky counterfeit scam. Sergeant Jones would appreciate it far more than Sam ever could. There had been cases of counterfeit ration books before, but this was something else entirely. Or so it seemed. Yet, the resolution remained just out of reach.

Mason's throat was parched, and his back was aching. But he didn't want to move away from the meticulous record keeping. It all quite surprised Mason. He'd always thought of Jones as a bit of a loose cannon, more interested in the thrill of the investigation than in actually resolving it. And worse, a terrible gossip, spilling the details of every case just to earn himself another pint from whoever he was regaling with the story at the local pub. More than once, Jones had been reprimanded for his loose tongue. Superintendent Smythe had been forced to remind Jones that, like the war, loose lips could cost lives when the work of the police was brought into disrepute.

Sam Mason knew that if he shifted away from the desk, he'd have to contend with the heated looks that Sergeant Jones was unsuccessfully trying not to throw his way from behind his desk that almost faced his own.

Not for the first time, Sam regretted not informing Superintendent Smythe that he didn't want the case file passed to him.

A white mug of something murky and indefinite slid onto his desk, and he risked looking up.

"Thought you could do with this," Sergeant Clara O'Rourke offered. He found a tired smile on greeting her cheerful look. She looked bright and alert, her hair as neatly braided as ever, held up from the neck of her blouse by some clever contraption, her uniform immaculate. If he looked down, he'd find her shoes were shinier than his, and he spent every evening buffing them. Sam Mason felt that he'd benefit from some of her unending enthusiasm, even for the mundane tasks of policing Erdington during the war.

"I could do with something that tasted like tea rather than just looked like it," he grumbled, but it was good-natured. Everyone was suffering under the same privations. They'd even been told only to use the police car if it was an important matter because of the lack of readily available petrol. When would the blasted war end?

The newspaper was filled with hope these days, but still, the enemy wasn't defeated, not yet, even if the Birmingham Post's leading headline was 'Brussels liberated in non-stop drive." Saturday's newspaper had been just as filled with optimism, 'Unchecked advance in 200 mile Front.' Sam Mason just hoped it wasn't all too good to be true. They could do with some cheering news.

"Did you see who arrived?" O'Rourke continued in an aside. She had her back to Smyth's office door, and it was as though a cloud passed before the sun. For a moment, Sam could forget about Jones and his fury.

"No, who's here?" Mason asked just as quietly, leaning back in his chair, pleased to have the opportunity to rest his aching back, and for once, delighted to be able to indulge in a bit of gossip. He wasn't typically one for gossip, but a man could only spend so much time mired in the bits of paperwork that made up the counterfeit case.

"That Chief Inspector Roberts, the one who helped us on the Robert McFarlane case, at the behest of the Chief Superintendent."

"What does he want?" Mason found himself shifting slightly to stare at his Superintendent's closed office door. He caught Jones' glare and ducked behind O'Rourke again. He was going to have to speak to Jones. He needed to know that Mason hadn't wanted the case. Jones might stop being so angry then.

"I've no idea. But they've been in there for about an hour now."

Sam shook his head. How had he not noticed? He'd not appreciated just how engrossed he'd been in his work. He glanced at O'Rourke. She'd been considering the problem for some time, her lips pursed and her forehead wrinkled so that one of her braids was threatening to fall over her nose.

"It'll be something tedious," Sam announced quickly, as though that solved the problem. He really couldn't see that it could be anything else. Certainly, there weren't any notable local cases to worry about, not at the moment. The court case concerning the youth shooting from the open window of a train carriage was proceeding as it should. Much of that was coming down to expert testimony from Doctor Lucey and other firearms specialists. It wasn't as though much could be said to disprove what was patently the truth.

Apart from the counterfeit case and the general feeling of raised alertness, the police station and the work of the men and women within it had returned to the normal levels of the pre-war years. People were concerned with lost dogs, stolen bicycles, and the constant problems with speeding motorists on the main road. If Mason closed his eyes, he could almost forget the war was even ongoing. Well, provided he didn't need a cup of tea or a biscuit, he could.

On duty at the front desk, Constable Williams had so far that day reunited a lost motorbike with its owner and helped a stray dog who'd wandered from the park at Pype Hayes all the way to the butchers. It was all routine, mundane, and just the way Sam liked it.

"I'd still rather know what it was. They work on all sorts of cases for the Chief Superintendent. It might be something really interesting."

"Or, they might just be discussing this counterfeit scam. Maybe they have one as well. I know that there's been a great deal in the newspapers about these 'squids' and their double-dealing."

But O'Rourke was already shaking her head, and then she stood quickly to attention, moving away to her immaculate desk and placing her hands on it as though about to pick something up and walk away, as the door to Smyth's office abruptly opened.

Roberts left the office first, the remnants of a smile on his face as he came to stand in front of Sam, as O'Rourke had just been doing. Smythe wasn't far behind.

"Sir. Roberts," Sam stated flatly, not standing because it would hurt his back too much. He imagined Smythe didn't expect it, and Roberts was only his equal anyway.

"Ah, Mason," Smythe began, a self-satisfied smirk on his face. "Roberts here has come to ask for your assistance with an extraordinary case."

"Has he?" Mason felt a spark of hope that he'd be pulled away from the counterfeiting even as he appreciated an 'extraordinary case,' probably meant a murder, somewhere. They'd been getting no end of telephone calls, and even letters, from other police stations, asking for Mason's help since they'd solved The Custard Corpses murders. So far, Smythe had refused all offers.

This one must be particularly exceptional.

"Yes, he has. And, on this occasion, I think that you would be just the person to help with it. The Chief Superintendent," and Smythe beamed ever wider. "Has specifically asked for you."

Mason looked down, suppressing a tight smirk. Of course, Smythe wasn't going to deny the Chief Superintendent if he asked for Mason's assistance. Smythe, for all the two of them rubbed along together well, still had his eye on achieving a higher post than that of Superintendent.

"Here," and Roberts passed a paper file over. It wasn't the thickest, in fact, as Sam opened it, having closed Jones file and moved it aside, he realised there was little more than a report from Doctor Lucey, the police pathologist he'd just been thinking about, concerning a body that had been found. There weren't even any crime scene photographs.

Sam cast his eyes over the report, noting that it was a recent find from Saturday night. The blackout times were slowly slipping towards autumn and winter when it hardly seemed worthwhile taking them down during the day. Already, Annie had been complaining about the quick onset of darkness after the long summer nights.

There was little of note contained within the file. If he didn't know better, Mason might have supposed that there was nothing suspicious about the death at all.

"No photographs?" he asked, thinking of how accurate scene of crime photographs would have helped him solve The Custard Corpses so much more quickly.

"Yes, but," and here, Roberts paused, glancing at a too interested O'Rourke before pressing on. "Well, it's a bizarre one. I don't want to be walking around with them. I wouldn't want anyone to discover them if I happen to mislay them."

Mason felt himself sitting up taller at this admission. Having worked on the Middlewick Murders together, Mason was intrigued to see what could be so much more bizarre than that.

"Bizarre in what way?"

"Now, Mason, this is nothing to do with the previous murders. This is something entirely different." Smythe barked a laugh. "Don't be thinking it's at all related because it isn't."

Sam nodded but kept his gaze on Roberts. He hadn't thought it was related anyway.

"You don't know who the dead person is? There were no identification papers on them?"

"No, nothing, and that's another problem. No one has been reported as missing, not that it tends to happen a great deal at the moment. But, no, we don't know who has been murdered, other than he was a male, about forty years old, and with few other distinguishing marks."

"So, there were some?" Mason pressed. He was becoming a bit frustrated with all this failure to address the matter.

"I think you should come with me, and I'll show you what I mean."

"What? Do you still have the body? It's not been released for burial?"

"We do still have the body, yes. So, no, it's not been released for burial. Not that we'd know to who we could release it. I want to show you, and then I think you might understand why the case is so peculiar."

Sam made to stand and then looked at O'Rourke.

"O'Rourke is coming as well," it wasn't so much a question as a statement.

"Oh yes, we need her on this too." In the background, Sam was aware of Jones listening to the conversation and the droop of his shoulders as he realised that he was to be overlooked once more. But he was about to get the counterfeiting case back, which he probably didn't want, even though he was angry at having it taken away from him.

Only at that moment, young Williams walked into the station, looking agitated. Mason wondered what item or person he'd been returning to their owner this time.

"What is it?" Smythe barked at him, not unkindly.

"Well, you'll have to excuse me here, but I believed that those," and everyone inhaled sharply, fearing what he might say next. "The Automobile Association officers," and everyone exhaled with relief.

Williams was usually very mild-mannered, but he seemed especially riled at the moment. "Weren't allowed to inform the motorcar users when we've set up a speed trap. You know we've got Hodkins and Bert from Birmingham police station monitoring the speed of the road users on Tyburn Road after that nasty accident. I've just seen them. I thought I'd check on them while I was returning Mrs Aldie's misplaced ration book to her, and there's only one of those," an inhale again. "Officers," and an exhale, "standing there not saluting the cars that don't display one of their badges on the front grill. I mean, I wouldn't object so much, but they're all travelling too fast, trying to enjoy the last dregs of petrol before there's none left, with no thought for pedestrians or cyclists."

Smythe's face clouded at the news. The problem with the car association people was becoming a bit of a regular occurrence. This wasn't the first time that their antics had upset the men and women who worked at Erdington police station.

"There was a court case, alright," and Smythe was riled by now as well. "Thirty years ago, it was, and they're not to interfere. Right, come on, lad, I want to meet this chap." Smythe was already shrugging on his coat as he made the announcement. Sam grimaced, pleased to be going out, even if it was to look at a dead body.

"Report back to me tomorrow, Mason," Smythe threw over his shoulder as he left the police station, the door banging shut in the wind, a loud shriek testifying to it being both opened and then closed. The door needed some attention. No one could think to sneak in or out of it at the moment.

Mason made to stand, doing so slowly, wincing at the same time, pleased when his feet obeyed him, and he could reach for his coat and slip it on over his smart grey suit. There was a fierce wind outside today. Certainly, not a day to be standing on the side of the road checking the motorcars and buses weren't travelling too fast.

"I've brought my car, but you should probably take your own. Otherwise, I'll have to send you back on the bus and the trams, and that might take much of the evening." Jones apologised.

"That's not a problem. O'Rourke will follow." The petrol rationing was starting to cause problems, just like the lack of tea and sugar, and all the other items they couldn't get at the moment. Sam was pleased that he and Annie had planted so many vegetables in the garden. He was looking forward to eating his potatoes, carrots and peas when they were ready to be harvested.

O'Rourke nodded smartly at being included in the trip to the mortuary, collecting the keys to the Wolseley before following them outside. Sam avoided looking at Jones as they left, the door squeaking once more. He didn't need to see that Jones was either relieved or angry at having the counterfeiting case returned to him.

Sam chose to travel with Roberts, not O'Rourke, on the way to the mortuary, hoping that the man might offer him some more information, but Roberts did no such thing. Instead, the conversation was all about the roadside officers and the challenging task they had trying to combat the overzealous will of the Automobile Association as they did whatever they could to prevent their members from being caught for speeding. Sam was amazed anyone would waste their fuel on travelling so fast, but then, he didn't own a car. And he wasn't as keen on driving as he once had been.

So, Sam gazed out of the window, watching the familiar landmarks pass by, the vast Dunlop factory, the tram station, the hospital and the football stadium, and only then did they come to a stop.

He'd been to this hospital before, and he wasn't a stranger to the mortuary, and still, he shivered as they pushed open the old double doors and entered the corridor that led to the mortuary in the basement of the hospital. It never helped that mortuaries were such unwelcoming places, even for the living.

At his back, O'Rourke dogged his steps. He didn't turn and ask her if she was comfortable in the mortuary. She wouldn't appreciate such words, especially after everything they'd gone through on The Custard Corpses case, but those deaths had been cold cases. This was a fresh death. And she'd see it, in the flesh, as well.

Two men looked up as they entered the room, huge steel lamps hanging down from the ceiling so that they only illuminated small areas, casting the rest of the space into near darkness.

"Ah, Roberts. Here at last," the younger man commented, his words sour, as though this was a big problem.

"Traffic was bad. My apologies Doctor Lucey," Roberts muttered by way of an apology, and Sam looked down. The traffic hadn't been bad at all. But the eyes of the tall man with a shimmering brown head kept straying to the large clock on the wall. The hands ticked loudly, marking the passage of each second. Sam thought such a steady tick would drive him bonkers in a very short amount of time. It seemed Doctor Lucey had places to be.

"Well, let's get on with it. Why you couldn't be content with photographs, I've no idea." Roberts turned a pleading look towards

Sam, and Sam surged forwards, but before he could introduce himself and O'Rourke, Doctor Lucey spoke.

"Here you go. You've got five minutes." He said as though such a statement was reasonable. Roberts nodded, even as Doctor Lucey turned to a table on which a blue sheet covered some sort of lump. Sam could feel the coldness of the body even from where he stood. He was glad he wore his coat even though he'd meant to take it off.

Sam stepped closer and then gasped as the sheet was pulled back by the man assisting Doctor Lucey.

Sam Mason swept the body before him and then looked at Roberts. Roberts shrugged one shoulder eloquently as if to say, 'see the problem now,' but it was O'Rourke who spoke.

"And he was found in such a, such a position?"

"Yes, just like this. It was difficult to get him here in the back of an ambulance, and he won't fit in any of the cold stores, no matter what we do."

"And, he won't lie flat?" Sam was pleased O'Rourke asked the questions. He felt words were beyond him.

"If he would lie flat, don't you think I'd have dealt with it by now. So no, he won't lie flat. And now you have four minutes." Doctor Lucey's tone was biting and filled with condescension.

Sam shared a look with O'Rourke for the harshness of the other man and bent closer. It was the most bizarre sight he'd ever seen. Here, lying on the table, was the naked body of a man, age impossible to tell with any surety, because his head was bent over his feet, his body neatly bent in two. All Sam could see was the back of the man's head, which was covered in a mass of dark curls, and the spikey hair that tumbled down his back, all the way to the pale flesh of the man's bottom.

Mason walked around the table, stopping at the man's feet, curled tightly. He bent down, just to be sure, but the man's nose rested on his lower legs.

"I couldn't even get in that position," the older man in the white doctor's cloak commented. Doctor Lucey huffed as he flicked through a clipboard he was holding, somehow making the action seem as loud as gunfire in the silent mortuary.

"Age, probably in his forties. Some markings to the feet and the toes have been scraped in mud or something like mud. I can't open him up enough to look at his face, not without cutting him in two, and Roberts here said that wasn't to be done. Not until you'd looked at the body. So, now you've looked at it, can I begin the next part of the process."

"So, you're going to cut him in two?" Mason couldn't keep the horror from his voice.

"Yes," there was nothing in Doctor Lucey's response that made Sam think what was about to happen was in any way unusual.

"What about the hands and nails?" Mason asked Roberts.

"Some markings, again, probably mud or something like that. We've taken fingerprints, but the local office has nothing on record to tell us who he might be. We'll send them on to London, but I don't hold out much hope. I don't think this man is a criminal. I can't see why we'd ever have needed to take his fingerprints in the past, and that's the only way to confirm his identity as there's nothing else on his body."

"Are we done here?" Dr Lucey pressed.

"Yes," Sam announced, keen to be away before the equipment being brought into the room by another figure shrouded in a white cloak could become clear enough for him to see the drills and blades.

"Good. I'll call you back in when I've cut the poor sod apart."

Sam nodded. He didn't trust himself to open his mouth and all but ran from the mortuary, all the way outside to the clear air of the day, hardly feeling the ache in his back and leg at all.

O'Rourke caught him first, Roberts coming along more slowly.

"Pleasant chap, isn't he?" Roberts asked with an arch of one eyebrow.

"Not really," Sam agreed. He didn't know what of his many questions to ask next.

"I know. I've no idea. He was found like that. Poor git."

"And where was he found?"

"Out the back of the aerodrome at Castle Bromwich, hidden in the woods."

"What? So he was an airman?"

"Impossible to tell as he was found as naked as you saw him. No one's been reported as missing, so we think it unlikely. And yet?"

Sam nodded. It seemed obvious to suspect something to do with the Royal Air Force. But perhaps that was what the person who'd killed the man had wanted them to think. It might be little more than a red herring, meant to force them to check every airman assigned to the RAF base painstakingly. It was undoubtedly a good way of distracting them. The higher authorities would insist on a thorough investigation. Just in case the man had been compromised in some way. There were spies and counterspies, allegedly, throughout Great Britain.

"It can't be dismissed, can it?" Sam twisted his lips in thought. It was indeed a bizarre case. The fact the body was naked was of note. The positioning of the body was something else entirely.

"Do you think he'd been crushed into a small space?" O'Rourke asked. "And that's why the body was like that?"

"It makes sense, but the body wasn't found in a confined space. It was hidden beneath the trees but easy enough to see. A dog walker found him. Put's you off getting a dog," Roberts commented good-naturedly. O'Rourke's face clouded in sympathy for the poor person who'd been greeted with such a sight when they were probably busy minding their own business.

"And you questioned them?"

"No, I didn't, but the first officer on the scene did. Said they couldn't be involved in any way. The body was cold and hard. No chance they might have done it and then pretended to find them. They have no car and no means of moving a body in such a position."

Sam hadn't expected the answer to be any different, but all the same, it would have been nice to have solved the case so easily.

Silence fell between the three of them. Roberts lit a cigarette and wandered away from the door, having offered them both one of the long, white sticks. But Sam had declined, and O'Rourke didn't like the things at all. She coughed, just to make a point. Sam looked down and smiled. O'Rourke was very particular about people who smoked. She disapproved, even if all the film stars were doing it. She said it was a filthy habit, and Sam was inclined to agree.

Sam rubbed his hands together and then settled them behind his back, holding the one with the other. O'Rourke noted him.

"You look like a proper copper now," she teased him.

"What? Don't I normally?"

"No, I'd say you look more like an accountant, or a clerk, than a copper."

Sam sniffed. He'd always thought he didn't suit the uniform, but now it seemed that even in just his coat, he didn't look like a police officer either, let alone a Chief Inspector. Not that he minded. When he looked at Jones, it was impossible to deny that he worked for the police. He'd rather there was something about him that meant people didn't immediately look contrite when they saw him.

"Come on. It's done." The voice at the door startled all three of them. Sam turned to see the white coat disappearing. He had no idea whether it was Doctor Lucey or not. He doubted it. Lucey wouldn't have left his mortuary to run such an errand, of that he was sure.

Steeling himself for what he might be forced to look at now, Sam sniffed once more of the fresher air and then followed O'Rourke inside. Her steps were firm, her stance slightly rigid. Behind them, Roberts huffed somewhat with each step he took. It seemed that none of them were keen to see what Doctor Lucey had done to the body of the dead man.

"This should be interesting," Roberts eventually broke the silence as O'Rourke pushed open the door to the mortuary. Sam didn't reply, neither did O'Rourke. Sam found his eyes trained on where they'd first seen the body. The trolley was no longer covered by a blue cloth, although a small piece of fabric had been placed over the man's genitalia, no doubt to spare O'Rourke from embarrassment. Perhaps Doctor Lucey wasn't quite as unfeeling as he seemed.

Sam's eyes flicked to the clock. It was 1.45 pm. It hadn't taken long to hack through the man's midriff because that was evidently what Doctor Lucey had been forced to do. Mason looked around, but the tray of medical implements had been moved aside, and although the smell was ripe with bleach, it did at least cover the scent of blood.

Doctor Lucey stood at the man's head, a quizzical look on his face.

"Well, I'd like to tell you that the mystery is solved, but of course, it isn't. Nothing of great note to report. He died from blunt force trauma to his chest. It's a welter of bruises. But there was this, on the forehead."

Roberts stepped closer than Mason wanted to, his eyes taking in everything he saw. O'Rourke wasn't far behind. Mason shook his head and moved nearer.

The man's dark hair had been pulled back so that the forehead was easy to see. The skin there was white, marbled and mottled, yet there was something to be seen—an imprint in the skin.

"What is it?" Roberts asked, almost touching it but then snapping his right hand back.

"I can't tell. It's an odd shape. Look, it's long here, and then it seems to be thin here." Doctor Lucey pointed as he spoke, and Mason appreciated that the shape was longer than he'd first thought. Even beneath the harsh electric lamps, he'd only seen the rounder shape on the right side of the forehead, not the thinner one at all.

"I would say the poor sod was lying on something that left that mark. How, I'm unsure, what with the body being as twisted as it is."

"So, we have a strange mark on the forehead and not much else?" Roberts asked Doctor Lucey.

"Yes." Doctor Lucey commented some interest in his voice now.

"It's certainly unusual," the other man in the room observed. He seemed to defer to Doctor Lucey, although he was the older of the two. "I've never seen anything like it before. I can't imagine that you have?" He peered at Mason through thick-lensed glasses, wild tufts of greying hair barely contained beneath the white cap he wore.

"No, nothing like this. Mind, I've seen some perplexing things in my time."

"Roberts here says you're the one who solved that case, the one they're calling The Custard Corpses?" There was grudging respect in Doctor Lucey's voice.

"Yes, that was me, but not alone. I couldn't have done it without O'Rourke, or my wife, to be entirely honest."

"You don't think this is somehow connected, do you? Is that why you're here?" But Roberts was shaking his head.

"Not at all. This is entirely separate, if just as bizarre. So, he was killed by blunt force trauma to his chest?" Mason was pleased that Roberts was eager to change the topic of conversation. Yes, he was relieved they'd solved the case of The Custard Corpses, but he didn't want to be always known as the 'Custard Copper' as some bright spark at The Daily Mail had decided to call him. He couldn't help thinking that some of the cartoons featured in the newspapers would have shown him in a yellow uniform if they could have printed them in colour. It was quite something to put a man in custard for life.

"Then what's he doing here?"

"A case such as this needs as many eyes on it as possible. And, of course, the body was found in his local area. If the Royal Air Force hadn't called us in, he'd have been given the case anyway." That neatly summarised everything, Mason hoped.

"Right," but Doctor Lucey didn't sound at all convinced.

"Anything else?" Roberts asked. Mason thought there was quite enough as there was.

"No. Nothing but mud beneath the nails. I found no marks on him, no tattoos, nothing at all. Poor man." The words sounded right, but they lacked any type of sympathy.

"Yes. And now, you can keep him here, in one of the cold stores, until we find out more. We don't even have a name to bury him with."

"We can keep him for seven days, at the most. After that, he'll have to go to one of the undertakers, name or no name."

"My thanks," Roberts confirmed, turning to leave.

"Tell me one thing," Doctor Lucey asked as Mason made to leave. "When you find out who he is or who did this, will you let me know? I'd sleep easier in my bed if I'm not worried there's some sort of multiple killer on the loose, and I was going to get another one of these bodies to tend to."

"Of course, Doctor Lucey," Roberts smoothed. "If we can tell you, then we will. Now, good day to you, both."

Mason took a final look at the body. The man was younger than him. He had an athletic build, or rather, he had. There were muscles in his arms and along his stomach that Mason hadn't owned for many years. But, other than the mark on his forehead, he was just another man. Mason bowed his head, offered a quick prayer for the dead man, and then turned aside.

He couldn't help wishing that Smythe hadn't thought to involve him in this.

Hadn't he solved enough inexplicable crimes recently?

"I took a drawing of the shape on the forehead," O'Rourke said to Mason as they made their way back to Erdington Police Station, having communicated their goodbyes to Roberts. He'd offered them both a wry smirk. "Do you see why I need some help, now?" he'd asked.

There wasn't a great deal of traffic on the roads. O'Rourke had swerved to avoid a few cyclists, as well as the odd bus belatedly stopping along its route.

"Good, but there should be photographs as well, soon enough."

"Yes, but I didn't think they'd quite show it as clearly as my eyes," O'Rourke continued. Mason grunted softly. She was probably right. After the problems with their previous case, it was better to have drawings and photographs. More evidence was better than not enough.

"Who do you think it was?" O'Rourke continued, her eyes on the road. Sam shook his head and then realised she couldn't see the movement as she was busy concentrating on the junction.

"I've no idea. But we'll go to Castle Bromwich aerodrome tomorrow. It's the only place we can start. There's no other information to hand."

"Will Roberts be coming with us?"

"No, he's spoken to the Flight Squadron Leader over the telephone today to inform him that we'll be visiting. We can do the more tedious footwork following up any conversations they might have had already."

"It's peculiar, though. Isn't it?" O'Rourke continued.

"Very. And we won't solve it by talking about it when we know so little about the man."

"No, and if he was a spy looking at the aircraft, which is the only conclusion I can draw at the moment, then I can't see that we'll ever know about him."

"You're right. But we need to try. In all honesty, I would have expected Roberts to keep it to himself if he was suspected to be a spy or something to do with military intelligence. I almost find it more extraordinary that they're handing the case back to us."

"You make a good point," O'Rourke mused, edging her way around a horse-drawn cart laden with coal-filled sacks.

"These horse-drawn carts are a menace," Mason mused as O'Rourke moved slowly past the horse so as not to startle the animal.

"They are, but at least they can't drive too fast."

"That's a good point." Mason agreed with a tight smile. The horse and carts couldn't cause them any problems with the Automobile Association and its determination to ensure not a single one of its members was ever caught for exceeding the speed limit, even if the speed limit had been put in place to protect pedestrians and cyclists.

CHAPTER 2
TUESDAY, SEPTEMBER 5TH 1944

The following morning, O'Rourke drove them to the Castle Bromwich aerodrome. It wasn't far, and it was threatening to be a pleasant September day. Above their heads, Mason could hear the rumble of the Hawker Hurricanes and Airspeed Oxfords. It was a rare day when the sound of engines in the sky didn't cause him to look up in fear, but today, there were merely newly built aircraft being tested before being deployed, or he assumed, from the fact they kept taking off and landing quite quickly. It had been many months since a bomb had fallen from a German plane over Birmingham. He hoped it lasted.

"Could you imagine flying one?" O'Rourke asked, bending her elbows low to the huge steering wheel to enable her to look through the windscreen at the aeroplanes overhead.

"I don't like heights," Mason admitted. "I admire them all, the men and the women, but it's not for me. Why, do you think you'd like it?"

"No idea, but I'd look flash in the uniform," O'Rourke offered with a chuckle. "And the flight officers certainly make dashing figures." Mason shook his head at her words.

"They'd be no good for you, flying off at a moment's notice and with you not knowing if they're going to come back."

"Well, maybe when all this is over then," O'Rourke mused. Mason watched her through the corner of his eye. She was young to be pining for a man. One day the right man would walk into her life, but until then, what harm was she doing in assessing all her options?

They pulled off the road into the area of the aerodrome surrounded by barbed wire, having avoided cyclists, a horse-rider, and a gaggle of children tearing down the street chasing a football. A smartly dressed flight-woman with her hair contained beneath her cap, blue uniform immaculate, and her shoes so shiny that Mason had to blink, approached and stopped them. But upon realising they were the police became far more friendly.

"You'll find the Flight Squadron Leader in there," she offered, her words light and breezy, directing them towards one of the low build-ings. "Ask anyone you see if you get lost, and keep your eyes on the sky. You never know who might be playing silly beggars up there." With that said, she stood aside to allow them entry.

The engine of the Wolseley thrummed to life once more as O'Rourke continued their journey through the restricted access of the gate. There was a wide road, but it was surrounded by colossal air hangers, some older than others, evident in the darker colours of the roofs. Aeroplanes, with their dull green paint, seemed to stretch as far as the eye could see in front of them.

The air rang with the sound of engines and was rife with the stink of petrol and oil. It was clear to see where all the fuel was going. Not into police cars but aeroplanes.

Mason didn't object at all. He'd rather know there was a Hurricane or an Oxford close to hand should the German planes return than be able to take a jaunt out into the countryside at a moment's notice.

"Cor, it reeks," O'Rourke complained as soon as they left the Wolseley close to the building towards which they'd been directed. O'Rourke didn't think she'd parked it in the way, but it wasn't very easy to tell with all the coming and going of military trucks, people and aeroplanes being pulled out of the hangars. Mason was braced for someone to order them to move, but the cry never came.

Ahead lay the low wooden building they'd been directed towards, the roof painted green, no doubt to blend in with the grass fields that surrounded them. That way, it wouldn't be possible to see it from high in the sky. The grass had been meticulously kept short on the fields. There were many men and women in smart Royal Air Force uniforms, the dark blue a stark change to the green of the army personnel Mason was more used to seeing. Either that, or they wore dirty overalls, which might once have been white, as they tinkered with engines and propellers, and no one seemed to give the two police officers a second thought as they walked amongst them all.

"Is this where we'll find the Flight Squadron Leader?" Mason asked of a uniformed man pushing through the double doors, his eyes on a piece of paper in his hands.

"What?" The man asked, only just looking up in time not to crash into O'Rourke.

"I'm Chief Inspector Mason, from Erdington Police Station, and this is Sergeant O'Rourke. Is this where we'll find the Flight Squadron Leader?"

"Oh, yes, yes, sorry, second door on the right. Mind, he's in a foul mood. Something about a missing uniform or some such. I couldn't really tell what he was complaining about. Oh, is that why you're here?"

Mason eyed the man intently.

"I can't say why we're here. Apologies. But thank you for your assistance."

"Oh, right, yes," the airman smiled and eyed O'Rourke with an appreciative look.

"Thank you," Mason reiterated, waiting for O'Rourke to follow him inside. She smiled at the young man, and then gave a funny giggle and walked into the building, looking behind her so that she almost collided with Mason.

"It's impossible to know where to look," she apologised, righting her path and pulling her eyes forward.

"Not really. Just remember why you're here," Mason spoke with a hint of iron.

"Well, yes, I haven't forgotten that. But, well, he looked at me first," she objected, the hint of a smile on her black cheeks.

Mason shook his head, standing before the indicated door, and swiftly knocked. A deep voice called, 'come in,' but it was rife with frustration.

"Now here, Arkwright, I told you to get on with it, not to come back here with more complaints." The man behind the desk didn't even look up from his desk, and Mason paused, waiting for the man to realise they weren't this Arkwright character.

"Well, don't just stand there." The voice continued, and yet they didn't move. Only then did sharp blue eyes look upwards, followed by a long drooping nose and a moustache almost as wide as the room.

"Well, you're not Arkwright," the voice began, taking in both Mason and O'Rourke as his head turned from side to side. From somewhere close by, the clacking of a typewriter could be heard until it was overlain by the grumble of yet another aeroplane engine.

"Chief Inspector Mason and Sergeant O'Rourke. Erdington Police Station," Mason introduced them both.

"Is this about that bloody body? I told the bod on Sunday that I had no idea who the poor sod was. Certainly, nothing to do with us." The man's hands didn't stop moving as he spoke, and Mason moved aside to see he was doing two things at once, filling in a report and moving some pieces around on his desk. They looked like model planes. Mason shook his head. The Flight Squadron Leader wasn't making any progress with either. He should just concentrate on one thing.

"So, you saw the victim then?" Mason asked. O'Rourke was staying quiet in the background, but he was aware she had her notebook out once more, pencil poised to note down anything of interest.

"Yes. They called me over, made me look at the poor sod. Like I say, no idea who it was."

"But you didn't see the face?" Mason continued, just to press home the point.

"No. Well, how could I? Why? Have you seen the face now?" The questions suddenly tumbled quickly, an edge to the Flight Squadron Leader's voice. The man hadn't introduced himself yet. Perhaps he didn't feel the need to, when there was a wooden name badge on his over-filled desk that read 'Smith-Johnson,' an unfortunate double-barrelled name, but probably not very common, Mason mused to himself, despite the two constituent parts being widespread.

"Yes, we have a clear image now. Would you like to see?" The photograph had been waiting for them when they'd arrived at Erdington Police Station that morning. The photographer had ensured only the top part of the body was visible. Mason was grateful for that.

Now, he slid the large photograph from the brown envelope it was in and showed it to Flight Squadron Leader Smith-Johnson. Smith-Johnson did at least take the time to peer at the black and white image from over his long nose, a slight wrinkle to his lips which forced his blonde moustache up, but he was shaking his head quickly enough.

"No idea who the poor fellow is. None at all. Never seen him before in my life. Is there something on his forehead?" He went on to ask, picking out the shape quickly, undoubtedly because of the shadows it caused beneath the bright lights of the camera. Mason was impressed by the man's sharp eyes. No doubt they were needed to become an airman.

"It looks like it, yes, not very easy to make out, though."

"No, it isn't. Something round. Maybe a coin or something," Flight Squadron Leader Smith-Johnson harrumphed to himself.

"Do we have your permission to ask around? See if anyone knows the man?"

Now Smith-Johnson paused, pulling his lips tightly together, his eyes losing focus.

"If you must, yes, but stay away from the airfield itself. If you plan on seeing the place the body was found, be careful as well. There's all sorts lands amongst those trees from the aeroplanes overhead. I've known my airmen and women to dump fuel and unwanted bombs. Go carefully. I keep telling the locals to stay away from there as well. Who knows what they might find? Bloody dog walkers, don't you know?" And again, his lips pursed.

Mason mumbled something in agreement, more sound than words, and turned to leave.

"And one more thing," Smith-Johnson stated, his eyes back down on his desk. "We're expecting Squadron 577 to return in an hour or two if you're still here then. It'll be noisy and busy. Keep an eye on the sky to keep yourself safe. If they're running low on fuel, they tend to skim the tree tops."

"Thank you," Mason almost warmed to the man for the concern, but Smith-Johnson was making shooing motions with his hands. Mason shook his head and moved away. He made sure to shut the door just loud enough for it to be construed as a purposeful action. Mason appreciated Smith-Johnson was busy with the war effort, but he could still have given them more of his time, and considered whether he knew the identity of the dead man for longer.

Mason finished returning the photograph to the brown envelope while O'Rourke stayed quiet. Only as they emerged back into the daylight did she speak.

"He wasn't lying, but he wasn't exactly overflowing with help."

"No, he wasn't. But he could have prevented us from asking our questions, so I won't be too harsh on the man. Still, it does help to engage with the police, especially when a body's been found."

"He noticed the mark on our victim's forehead quickly enough," O'Rourke mused as they took in the view before them. Where to start? Mason didn't believe the answer lay here, but all the same, it was the only clue they had to the man's identity.

"Shall we go down to the woodlands first," and he pointed in the far distance, where a smattering of trees could be seen beneath the blue sky, soft clouds moving slowly across it.

"May as well, and then work our way backwards," O'Rourke agreed. Mason looked down at his feet. He'd put on his good boots for this, the ones that didn't make his back ache as his police-issue ones did. He grimaced slightly at the task he faced. He didn't like to be constrained by his injury, but sometimes, such as now, it wasn't the easiest.

"Come on then," he encouraged O'Rourke. She also had her boots on. It seemed they were both prepared to traipse through the undergrowth and woodland.

It turned out that there were many more trees than Mason thought there would be. A thin wire fence attempted to demarcate the aerodrome from the wooded area beyond, but it was too easy to hop over, even for Mason. He could see why people continued to walk their dogs there.

As soon as he was a few tree lengths beneath the moving boughs above his head, it was easy to forget that close by, there were any aircraft. It was almost pleasant.

"Do you have the map that Roberts gave us?" he asked O'Rourke. Roberts had ensured they had all the information they needed now that they were assisting with identifying the dead man.

"I do, yes. It's this way," and she led him further under the trees. Mason took his time, being careful where he placed his feet on the rugged terrain. He didn't want to have to hobble back to the Wolseley, not beneath the watching eyes of all the airmen and women about their tasks. They exuded youth and vigour. He'd not had that for many years, and while he accepted it, sometimes it was unpleasant to be faced with the judgement on young faces. They never thought they'd be old. Time would show them the truth of that.

But, he thought, what did they know about him, after all? He was unsure whether it was because of his pronounced limp or because he wasn't wearing a military uniform that he garnered such interest. He tried to dismiss it from his thoughts. After all, these young men and women were putting themselves in danger on an almost daily basis for him. Even just being at the aerodrome was a risk. In recent years, it had been struck by enough enemy bombs that eleven of their number had been killed just going about their typical day-to-day business.

Mason hadn't been called in on those occasions. Those crimes hadn't needed solving. It had been too easy to say who was responsible—the enemy.

"Here you go," O'Rourke announced with a flourish. Mason stopped and looked around him.

"How do you know?" he asked. Everything looked the same. There were no genuinely identifiable markers beneath the trees. They all looked identical to him.

"The notes say it was twenty-three and a half feet from the wire fence and three and a half feet from a large tree with a hollow just about head height." She pointed to it. "It also helps that there are lots of footprints, tyre marks, and here, some paw prints left by dogs."

Mason nodded and tried not to look as confused as he felt by how easy she'd found it to decipher the pencil-drawn map that she'd copied from the original one left with the photograph of the victim. Mason knew he would have spent the day wandering around, probably falling over his own feet, and would never have found this place.

"It's very secluded," he stated.

"Yes, not sure how you'd have got a body here, though, and certainly not one in such a position either. It would have taken more than one person to carry it. I can't see that they'd have risked dragging it. That would have left a very definite trail." O'Rourke was bent over, carefully examining the ground, but a distant rumble had Mason looking upwards. Through the few breaks in the branches of the summer-green trees, he just caught a glimpse of the underneath of one of the aircraft. A Hurricane, he was almost sure. He doubted that any flight crew would be able to see where he stood. So, yes, it was an isolated location, but it answered none of his questions.

O'Rourke was down on her hands and knees now.

"What have you found?"

"Nothing. But I wanted to see if that object was here, the one that's left a mark on the victim's forehead. They might have missed it when they collected the body."

"Here, I'll help you." But O'Rourke was shaking her head.

"No, I don't want to have to get you back on your feet again, if you don't mind me saying so, Sir." It wasn't like O'Rourke to call him sir, and he nodded. She'd not wanted to have to say that.

"Point taken, and a well-made argument, at that." Leaving her to the task, he began to walk in slow circles that slowly got wider and wider, around the point where she scrabbled around on the floor. He kept his eyes on the ground just in front of his feet, noting that the earth was dry now and that his passage made minimal impact.

He tried to remember when it had last rained. Had it been this week? Or last week? It was the summer, well, starting to turn to autumn, yes, but still, it didn't stop it from raining. But he was struck by the thought of how much rain would hit the ground beneath the thick branches. It was more likely to seep along the ground, perhaps from the higher ground of the aerodrome.

Mason didn't expect to find anything. After all, when they collected the body, the police officers under Roberts command would have searched vigilantly. Still, it gave him something to do while O'Rourke continued to run her hand over the place where the body had been found. He didn't expect her to see anything new, either.

Mason didn't believe that the man had been killed here. No, this was just a handy location to leave the body. Not that it would have been handy to get to, no, but it would have hidden the body. Perhaps whoever had committed the crime had seen the signs left by the Ministry of Defence warning dog walkers away from the aerodrome and had hoped it would be a long time until the body was found.

"Nothing," O'Rourke sagged with disappointment as she returned to her feet, running her hands over her skirt to try and dislodge the mud and detritus from her hands.

"Can we walk out that way?" Mason asked, keen to see where the woodlands ended. If he remembered correctly, there was a playing field.

"Yes, but we'll have to come back this way or fight to gain access to the aerodrome again and the police car."

Mason nodded. He'd already done more walking than he liked. But it needed to be done.

But before they came to the playing fields, there was a road to cross, and before that, yet more wire fencing.

"I don't think we'll get through it this time," O'Rourke mused. Mason nodded unhappily. Here the fencing was far more elaborate and topped with barbed wire. Certainly, not at all welcoming. It would put him off trying to get inside. But all the same, he was able to see what he wanted to see.

"So, there's a road through here, the fields over there," and he pointed. "And the train line runs in the far distance, and there's the River Tame to the south. It's not as if the murderer was struck for ways to make it here."

O'Rourke looked down at the pencil-drawn map on her notebook she'd constructed to show their approach to the site and added a few more details. Mason turned on the spot, looking all around him. He could see the more built-up area off to the northwest, where Erdington lay, from where he stood. The hangars where the aeroplanes were stored were also visible, and the buildings in which the aircrew lived and the factory to the side, turning out the aeroplanes as quickly as it could. The aerodrome wasn't here by chance.

It was an open area, all things considered. The trains travelled as regularly as they could around the Castle Bromwich Curve, and many roads could bring someone here.

O'Rourke stayed quiet at his side, only the sound of her pencil moving over the paper and her soft breathing making him feel as though he wasn't alone. He sighed. None of this made any sense, and then he ducked low, the sudden rumble of the aeroplanes coming into land startling him, for all he'd been warned about the return of Squadron 577.

"Bloody hell," he exclaimed, holding onto his hat. It felt as though the aeroplanes were trying to land on him. "Come on, let's make our way back." O'Rourke's mouth opened as she watched two aeroplanes seeming to land, one on top of the other.

"No," she said softly at Mason's side. "No, I don't think I'd like to do that at all."

It was an effort to retrace their steps back to the hangars where they'd left the car. O'Rourke matched his pace, and Mason tried not to slow as much as he wanted to. By the time they were back close to the airfield, they'd witnessed no end of aeroplanes coming into land, and Mason had begun to wish that one of them might give him a lift back to the Wolseley.

It was challenging to keep his eyes on where his feet should be going, as they strayed too often to watch the heavy-bellied aircraft landing.

In sight of the hangar, Mason held out his hand, puffing through his cheeks.

"Let's wait a minute or two, catch our breaths. I don't want them looking at me when I'm all pink-cheeked and puffing." He wasn't usually a proud man, but watching the men and women run or walk really quickly around the airfield was making him feel all of his years and all of his injuries.

"I don't know how they don't all fly into one another or roll into one another. There's just so much happening." Mason agreed but didn't have the breath to tell her exactly what he felt watching it all. Not yet.

"Oye, don't stand there," the voice that shouted from close to the nearest hangar door was filled with fury. Mason shared a look with O'Rourke and then began moving again. Somehow, it was impossible to think the words weren't directed at them.

The bearer of the voice, a man probably a similar age to Mason, began to run towards them, hands beckoning frantically. Mason could see the fury on his face.

"What on earth are you doing here," the man exploded, only then seeming to notice O'Rourke's uniform.

"Ah, you're here about the body? Aren't you? Didn't Smith-Johnson tell you about the squadron coming back? It's bloody dangerous to stand there."

"He did, yes," O'Rourke offered with a smile. Mason was still finding it hard going. "We didn't realise how long we'd been having a good look around for."

"Well, come over here, out of the way. The pilots try and look everywhere at once, but it's not the easiest. I'm Flying Officer Thompson, by the way." And he held his hand out to Mason and then O'Rourke. Now he knew who they were, his fury seemed to have disappeared.

"Apologies for that. The youngsters are always cutting through the fences. I've told Smith-Johnson enough times that there'll be an accident, but he has other things on his mind. Or so it seems, to do anything about it."

Close to the hangar doors now, Thompson slowed his steps.

"So, have you found out who the poor sod was? What a way to go? And to be found like that. Very strange indeed. I had wondered if it was some poor bugger jettisoned out of one of the aeroplanes, but I can't see how they'd get in such a position. You certainly wouldn't want to be naked up there. It gets frigid."

O'Rourke hesitated before replying, and Mason found he had the breath now.

Flying Officer Thompson was a tall man, smart in his blue uniform, and with a full head of dark brown hair. He'd cut himself shaving that day, and a slither of blood was just evident on his long neck.

"No, not yet. Enquiries are continuing," Mason said. "Here," and he slid the photograph from the envelope. "Have you ever seen him before?"

"Ah, you opened him up then," Thompson muttered, peering closely at the photograph, casually referencing how the dead man had been found. It was evidently common knowledge for all Roberts hadn't wanted to speak candidly about it even in Erdington Police Station.

"No, I've never seen him in my life, and I do know all the air personnel and most of the locals as well. You can ask around, but I don't think anyone will know him if I don't." There was a slight depreciating quality to his tone. Mason almost felt his eyes narrow at the man. Was he really so sure, or did he just want to put them off asking the others?

"We have permission to ask around," Mason confirmed. For a moment, Thompson looked like he might argue, but then he found a smile on his face again.

"That way to the canteen then. You'll find most people in there, and you can help yourself to a cup of tea as well if you can call the muck they're serving tea." And Thompson dipped his chin and turned to walk inside the hangar. As he went, his head remained up, surveying all before him, and Mason had to admit, as Thompson called someone to his side and began berating them for an oil spill on the floor, that the man probably didn't miss a great deal. Still, if there were people in the canteen when he helped himself to a cup of tea, there was no harm in asking. And he did need a cup of tea after their trek.

The canteen was in a small building, to the side of two of the aeroplane hangars. It wasn't a permanent building, and Mason noted the corrugated iron roof with a grimace. It wasn't a problem when the weather was fair, but come the rain, it would be so noisy they might not even hear the aeroplanes coming into land.

O'Rourke went in first, hopping up the three concrete steps and then pausing. O'Rourke's appearance occasioned silence inside the canteen, and Mason hobbled quickly to join her.

He eyed the men and women whose attention O'Rourke had caught and offered them a firm nod of his head. He knew that they would respect his authority, if not O'Rourke's.

"Cup of tea, love?" the voice from behind the counter broke the prolonged silence.

"Yes, please, two if you don't mind."

Quickly, two white mugs were placed on the counter, and O'Rourke went to collect them. Mason found himself a chair and sank into it gratefully. All the walking was taking its toll on him.

"Are you here about the body?" the woman continued. Her broad face was framed by white hair, although she wore a brightly covered scarf over it.

"Yes, we are. Why do you know anything?" O'Rourke asked, her tone bright and polite.

"No, the poor sod. It's just everyone's been gossiping about it," the woman continued her tone cajoling.

"Well, we have nothing further to add," O'Rourke quickly informed her. "If anything, we need all the information you know."

"No good speaking to me, love." The woman continued, her enthusiasm dimming a little. "We've no idea who he was either."

"Well, if you think of anything, do let us know, and thank you for the tea," O'Rourke offered, lifting the two mugs and bringing them to Mason.

Now there was a hubbub of conversation in the room. There were seven other people in the canteen. Four airmen sat together, heads bowed, two women having a natter, laughing softly at something, and an officer sitting alone, nursing a mug of tea, and reading the local newspaper, his forehead furrowed.

"There's been nothing in the newspaper," the man stated, pointing to it, although he didn't look up from what he was reading.

"I'm sure there will be when we know who he is," Mason explained.

"If you ever do," the man added darkly. Mason narrowed his eyes at him.

"Ignore Carruthers," one of the women called. "He's all doom and gloom today. But I can tell you we don't know who the man was. No one is missing from here." She had bright eyes and wavy auburn hair. She was as young as O'Rourke and smiled towards her.

"And none of you heard anything on Saturday night?" Mason asked. The woman was the most friendly member of the aerodrome that they'd met so far.

"We had a dance on Saturday night," she explained. "There was loud music for much of the night, and if I remember correctly, there was no moon. Wasn't it cloudy?" this she asked the woman to whom she was speaking.

"Oh yes. It was really dark. I fell over on the way back to my bunk," as she spoke, she bent to rub at her calf.

"So, you don't believe anyone could have seen anything, then?"

"No. As far as I know, everyone was at the dance. Sorry. We've all been asking these questions to each other." Mason nodded, lifting his mug to sip from it. He was startled at realising that the tea wasn't half bad. Perhaps they had access to better supplies than the police. Or maybe he was just so thirsty that he didn't notice.

"Thank you for your help," he called to the wavy-haired woman. She smiled and quickly returned to her conversation.

O'Rourke looked at Mason, eyebrows high as she indicated the tea, and Mason nodded. Why not have another cup while they were there.

CHAPTER 3

Smythe appeared the moment they returned to Erdington Police Station.

"I take it no one knew anything?" he asked without preamble.

Mason noted that Jones was still behind his wall of paperwork. He felt a pang of sympathy for him.

"No. No one knows who he is, certainly not amongst those we were able to speak to, in the canteen and the few officers as well. And the place is open to all sides. The body could have got there by boat, or even train, although that's improbable. Mind with the shotgun from the train case; it might be worthwhile not dismissing it quite so out of hand. It could have fallen from one of the aircraft, although I find that highly unlikely. Even the playing fields are in easy distance, and roads crisscross the aerodrome. There's good barbed wire in some places, but in others, such as the woodlands, there's barely a single piece of wire to show people shouldn't be there. And the signs aren't much use either."

Smythe nodded, clearly unsurprised, but his eyes did alight at the mention of the word 'sign.'

"Well, we've done what we can for now. I think you'll just have to ruminate over it and be patient. At some point, there'll be an uproar about the missing man, and that might help. But, in the meantime, these bloody Automobile Association people have been making a fuss."

Mason suppressed a sigh, considering what he was about to be asked to do now.

"There's a few of the chaps, all on their smart motorbikes, decked out in camouflage green. They're down at the Mile Oak raising a right old stink about some signposts that they say have been meddled with by someone. I said we'd send someone down, and it's better if it's you than anyone else. They'll respect your position as a Chief Inspector. They're all very disciplined with their patrols and officer and what-not. Poor Jones had a proper telling off yesterday from the patrolman who came to report the problem after you'd gone to the mortuary. And he was only a patrolman."

Mason detected a stiffening in Jones' shoulders at the words, and he mumbled something that would hopefully be taken as an agreement. He'd have liked nothing better than to get back to helping Jones with his counterfeiting investigation. Still, it seemed that 'meddled' road signs were worthy of a Chief Inspector's time when it involved the dreaded Automobile Association and their long-running determination to undermine the work of the police.

"They've got one of those little boxes at Mile Oak. Have you seen it? It looks better cared for than most of the allotments around here." With that, Smythe headed back for his office, and O'Rourke flashed him a bright grin. Mason would have liked to eat his lunch and enjoy another cup of tea, but perhaps it would be better done out on the road, after all.

"Come on then," and Sam reached for his only just discarded coat and hat.

"Jones, I'll be back to you when I return."

A head appeared from behind the piles of paperwork, an undecipherable expression on it. Jones could be a contrary git when he wanted to be, but this counterfeit claim was way beyond him, even though he'd done all of the door-knocking and foot-wearying work to get to where he was. He was also the one who'd been tasked with speaking to the local government officials and the shopkeepers. Mason could well understand why he both wanted assistance and was loathe to share his findings.

Outside, thick white clouds scudded in front of the sun at great speed, and Mason was pleased for his coat once more.

"Bloody road signs," he muttered to O'Rourke. She grinned at him, sharing his frustration, but pleased to have an excuse to drive the Wolseley once more.

"I thought they'd all been taken down? Don't want the Jerrys knowing how to reach Coventry and so on."

"I did as well, but they're a peculiar bunch. Maybe they have permission to keep some of the other signs up. After all, the army convoys need to know their way to the aerodrome and Dunlop's."

O'Rourke fell into step beside him as they made their way to the police car. They couldn't walk the distance to Mile Oak. Mason wished he'd asked now why it had to be an officer from Erdington Police Station that went out to Mile Oak. Surely it should have been the job of the Sutton Coldfield branch or the Tamworth one. For a moment, he considered turning back, asking Smythe about it, but changed his mind. Perhaps it was better to be away so he could think about the unknown man who'd been murdered.

"I've been thinking about our unidentified victim."

"Me too," O'Rourke agreed. "I've been considering why he was bent like that. It must have been to fit him into a small space. One that people wouldn't necessarily think had a body in it."

"That's a good thought," Mason agreed, stepping into the front seat of the Wolseley. "Perhaps if we could determine just what object a grown man's body could be twisted into, we might have an idea of where to look. Could it be a packing crate or something like that? They must have a lot at the Dunlop factory and the aerodrome. They're probably not as hard to get hold of as we might think."

"But a packing crate would be large enough for a body? Surely?" O'Rourke spoke as she waited for a gap in the traffic to allow her to turn towards Walmley.

"If he were in a packing crate, they wouldn't have needed to bend him quite so much. That's what I'm thinking."

"So, smaller than a packing crate, then?"

"Yes, much smaller."

As he watched the landscape flash by, Mason considered O'Rourke's suggestion.

"Then why crush him up small and then leave him out in the open to be found?"

"Now that," and she shook her head ruefully. "I don't know the answer to."

In front of them, Mason could see old Watling Street coming into view as they travelled along Sutton Road. He caught a first glimpse of the unmistakable Automobile Association telephone box. Even it had been repainted in less lurid colours than usual because of the war effort. All the same, the road sign placed above the box was a monstrous thing, as it sat atop the sentry box, decked out in camou-flage green and black stripes. It drew the eye easily enough.

To the bottom, the set of double signs directed the motorcar driver, or bus or motorcycle rider towards Fazeley or Hints. The higher up signs led the traveller towards Tamworth or Lichfield, depending on which was you wanted to travel.

The signs were the same green as the telephone box was edged in, with the writing in black on them and the distance given in miles. He smirked on seeing it. He well remembered when he was a much younger man, and the signs had been more simplistic, simply high-lighting the ancient milestones used for so many decades, if not centuries, and often written on what was little more than lumps of handy stone.

That had been changing before the war. Now everything had been set back until the bloody war was over.

If they ever ended petrol rationing, he could see a growth in the use of motorcars. And not just for the men. Women had been driving lorries and ambulances as well, just as O'Rourke drove the Wolseley. The future, when it arrived, promised a great many changes, and he welcomed it.

He had to admit, the patrolmen had done an excellent job of main-taining the small building. He'd never needed to access one of the tele-phone boxes before. He doubted few did, not here. The route the patrols took each day took them routinely past this place. He knew that because he'd seen them often enough. Before the war, most of the patrols had ridden bicycles. The change to motorbikes had been welcome but slow. The routes, he appreciated, could be longer ones when the patrols had motorbikes and not just peddle power.

If anyone happened to break down between Mile Oak and Erdington, and the breakdown wasn't caused by lack of petrol, they would get found soon enough. Still, the cables above the telephone box showed that the telephone was connected to the switchboard run by the Automobile Association from their head office.

It would be strange, he thought, to pick up the handset and have it answered by someone in faraway Leicester Square, London, when the person who called had broken down here, in Mile Oak, over a hundred miles away. Still, the switchboard operator would ensure help came soon enough.

Mason wasn't expecting to see the collection of roses and geraniums surrounding the Automobile Association box, the colours bright; the roses an array of reds and whites, the geraniums a darker red.

"Have they always been there?" he thought to ask.

O'Rourke nodded. "Oh yes. They're very proud of their flowers and the good condition they keep their little box in."

Mason didn't know what to say. Bad enough the camouflage green without the flowers as well. They were going to extraordinary lengths to showcase the Automobile Association. And then he groaned because there were two roadside patrolmen, with their motorbikes pulled up on the side of the road, standing, one either side of the road, watching the traffic flow.

"I wonder if the Tamworth police have a speed trap out today?" Mason asked O'Rourke. He couldn't think of another reason why two of the patrolmen would be stood in such an odd arrangement.

"I can't see one," O'Rourke replied quickly.

"Then what are they doing?"

Mason eyed the two men as O'Rourke pulled the Wolseley over to the side of the crossroads. They were dressed nattily in their uniforms. They looked as though they were in the army or the navy. The trousers and jacket were near-identical, in colour as well as cut. Mason was always surprised how people tasked with fixing motor engines could keep themselves looking so smart. Surely, he thought, they should have oily hands and oil stains on their trousers? But, of course, they no doubt had overalls to ensure such didn't happen.

Instead, they wore their brown trousers and smart long socks, trousers tucked into them, and beneath he didn't doubt that their knee-high boots were buffed so that they shone just as brightly as the angular Automobile Association badges on their jackets. He noted that they wore steel helmets and not the usual flat caps they'd worn before the war. The motorcycles had also been painted the same shade as the sentry boxes to stop them from being so easily identifiable.

Mason could tell that the approach of the Wolseley had been noted, but neither of the men moved from their positions where they were saluting the few automobiles and motorbikes that passed them in either direction. Mason thought their salute a little odd, hand held flat to the side of their faces and reaching up to touch the top of their steel helmets. No doubt that had been some bigwigs idea to differentiate them apart from military salutes.

As soon as O'Rourke had stopped the car, Mason walked towards the Automobile Association telephone box, keen to look more closely at it. This was a particularly good example, much larger than some he'd seen. Still, it only held the one door, and it wasn't open. He noted that it was a stable door design.

He waited, sure that one of the patrolmen would feel compelled to come and speak to him.

As the few buses and motorcars thundered through the junction, the gentle pips of horns sounded as well. But he didn't turn aside, instead bending to smell some of the red roses. They were a particularly dark shade. His father would have appreciated them. He didn't. He thought plants should be grown for the food they could provide, not for the thorns on their sides.

"Ah, you must be from Erdington police station." The voice was rich, brokering no argument. Mason was almost tempted to say that no, he wasn't from the police station at all. But managed to stop himself.

"My name is Patrolman Grant. Now, that chap at the police station didn't seem to know what I was talking about, but of course, you've already seen it, haven't you? And Patrolman Grant pointed upwards, towards the Automobile Association telephone box. Again, Mason was perplexed. He didn't understand what he was being shown either. He waited, hoping the patrolman would offer something further.

A soft sigh came from the neatly dressed man, with his black moustache and short-cut hair. He had a broad face, thin lips and ears that looked as though they held his large steel cap up.

"The top signs on the sentry box should direct the road user to the minor roads, and the bottom signs to the major roads. Look." There was outrage in the man's voice. Mason's brow furrowed, and then he realised.

"Ah, so the signs have been switched over." Mason had noted that Grant called it a sentry box, not a telephone box.

"Yes, of course, they have. Fazeley and Hints should be on the top, the Tamworth and Lichfield one, lower down. There should only ever be four signposts on top of our sentry boxes."

Mason was perplexed. He couldn't say that a crime was being committed.

"When did you notice it?"

"Yesterday. I hope it wasn't like that before. It's not good if we've been standing here and haven't noticed something as significant as that. I'm sure our members will have written to head office in London if such a thing has happened. I don't want them coming down on us. They've not long opened a regional office in Birmingham as well. I don't want this to be the sort of thing that gets me called before the regional manager. Not at all what we were hoping for."

Mason didn't think it particularly important, but then, he wasn't a road patrolman. As he considered it, Mason realised that provided it told you which way to go, it didn't matter if the major destinations were on the top of the pole extended above the sentry box or on the bottom of it. But perhaps they got graded on such things. Surely, the roses and geraniums would distract the eye from the road signs?

"Why are the signs even up?" O'Rourke asked. "I understood they were all to be taken down so the enemy couldn't find their way around."

"Ah-ha," now Grant eyed O'Rourke as though she'd just won a prize. "That's also part of the problem. These signs shouldn't be up, but someone has put them up, and in doing so, made a total hash of it."

Mason didn't dare look to O'Rourke. She might be pleased to have asked the question, but she wouldn't be happy at the condescending tone of the patrolman. He thought to draw attention back to himself.

"So, the signs have been swapped around. Aren't you going to change them back?"

"Well," and Grant looked most displeased. "My understanding was that nothing should be touched until the police attended a crime scene. Surely you need to check for fingerprints or something like that? We've had no word from head office or the regional office that the signs were to be put up once more, and so someone is up to no good, and they must be caught. For the security of the country, if not for confusing our poor members."

"Well," and here, Mason paused. He could have the signs checked for fingerprints, but he wasn't sure it would be beneficial. Still, it seemed that Smythe was keen to appease the Automobile Association patrolmen, so perhaps he should.

"I can get the kit from the Wolseley," O'Rourke offered helpfully. "The camera as well."

Mason nodded to show she should do so.

As she moved back to the Wolseley, Mason became aware of a thrumming noise amongst the small number of motorcars, bicycles and buses, and turned to see the other motorbike heading off into the traffic. The other patrolman hadn't even spoken to Mason.

"Where's he going?" It wasn't that Mason had necessarily wanted to speak to the rider about the problem of the signs, but now he was curious all the same as to why the man hadn't shown such outrage as Grant.

"Just out on his route. We take it in turns to ride our circuit. Today there's three of us. The other chap, Richardson, will be back soon, and then I'll go out this evening before the blackout. Just in case someone needs our assistance and can't get to one of the sentry boxes. There aren't as many of them as you might think, and our route is extensive. It takes us into Erdington, and that's why I reported the crime there. We go all the way to Tamworth as well."

"And how long does it take you to ride your circuit?"

"About four hours, if we don't meet anyone needing our help. Then it can take much longer. We ride out in a specific order."

"Every day?" Mason asked, just to be sure. "Even on a Sunday?"

"Oh yes. Every day. We take it in turns to have Sundays off."

"So three of you, on the same route, every working day, including Saturday mornings?"

"Yes, that's how it works. Of course, before the war started, the routes used to be shorter, and there were more of us. We used to use bicycles as well. It's been a difficult few years. Many patrolmen signed up for the war efforts, and with petrol rationing, many people have simply cancelled their subscriptions. It's an expense that can be avoided when you can't drive anywhere. The government aren't about to lift rationing anytime soon. Even if there's a victory tomorrow, I think petrol rationing will continue. The government detest the everyday motorist."

Mason grunted, allowing Grant to interpret as he wanted to. It had been difficult in recent years, and not just for the members of the Automobile Association. Mason wasn't blind to the complaints about the government and motorists. But, until motorists learned to observe speed limits, he was with the government.

"So," and Mason brought the subject back to the matter at hand. "Why do you think someone meddled with the signs?" He couldn't quite explain why someone would replace the signs if they'd all been taken down, and certainly not why they'd do it in the wrong order. Unless, of course, it had been done by someone who knew it would upset the patrolmen. Perhaps it was just someone playing a prank on the meddlesome patrolman. Mason admitted even he might have been tempted, what with Grant's officious nature.

"Well, it's obvious, isn't it?"

Sam turned to face the man. His dark eyes were bright with conviction.

"Someone replaced the signs. I mean, look at this place, if you didn't know the area well, and you didn't have one of our route maps, which we can't currently give out to anyone for fear they might be one of the enemy, you wouldn't know which way to go. You might be heading for Birmingham but end up going north, towards Lichfield or even further afield. They put the signs up to stop that from happening but made a huge mistake. And to think, they might have been successful in their deception if not for making such a colossal mistake of putting the signs back up in the wrong order."

Mason wanted to dismiss the suggestion, but his eyebrows furrowed in thought. It sounded ridiculous to his ears, but perhaps it wasn't. There was a great deal of paranoia at the moment that the enemy might appear from anywhere to undermine the successes in Europe. Road signs, whatever their order, would no doubt come in handy to anyone who didn't know the area well. And here, on the outskirts of an area known for its manufacturing, Grant's suspicions might just ring true.

"So, you noticed this when?" Sam asked, pulling his notebook and pencil out from his inside pocket. His sudden interest didn't go unnoticed.

"We realised yesterday and reported it, but no one came down. Your Smythe said he'd send you today, or rather, someone like you. There was a bit of an upset as well. You might have heard." Sam nodded. He didn't want to discuss the legality of the patrolmen's desire to protect their members from the speed traps. That was for Smythe and the higher up echelons to contend with, not him.

"And do you know how long it might have been like that?"

Now Patrol Member Grant looked uncomfortable.

"Well, I can't rightly say. Montgomery and Richardson aren't the most observant, I must confess, and I've been on holiday for five days. If you can call it a holiday when you've been busy in the allotment making sure the vegetables don't get overwhelmed by the weeds. But the signs weren't up before I went on holiday. So, at the most seven days, at the least, just the two." Grant nodded, but Mason could tell it sat ill with him to have to admit to the mistake.

"Why? What are you thinking?"

"Well, I have no idea. I was just curious. If, as you suggest, it's because someone replaced the signs, then I'm intrigued as to why that would happen."

"So, what, you think the bloody Jerrys did it?" Grant asked, his thin lips tight with fury. But Sam was already shaking his head.

"I have no idea who did it. It might be some trouble-makers looking for a bit of fun. Not that climbing up there and hanging over the road sounds like much fun to me, but you never know. Tell me, how would you get up so high?"

"Well, there's never really a great need to change the signs, not unless there's some special event on in the vicinity, and there's been nothing like that for a long time. On those occasions, we might affix an additional sign or just place one in front of the sentry box." Grant paused, opened his mouth and then shut it again. "But that wasn't what you asked, was it? No, there's a small ladder we could use, stored inside the sentry box, but it wouldn't get you so high. See, I've brought along a taller one today from our new regional office because I knew we'd need to right this problem."

"Is your regional office in Birmingham?" Sam continued to pursue.

"Yes, somewhere to keep the motorbikes and our supplies, and for repairs to be carried out. We're not all allowed to keep our equipment at our home addresses. It annoys me. I have to get the tram into the city centre, only to ride back out on my motorbike again. But it doesn't matter how much I decry the inefficiency of it all. They won't be moved about the matter. It's only been six months since they opened the regional office, and it's not been an easy six months."

"I'll need the address," Mason asked.

"Of course you will," Grant couldn't entirely hide his delight that the matter was being taken seriously. "It's on Hagley Road. You can't miss it." At that moment, a thrum filled the air, and Mason turned aside from examining the sentry box, a question on his lips, only for Grant to smile in delight.

"Ah, there you go. Almost perfect timing. That'll be Montgomery back from his patrol." He raised his arm to hail the other patrolman. The man pulled his motorbike into the same space as the other motorbike and raised his arm in salute. Mason tried to pick out details of the man's face, but he seemed to be busy, checking his machine was still in good order, and his head remained bowed. Not even Grant moved to speak to him. Quickly, Mason turned aside.

Grant leaned over as though to impart something significant.

"He's a funny sort, Montgomery. He knows his stuff but doesn't enjoy the front-facing role. Sometimes it's even a struggle for him to salute the members. His wife died in the bombing two years ago. She was the one who could make him smile. I've not seen it since. No matter what. Poor sod. I pity him. But he's an excellent patrolman. He was in the Military Police Supplementary Reserve when the war started, helped with the landing of the British Expeditionary Force in France at the beginning of the war, but they brought him back after his wife died."

Sam listened attentively, but he didn't see how Montgomery's personal life was relevant to the case. Luckily, at that moment, O'Rourke arrived with the camera.

"I've brought everything you asked for." The few buses and bicycles were carefully making their way around the Wolseley eyes forward, even as Grant watched them, saluting those who displayed the Automobile Association badge on the front grill of their car. The badge was easy to see, being the bright green that had been prevalent before the war.

Mason moved to help O'Rourke with the camera and bag filled with the supplies to take fingerprints.

Grant was watching the traffic, a mild look of panic on his face as he realised O'Rourke had brought the car closer to the telephone box. Mason admitted it wasn't the best place to park the police car, but he wasn't about to suggest it was moved. They wouldn't be long, and traffic at this time of the day was light.

"I had assumed you'd just dust for prints, or whatever it is you do, once the signs were removed."

"But then we might miss something," O'Rourke smiled, despite Grant's tone, but Mason was aware that she wasn't enjoying Grant's scrutiny. Neither was he.

"We'll be fine from here on," he offered, hoping that Grant would return to his duties. But it seemed impossible.

"Here, you don't want to put it there," Grant had his hands on the wooden ladder he'd pulled from beside the sentry box. "We would always go up from here, see. There are even little marks where the ladder has leant on the sentry box before."

"Thank you, Patrolman Grant, but if you could leave us to our task now."

Grant failed to detect the iron in Mason's voice, and O'Rourke couldn't look at him. The patrolman was obviously a meddler, and Mason didn't appreciate it.

"Mr Grant," he raised his voice, as Grant still fiddled with the ladder, clearly trying to avoid some of the flowers surrounding the sentry box but succeeding only in making the ladder too short for the task.

"Chief Inspector Mason, if you'll just bear with me, I'll get up there in no time at all."

"Mr Grant," and Mason spoke even more firmly. "You asked the police to investigate, and the police are now here to do just that. If you could leave us to our task while you return to yours, this will all go far more smoothly."

Finally, Grant detected the threat in the words and blinked rapidly, meeting Mason's eyes.

"Ah, yes, of course. I'll just leave you to it. I need to check on Montgomery. Ensure the roads are clear, and he's not had to help any waylaid motorists."

Mason and O'Rourke watched Grant walk away. He took his time checking the way was clear before striding across the wide road.

"Goodness me," O'Rourke exclaimed. "What a funny man."

"You could say that," Mason countered. "Now, let's get this done and then we can leave Patrolman Grant to his duties."

With practised ease, O'Rourke shot up the ladder.

"Oh, sir, you might want to see this," she commented a short time later. Mason was holding the base of the ladder, careful to keep his eyes on the roses at his feet. He'd been distracted by the sound of a motorbike, and looked perplexed as the one that had only just arrived, left just as quickly before Grant could even so much as say hello.

Mason could hear Grant chuntering to himself, even as he resumed his salutes to the passing motorists.

"Why, what is it?"

"If you can, I think you should look," Mason felt the movement of her coming down the ladder, one sensible shoe after another. Her skirt was long, covering most of her legs down below her knees. It was a good and sensible uniform, but not for climbing ladders besides a busy crossroads.

Mason moved aside when he hoped she couldn't possibly fall and injure herself.

"What is it?" Mason asked of her, but she shook her head.

"I want you to look. Tell me what you see, without me telling you what I see."

Mason shook his head at her tongue-twisting logic but grunted his agreement all the same.

The first step up the rung of the ladder made his back hurt, and he almost changed his mind. Surely, O'Rourke could have taken a photograph, but then when he got to the top of the sentry box, he understood why she'd insisted on him seeing it.

While the signpost extended far above the roof of the sloping roof, the two sets of signs the wrong way round, as Grant had explained to them, that wasn't what concerned O'Rourke. No. Instead, it was the way the roof of the sentry box had been changed, and quite recently as well. There were some stray wood shavings and even places where the two green paint colours weren't quite the same. He could smell the fresh-cut wood as well. What intrigued him most was the fact it seemed to be the perfect hiding place for something, although what, he wasn't sure.

Mason shook his head.

"Do you see what I mean?" O'Rourke called to him.

"I do, yes. I certainly do."

CHAPTER 4

Mason passed up the items that O'Rourke needed to complete her fingerprinting, and all the while, his thoughts were far away. He'd come down the ladder quickly, having seen the adjustments that had been made.

Suddenly, he appreciated there was a war on, and abruptly, he was genuinely fearful that something untoward might be happening, and almost beneath his nose. It didn't sit well with him.

It took Mason some time to realise that Patrolman Grant had returned and was busy talking to him.

"And when you're done, I'm taking all the signs down. Better that than word getting back to head office that we have incorrect signs on our sentry box. It's all the new man in charge needs." Mason furrowed his brow. Of course, he knew that Stenson Cooke had died two years before, the man who'd been in charge of the Automobile Association since its inception, but what he couldn't quite work out was why his successor would be so concerned with this small matter in Mile Oak, miles away from London.

The men and women who worked for the organisation had far more critical things to concern themselves. They'd played an essential part in the war effort, even going so far as to be asked to retrieve the cars of those members who'd abandoned them in France in 1939 when war had been declared. Some of the stories had made it into the local and national newspapers.

Mason also knew that the local patrolmen and women had been assisting the army with their detailed knowledge of local areas.

"Tell me, where else are there sentry boxes, close to here? Is there a box number forty-one and a forty-three?" Mason had noticed the number, forty-two, on the front of the sentry box. He was sure that an organisation such as the Automobile Association would have been logical in assigning its numbers.

"Well, now. I'm afraid it doesn't work like that. Not at all. The sentry boxes all have numbers, but the numbers you're asking about aren't close by; they're in the south. Many miles from here."

"So, there aren't any other sentry boxes close by?" Now Mason thought about it, he wasn't entirely sure whether or not he knew of any others apart from this one, here, at Mile Oak. Well, maybe there was one, but he couldn't place it, not right now.

"Well, yes, there are, but not in numerical order. The one numbered one hundred and fifty-four is close to Warwick, the three hundred and thirty-five at Moxhull and the three hundred and forty-one at Appleby Fields Crossroads on the way to Ashby. Oh, wait. The seven hundred and eighty-three is also close to Warwick. Sorry, I almost forgot that one. And of course, there's the three hundred and fourteen at Beech Lanes, where the A456 meets the A4123, close to the centre of Birmingham." Sam didn't think to ask how Grant could remember the locations and the numbers. It somehow seemed only natural that he would know them.

"And these sentry boxes aren't on your route?"

"No, not those ones. Sorry. Why?" Grant thought to ask, but Mason distracted himself with helping O'Rourke as she handed back down her supplies from where she'd been seeing if there were any fingerprints left on the roof of the sentry box or on the signposts that were still up there, all be it, the wrong way round, according to Grant.

"I've finished," she announced cheerfully to Grant, but Grant hardly heard her. His gaze was fixed only on the signs.

"So," Grant eventually asked. "Do you think you'll find the

culprits?" The words sounded like a question but were more an accusation.

"We'll certainly do our best to do so," Mason assured the other man, thinking that as much as Grant annoyed him with his officious manner, if not for him, these perplexing signs wouldn't have been found at all.

"Check-in at the police station in a few days, and I'll ensure an update is left for you." Grant muttered an agreement but was already climbing the ladder to remove the offending road signs.

"And of course," and Grant said this as an afterthought. "If you could keep the regional office informed as well, that would assist me."

Mason made hurry up motions with his hands so that he and O'Rourke could be long gone before Grant thought to ask anything else, but as he walked away, Mason thought to poke his head into the now open sentry box. As he'd thought, it contained little more than a black telephone, the number written on it, Tamworth 2044. He also saw a small container, which he suspected must contain some emergency petrol for motorists and motorcyclists. He wasn't sure where the local garage was but imagined it was some distance away.

"What are you thinking?" O'Rourke asked as she successfully steered the Wolseley back onto the road to return to Erdington once she and Mason were inside. They'd left Grant trying to remove the signs, even while saluting the members who drove past. He needed to be careful, or he'd fall into his precious roses. Mason wondered whether one of the members would write to head office about Grant's antics.

"I don't really know. It could be something, but equally, it might not be."

"I think we should probably check the other sentry boxes," O'Rourke announced as Mason nodded in agreement.

"I do as well, but first, I'm going to run it by Smythe, make sure we're not barking up the wrong tree, as it were."

O'Rourke concentrated on driving carefully along the road on the way back, and Mason made a decision.

"But that one, the three hundred and thirty-five sentry box, that's almost on the way back to Erdington, at Moxhull. We should go there first, just to see if we can find anything strange."

O'Rourke's lips widened in a grin, and she expertly moved to take the road that led there. Mason wasn't entirely sure what he was thinking, but all the same, it was puzzling. More than perplexing.

In no time at all, the second camouflaged sentry box came into view before them. It was located on a quiet stretch of road, at a T-junction where it would be easy to get lost. It was straightforward to pull the Wolseley over to the side once Mason had made sure there were no patrolmen or women nearby to disturb them. In the far distance, Mason could see the new Moxhull Hall, while to the side of him were the remains of the old house, most of which had burnt down over forty years before.

This sentry box was just as elaborately fashioned like the one at Mile Oak. What it lacked in carefully placed flowers it made up for by having some sort of small wooden building on the immaculately cut grass.

"Is that a well?" he asked O'Rourke in surprise as he stepped from the car. Above, he could see that there were no road signs.

"It looks like it," O'Rourke commented, striding up the slight incline to take a good look at it.

"It's even got water in it, and the handle works," she exclaimed as she twirled the wooden handle. Mason chuckled at the surprise in her voice as a small bucket appeared from the depths of the well.

"I wish we could do up the police station in the same way," O'Rourke commented. "I'd quite like some pretty flowers and a well outside."

"I suggest you ask Smythe," Mason offered, and she rolled her eyes and shook her head so that her black braids moved and softly chimed together.

"I don't think Smythe is much for the aesthetically pleasing," she muttered, turning aside from the well to look up at the top of the sentry box.

"Do you think the roof has been changed, as at Mile Oak?"

"We'll only know that if we take a look." Mason looked around.

They had no ladder here because they'd not thought to bring one with them, and the sentry box was almost two metres tall.

"We can't climb it," he announced, annoyed at being stumped by the lack of something to stand on. It seemed that Grant had thought of everything. Sometimes, being a bit of a know it all did have its advantages.

"No, we can't, but look, there's a tree, and I can climb the first few branches and get high enough."

Mason looked at her aghast.

"I was younger once," she stated matter of factly. "I can climb trees. I imagine you used to as well." Without waiting for him to argue with her, O'Rourke moved to the lowest hanging branch on the ancient oak tree and hauled herself up. Mason shook his head, wishing she wasn't doing this on the main road and that they'd parked the car some distance away. But she quickly moved up to the next branch and then the next one and began to shuffle herself forward, on her hands and knees.

The branch moved with the action, and Mason bit back an order to get down because she cried with triumph.

"It's the same," she called.

"We'll have to come back with a ladder," Mason announced as O'Rourke stretched out.

"We will, yes. No chance of me reaching, not from here."

A honk of a horn, and Mason turned to glare at the driver of a delivery lorry who was watching them, mouth open in shock. He gave the driver his sternest look. The woman should have her eyes on the road.

"Get down, O'Rourke, before anyone else sees you up there."

"Right. Hold on, and I'll be there in a moment or two." Her voice sounded a little strained, and Mason thought it better not to watch her as she made her way back to ground level. Instead, he examined the sentry box. As with the other one, it was painted a striking camouflage green on the sides and edges, the majority of the wood black, with the organisation's emblem showing on the front. The two A's were linked but were angular, one line being used to cross both A's.

The door to the sentry box was firmly closed, but he could see where keys had been used to open the door wide. It had left a scrape in the encroaching grass, and there were some chips of paint missing from around the lock as well. For all that, the colours were fresh, if not bright. As with Patrolman Grant at Mile Oak, it seemed that the patrolmen and women who called this sentry box their own, endeavoured to keep it in good condition, despite the deprivations of the war.

A soft huff and O'Rourke appeared before him, dusting down her hands and long skirt. He noticed that her black shoes were scuffed as well. She was a little out of breath, but nothing too serious.

"Shall we just go and see the other sentry boxes?" O'Rourke asked, her enthusiasm difficult to ignore.

"No, we need to speak to Smythe about this. And get a ladder," Mason admitted reluctantly. This was undoubtedly intriguing him but, there was little point going about it with only half the resources.

"We'll come back with a ladder," he announced firmly. "Now come on. Let's get back before one of the patrol people turns up. I'm sure they must all gossip about these things, and I don't want Patrolman Grant sticking his nose in where it's not wanted."

O'Rourke looked slightly crestfallen, but then her eyes gleamed.

"Wouldn't this be something if we'd uncovered some spying activity because of this? Your name would be in the national newspapers again." And she laughed as she jumped back into the Wolseley. Mason didn't much like the thought of drawing attention to himself once more, but he was beginning to think, as O'Rourke was, that there was something mighty intriguing going on. And, he admitted, perhaps it would be good not to be known as the custard copper.

"So tell me again," Smythe demanded when Sam knocked on his door and began to explain what they'd discovered, having been beckoned to take a seat in the hard-backed wooden chair that awaited people there. Sam opened his mouth to do just that, only for Smythe to interject. His Superintendent had flushed cheeks and looked far from happy.

"So, this obnoxious Patrolman, Grant, and their flouting of the speeding laws might be on to something?" Smythe demanded. He was sitting behind his desk, but Sam was convinced that beneath the wooden desk, his feet were moving as though pacing.

Mason nodded and then grunted his agreement as Smythe didn't see his nod.

"So you went all the way to Mile Oak, and sentry box number forty-two, and then back to this box number three hundred and thirty-five. Why on earth these aren't numbered concurrently, I simply don't know," Smythe interrupted himself, a sign of his frustration. "And you found the same thing at both of them, apart from the lack of direction signs on the second one."

"But you couldn't see anything else on the top of sentry box three hundred and thirty-five?"

"No, we need to go back with a ladder."

"Then I suggest you get on with it, and if you come across the same thing, you'll have to go to the other local sentry boxes as well. I'm sure you can find them. They are quite distinctive with their little gardens and black and green paint. See if they have the same on them. I'll be damned if I know what it's all about, but I don't like it. Not at all. And certainly not when we're at war."

Mason, eager to be gone now he had the support of Smythe, was working his way back to a standing position. It was awkward. He'd been in the car for a long time that day and walking around on the uneven side of the road. It did his back no good at all.

"And the murdered man? You've had no flashes of insight as to what that might be about?" Smythe asked this with a gleam in his eye. Mason appreciated he was keen to have something to report back to Roberts and, more importantly, the Chief Superintendent.

"Not at the moment, no. I'm trying to determine what he might have been put in and why it had to be so small."

"Yes, I'm sure you are. Well, if you think of something, let me know, and I'll pass it on to Roberts. It'd be good if we helped them solve this one, as well."

Mason mumbled an agreement with his hand on the door, but his mind was on the sentry boxes. That was a mystery he felt was more in his power to solve than the identity of a dead man who had no finger-prints on record and therefore couldn't be traced that way. Smythe had shared that information with him before Mason had managed to inform him about the strange events at the sentry boxes.

In the main office, Jones remained stuck behind his pile of paperwork, his head barely visible, and Mason knew a moment of sympathy for him.

"I'll help with that tomorrow," he announced, moving as quickly as he dared to where O'Rourke was busy chatting to Constable Williams as he lingered behind the desk. She had a wooden ladder beneath her arm that had five rungs on it, and Mason bent to help her carry it.

"I'll do that," Constable Williams announced cheerfully. "It'll give me something to do. I've been quiet all day," he complained, although still with a smile on his face. "Smythe is interested in any missing person cases, but we get one of those so rarely, I'm not expecting one to arrive today just because Smythe wants one."

There was no complaint to Williams words, none at all, just a colleague sharing his thoughts about Smythe. Mason appreciated he was probably just pleased to have someone to talk to as he held the door open for him, a loud squeak of protest filling the air. O'Rourke had gone on ahead, and Mason risked a glance along the roadway, but there was no one making a beeline for the police station. The front desk would be safe for the few moments it would take Williams to load the ladder into the Wolseley.

"Has Smythe asked you for anything else?" Mason asked, curious to see how his Superintendent's mind was working.

"Only to let him know if I see those Automobile Association patrol men again, with their smart salutes. There's no speed trapping going on today because the Birmingham crew have the day off, but all the same, I think Smythe is keen to avoid them all."

"As am I," Mason confirmed, watching as Williams and O'Rourke attempted to force the short ladder into the back of the police car.

They'd not yet had time to do anything with the fingerprints they'd taken from sentry box forty-two, but Mason was inclined to think that if the prints from sentry box number three hundred and thirty-five didn't match, then they were probably looking for trouble where none existed. Mason didn't think he should be giving too much of his time to solving something that might not even be a crime with the counter-feit case to solve.

"Thank you, Constable Williams," he called to the younger man as he began to lope back towards the front desk. Even with the promise of nothing but answering the telephone and helping people who'd mislaid their purse or coat, Williams exuded eagerness, even if he didn't feel it.

"What did Smythe say?" O'Rourke asked as she pulled left onto Sutton New Road. It was long after lunchtime, and Mason realised that neither of them had thought to eat, too caught up in what was happening.

"He's desperate for me to determine who the dead man was, but he thinks we should find out if there's a connection between the two sentry boxes, all the same."

At the crossroads, O'Rourke turned right onto Chester Road, and Mason mused as he watched the landscape flash by the window. At the next crossroads, at Pype Hayes Park, O'Rourke took the turning for Walmley. Overhead, Mason could hear the thrum of the aeroplanes from the aerodrome and spared a thought for the dead man. It was a pity they didn't know who he was, where he came from, or how he came to be on the land so close to the aerodrome.

In no time at all, they arrived at sentry box number three hundred and thirty-five once more. O'Rourke pulled the car up almost onto the grassy verge, tipping the Wolseley alarmingly to one side. Mason was just about to suggest they leave the car somewhere else, but O'Rourke already had the ladder out the back of the vehicle. Mason knew when it was better to hold his tongue.

Carefully, he exited the car, making sure no cars or lorries were coming and went to join her. She was dragging the ladder onto the grass, and he bent to pick up the one end of it.

"Slow down, or you'll ruin the garden," he called to her.

"Oh, yes, sorry, Sir," but there was no repentance in the words. Mason shook his head. O'Rourke liked the thrill of the investigation as much as he did.

Carefully, they leaned the ladder against the back of the black and camouflage green sentry box, shimmering brightly beneath the bright sun because of the gloss paint, and O'Rourke rushed up the rungs before Mason could say he wanted to do it.

"It's the same," she called down to him also immediately. "They've changed the roof, so you can't tell there's anything up there, but there is. And here," and she went quiet. He could hear her huffing and puffing, but he kept his eyes firmly in front of him. The police skirts weren't designed for all this climbing. It would be better, he thought, if they allowed women to wear trousers, as the men did. "It looks as though something's been stuffed inside it, but it's not here anymore. There are some wood shavings up there as well. You can see where the work's been done. I might be wrong, but I think the paint smells quite fresh."

Just as quickly, she stood on the ground beside him, looking up at the roof of the sentry box.

Mason shook his head, forehead furrowed as he glared upwards.

"I think we need some photographs," he commented.

"I'll get the camera," O'Rourke agreed, rushing back to the Wolseley. As she went, Mason was distracted by the noise of someone huffing and puffing, footsteps sharp on the road, no doubt from some very expensively heeled shoes. He looked up and met the eyes of a startled gentleman wearing a brown hat and long coat, profusely sweating, although it wasn't that warm. It just looked it.

"I say," he called. "You're not one of the Automobile Association patrol people, are you? If you are, you should be saluting me?"

"No," Mason replied quickly, keen to disabuse the man of the notion. "The police," and he indicated the car, and O'Rourke in her smart uniform, with the same action.

"Damn and blast," the man said, his bushy eyebrows high up on his face, where they just about disappeared beneath his hat.

"Well, let's hope the telephone connection is good today. I pay all this money for the service, and now I need them." Mason didn't have a response for that. He found a smile for his face.

But the man wasn't looking at Mason. He was fumbling around in his coat pocket, muttering to himself.

"I know I put it in here before I left the car on the side of the road. Now, where is the blasted key?"

By now, O'Rourke had seen that they had company and was taking her time finding the camera.

"Is your car parked in a safe place?" Mason thought to ask as a military lorry thundered past them quite fast for all there was a tight bend coming up.

"Yes, off the road, as much as I can make it. Now, I just need to find the... Ah, here it is?" And the man pulled a bronze-coloured key from his pocket. It was no more than two inches long. Mason saw it as it caught the afternoon sunlight. He watched, intrigued, as the man inserted the key into the lock on the sentry box to swing open the top half of the stable door, and lean in to use the black telephone inside.

But Mason wasn't listening to the words the man said to the operator who answered his call, rumbling with frustration that the blasted Morris Minor had broken down on the side of the A446. He didn't hear O'Rourke asking if it was alright to take the photographs now either. No, his mind was focused on the key.

"Excuse me," Mason called to the man when he'd finished making his call and had hung up the black receiver with an only partially satisfied mutter. "Would you allow me to examine your key for a moment? I don't think I've ever seen one before." Mason offered the request with a hint of humour in his words that he certainly wasn't feeling.

"Of course, here," and the man, Mason had heard him tell the operator he was Mr Foreshaw, took the key from the lock and handed it to him. Mason was aware of O'Rourke looking at him in surprise as he turned the key end over end, running it through his fingers, testing the length of it, the image running through his mind.

"Tell me how the key works," he asked Mr Foreshaw. "If you have the time to tell me and don't mind doing so." Mason opted for deference but also firm command in his voice.

"Yes, of course, I do. I'm to wait for the next patrol person. They'll be along shortly," Mr Foreshaw sounded pleased by the news. "Members all have a key, and then we can access any of the sentry boxes. If you look at the key, it has the Automobile Association emblem on it. All a bit straight-edged for my liking, but at least you don't forget and accidentally pop it in one of the RAC sentry boxes. That wouldn't go down well. It would get stuck, and then you'd had to tell the RAC what you'd done." Mr Foreshaw guffawed as he spoke.

"So every member has one of these?" Mason pressed. He didn't know a great deal about the way the Automobile Association worked. He knew there was a subscription fee, but much beyond that, he wasn't sure about the details.

"Oh yes, and if you decide to cancel your membership, then you have to return it. Of course, with the petrol shortages, many people don't need their membership, but rather than have the company collapse, we've all continued to pay our subscriptions if we can afford to do so. It's the right thing to do. They do good work for motorists. I'm sure you know." And again, Mr Foreshaw guffawed. "You know," and he elucidated, "when people get in bother for driving too fast and that sort of thing." Mason tried not to show his disapproval.

"And what, do you have maps that show you where all the sentry boxes are?" Mason asked instead.

"Yes, yes we do. I have one in my car, and I know this route well, anyway. I know there's the one here, and there's another one a little further on as well." Mr Foreshaw pointed northwards. No doubt, Mason decided, he meant the one at Mile Oak.

"Thank you," and Mason handed the key back to Mr Foreshaw, having run his hand over the indentations on the key, gotten a feel for the shape of the key in his hand, for the lumpiness of the decoration on the rounded end of it. Mason couldn't quite believe what he was thinking, but he might just have solved what it was that had left a mark on the dead man's forehead. If nothing else, the angular letters gave it away.

But and this thought consumed him, why would the man have the markings of one of the Automobile Association keys impressed on his forehead?

CHAPTER 5

After Mr Foreshaw had returned to his beleaguered Morris Minor, having locked the sentry box once more, O'Rourke quickly took the required photographs. And although the wind had begun to pick up, making it almost impossible, had also checked for fingerprints.

Mason hadn't told O'Rourke of his suspicions, but once they were back in the car, she turned to him.

"What have you discovered?" Her voice filled with impatience. Mason shook his head, thinking it was strange how quickly she'd learned to read his moods.

"A key? I believe it was one of the keys imprinted on the forehead of the dead man."

"One of the Automobile Association keys?" O'Rourke sounded incredulous, but Mason was nodding vigorously.

"Yes, the shape was similar. I'm sure of it. Little was truly visible, but I believe if we compared it, we'd see that the angular Automobile Association emblem was discernible as an impression on the skin."

"Well, I never," O'Rourke drove carefully along the road, and they quickly passed Mr Foreshaw and his broken-down Morris Minor. Mason was pleased to see it wasn't an open-top car. He could scent rain in the air, and he didn't know how long it might take the patrol person to reach Mr Foreshaw. But still, he had places to be, and it wasn't his job to stop beleaguered motorists who probably shouldn't be out on the road anyway.

The wooden ladder, now returned to the car, was making a racket in the back, but they needed it to investigate the other sentry boxes that were local to them, to see if there was indeed something strange going on or not.

"Where are we headed now?" O'Rourke asked, coming to a junction.

"It's not as close as I'd like, but Beech Lanes, or number three hundred and fourteen. You can head back the way we came from Erdington, and then we'll drive through the centre of Birmingham."

O'Rourke bit her bottom lip with concentration and then slowly pulled out onto the road. Mason was thinking hard.

"Maybe, if we have time, we can even go to the regional office of the Automobile Association in Birmingham. They might lend us a key so that we can try out the theory."

"And what reason would you give them? Can you lend me a key so I can see if a dead man has it on his forehead?" She flicked her eyes towards him, incredulous, but Mason nodded.

"Probably not the wisest to say that. I'll just say that we want to do some investigating into these mixed up signs."

"And do you think they'll just give you one?"

"I am a police officer," Mason stated, but perhaps O'Rourke was correct to worry. "Either that or we'll have to ask Patrolman Grant, and I don't much want him to know that we're taking his concerns even more seriously than he might think. He strikes me as the sort of character who'll come into the police station every day for an update and will insist on telling us every little thing he sees that concerns him. I'm all for people being suspicious, but some people think the milk being delivered late is cause for trouble."

O'Rourke lapsed into silence as she negotiated the flow of traffic.

"But why?" she eventually asked. "And more importantly, where?"

"I have no idea as to the why or the where. A small space with a key on the ground. But what that small space would have been, I've no idea."

They travelled in silence until Mason spied the sentry box ahead.

"There it is," he called, noting that it was almost identical to the sentry box at Mile Oak but that it wasn't entirely on a crossroads. However, the road layout was complicated enough, with one road leading to Wolverhampton and the other towards Edgbaston and the centre of Birmingham.

"We should park up there," and Mason pointed to a residential road. "Better to be off the main road." With the number of buses using the route, Mason thought it wise to avoid them altogether. Smythe wouldn't be pleased if they lost one of the wing mirrors or had a bash on the side. Smythe liked everything to look smart and to be well-cared.

"Shall we take the ladder with us?" O'Rourke asked. Mason could understand why. This sentry box was in a far more built-up area than the two they'd already visited. They might well get asked what they were up to, and yet, they'd come all this way through the slightly heavier traffic of the end of the school and working day, for many people.

"Yes, and the camera, just in case. I'll carry it," Mason offered, but O'Rourke was already hauling it out the back of the Wolseley.

"You can take the camera," she offered brightly. Mason knew better than to argue with her.

Quickly, they walked towards the sentry box, O'Rourke being careful not to knock anyone with the ladder.

Mason glanced at it, noting the sentry box was number three hundred and fourteen.

"There's no logic to these numbers," he complained to himself. Just like Smythe, he couldn't understand the numbering system they'd employed.

The sentry box was locked up tightly, the camouflage green and black paintwork just as bright as at Mile Oak and Moxhull, although there was no attempt to plant flowers here or even to have small ornaments. Still, the grass was cut, and it looked tidy enough.

Quickly, O'Rourke angled the ladder against the wood of the box and scrambled upwards. Mason nodded to a few passers-by. He pursed his lips as he stepped smartly to avoid a young girl wobbling along on her peddle cycle. A slightly older child rushed past as well.

"Be careful, Maud, or you'll be in the road, and mother will have something to say to me."

Mason shook his head. Why they were practising on the main road when they had not one but three local parks to choose from, he really didn't know.

Behind the older girl came a young woman pushing a large pram. And he swerved to avoid the black contraption from which querulous grumbling could be heard.

"Oh," he heard the disappointment in O'Rourke's voice and knew that there was nothing to be seen here.

"Nothing?" he called, just to be sure.

"Nothing at all. There's no sign of the roof being reconfigured."

"Hum," Mason wasn't sure what to make of that. Again, he examined the area. It was, he realised, filled with residential homes. He supposed it was a bit like having a sentry box on the confluence with Sutton New Road and Tyburn Road in Erdington. It was difficult not to know which way to go there.

O'Rourke joined him back on the ground, disappointment on her young face.

"Too busy," Mason offered. "Too busy to alter and hope no one noticed." He continued when O'Rourke gave him a perplexed look. "Homes didn't surround those other two boxes. In fact, the last one was almost deserted. I don't even know if anyone is living in the fire-damaged Moxhull Hall anymore. It was probably too much of a risk to make any changes here."

O'Rourke tilted her head from side to side, considering his words carefully.

"Perhaps," she eventually admitted, but she still sounded unhappy with the assumption.

"We'll go to the Hagley Road offices of the Automobile Association, ask for a key. I'm curious to see what's inside the sentry boxes as well as if it is the imprint of one of the keys on the face of the dead man. I might even ask them if anyone's been reported missing of late. It could be as simple as one of the patrolmen who's been killed."

"But why?"

"No idea, but if we could identify the body, we might stand a chance of discovering that."

O'Rourke mumbled an agreement as they collapsed the ladder and made their way back to the Wolseley. It wasn't satisfactory, but Mason couldn't help but think he had two strange occurrences on his hands. He didn't think they'd be connected, not at all, and yet, it was worth pursuing, especially if he found an answer for Smythe, who could, in turn, inform the Chief Superintendent.

It wasn't far to the Automobile Association office on Hagley Road from sentry box number three hundred and fourteen. They didn't even need to move from the main road. Mason eyed the building as O'Rourke attempted to find somewhere to park. The Plough and Harrow hotel seemed to take up much of the room on the main road, but then Mason spied a large area to the rear of the building.

They drove to the barrier blocking the way, and Mason expected O'Rourke to have no problems gaining admittance. But despite the police car and the prominent police uniform that O'Rourke wore, the patrolman on duty didn't seem keen to allow them entry.

"You can't come in here," the man complained through O'Rourke's open window. "This is for 'official' Automobile Association vehicles only."

"We're here on 'official' police business," Mason said to the man, his tone as officious as his. But still, the barrier remained down.

Frustrated, Mason opened the car door and got out, calling over his shoulder loud enough for the man to hear, "Come on, O'Rourke. If we're not allowed inside, we'll just leave the Wolseley here."

The patrolman, an older man, who seemed shrunken inside his smart uniform, complete with his steel cap, even here, looked aghast as O'Rourke ventured out of the car as well. Mason turned to watch him, scrutinising the play of emotions over the man's face.

"Alright, if you're going to be like that about it," the man said in a rich Brummie accent, "I'll just have to allow you entry, won't I?" He didn't seem pleased, but O'Rourke flashed Mason a grateful look and crouched back behind the steering wheel. Mason went to join her but then paused.

"Tell me, is this where all the local patrol people come to each day?" He asked the man instead. He was in the process of swinging open the camouflage green and black striped gateway.

"Some of 'em," the man offered, his tone sullen, his accent somehow even more pronounced. "They only relocated here about six months ago. Not everyone is as keen to have a central meeting place as others."

"So, you know most people?" Mason persisted.

"I might, yes. Why? What's it to you? Are you just here to complain about the patrolmen and women and their salutes?" Defiance in the words almost had Mason smiling, but he held on to his severe demeanour.

"Anyone missing, of late?" Mason had decided this man on the gate might just stand more chance of knowing than whoever was inside, managing the patrol personnel.

"No. Well, apart from those who've gone off to war. I can account for everyone else. I've seen them all in the last few days. I stand here, and I wave them in, and then I wave them out again. Most of them arrive with a pedal bicycle and then leave with an RSO."

"RSO?" Mason asked, confused by the initials.

"Roadside Service Outfit," the man said condescendingly. Mason nodded. "My thanks," he said, ducking back inside the car, now that the gate mechanism had been wound open.

"My thanks," O'Rourke called jauntily, in defiance of the guard's ill-temper, driving through quickly, only to stamp on her brakes.

There were many motorbikes and sidecars stationed just inside the gateway, and where there weren't motorbikes, there were bicycles and even a handful of lorries. The majority of them were painted with the same green camouflage and black detailing, although not all of them. A few, it seemed, had missed being repainted, and their almost too bright green colour shone brightly.

"Wow," O'Rourke breathed. Mason had to admit to some surprise as well. With rationing as it was, he wasn't expecting there to be quite so many motorbikes available. Two men with oil-stained hands glared at the car before indicating they should pull up in front of a wide-open garage door, inside which Mason could see equipment needed to keep the fleet of vehicles in good condition.

"Did old Fergus let you inside?" the first man demanded to know. He was holding an oily wrench as Mason exited the car again, and he looked far from friendly in his oil-stained overalls, not at all the smart uniform that Mason was becoming used to seeing on the patrolmen.

"Yes, he did, and I'd thank you for stopping waving that about in such a threatening manner. We're here on official police duty. Now, how do we get inside your offices?"

"Why, what's it to do with you? Any legal matters should be telephoned through to Fanum House. You can't come here, causing a fuss. It's the head office lot who'll deal with all the complaints from the police."

"This isn't a speeding matter," Mason commented, surprised at seeing such resentment to the appearance of the police. Most of the time, and even when he didn't want it, the arrival of a police officer occasioned respect from just about everyone.

"Then there's no need for you to be here," the other man commented. He was younger but missing much of his hair, where his skin was puckered and red. The youngster had been burned at some point. No doubt allowed to leave whichever military service he'd been a member of because of them. Mason noticed how he kept his one hand covered with a long sleeve, although the other arm was bare, his sleeve bunched over the elbow. He stood a little straighter and then regretted it.

"It won't take me long if you could just show me where the door is." Mason bit back his 'please.' He was a chief inspector. These men needed to show him some regard. But for a long moment, he didn't think they were going to do so. Only then Fergus appeared, coming from the other side of the building that faced the main road.

"Mr Wheelwright says he'll see you in his office. Follow me."

So, Fergus had made a hasty beeline inside, even as he'd dragged his feet about allowing them access to the service area. Mason shook his head. It wasn't as though he'd come to do anything other than ask for some help. He was almost pleased he wasn't about to demand answers to some outrage and take them to task for the speed trap that had been placed along the Tyburn Road.

Mason and O'Rourke followed Fergus, who stopped at the bottom of a short flight of cement steps.

"Up there and through the door. The receptionist is waiting for you."

"My thanks," Mason muttered, even though his heart wasn't in it.

Craning his head back, he looked up and saw a large Automobile Association badge above the revolving door. It, too, had been painted in camouflage green, and yet, the black letters of the two 'A's, as angular and slanting as they were, only made him all the more convinced that he was right in thinking it was that shape imprinted on the dead man's forehead.

"Good day," stepping inside, he removed his hat as he spoke to the receptionist. She was watching him with cold eyes, iron-grey hair held back in a severe bun that did nothing to draw the attention away from her lined and wrinkled face. She was well into her fifties, of that, he was sure. She watched him just as carefully as he observed her.

"Mr Wheelwright is a very busy man," she exclaimed. Behind her, Mason could see a collection of men and women busy typing, filling and sealing envelopes for posting contained within an area that this woman clearly had control over. It seemed very busy.

"Well, I'm pleased he could make time to speak to me on such a simple matter," Mason offered, hoping the sarcasm wasn't too evident in his tone.

"Follow me," the woman barked, without introducing herself, and Mason found his feet doing just that, as much as he'd have liked to take his time. He was curious as to what the men and women behind the desk were doing. He could see that there were four typewriters, but only two of them were being used.

She led them across an open expanse of wooden floorboards before stopping in front of a dark wooden door and knocking with a peremptory tone. O'Rourke rolled her eyes at Mason at the actions, but quickly they were welcomed inside.

As expected, the door led into a pleasant office. Perhaps not on a scale of the one at the custard factory they'd been inside a few months ago, but certainly charming enough.

Behind the desk, and now standing, was a tall man with a full head of brown hair and sharp eyes behind small glasses perched on a broad nose. It wasn't easy to tell his age, but Mason quickly decided the man carried his years lightly. Either that, or he'd been excused from war duty for some other reason that wasn't immediately identifiable. He couldn't see that managing the regional office of the Automobile Association would place him in a reserved occupation, but Mason had known stranger things.

"Thank you, Bettie," Mr Wheelwright called, and the sharp snick of the door closing informed them all of what Bettie thought of being dismissed in such a way.

"Good day, and please accept my apologies for your hostile welcome. It really isn't our way of doing things, but it's all so new, and everyone is keen to protect what they see as 'their' ground. Now, how can I help you?"

For a moment, Mason doubted all of his assumptions to date but decided as he was there, he'd ask all the same.

"A strange thing. I was hoping we might be able to borrow one of the keys to your sentry boxes. I believe, in some small way, it might help me solve a case I'm working on."

"Oh," a flurry of confusion crossed Mr Wheelwright's face at the pleasantly given request. "I'm sure that wouldn't be a problem. You can probably keep the key we give you. It's perhaps good if you can access the sentry boxes. I would have thought you might have already had a key, being the police?" Wheelwright asked the question with one of his brown eyebrows arched high into his hairline.

Mason didn't answer the question about the key. It seemed evident to him that if they had one, they wouldn't be here, now, asking the question.

"The Army does have keys. I'm sure you know that. It's good for the association to help the war effort. But of course, you must keep the key safely locked up if you don't use it. The Government has been very strict about our keys, maps and road signs. They're all secured here, away from anyone who might think to use them for nefarious reasons. As much as we bash heads with our government about motorcar privileges, for now, that's all forgotten about."

Mason wasn't surprised to hear that. It made him question the signposts being on display all over again. If what Mr Wheelwright said was true, then the signs at Mile Oak shouldn't even be there, let alone on show.

"So tell me, the keys open every sentry box in the country?" This was what he wanted to know.

"Well, yes, they do. All the ones for the Automobile Association, anyway. The Royal Automobile Club has been very slow to agree to combining our resources there. But that's not for you to know." Mr Wheelwright spoke as though sharing a great secret with them and one he was enjoying sharing. It seemed there was no love lost between the two motoring organisations.

"A bit of a bother sometimes, the keys, when people don't pay their two-guinea subscriptions but keep the keys all the same, and then think to call us when they break down. I mean, if they can't afford their two guineas, then how are they keeping their motorcar or motorbike running?" Mason opened his mouth to speak, but Mr Wheelwright barrelled right on, toying with a gold pen in his right hand.

"Our membership has plummeted during the war years. I probably shouldn't share as much with you, but well, if it's not common knowledge by now, I'd be surprised. We had over half a million members at the beginning of the war. We don't have anywhere near that number at the moment. And our staff? Well, we have so few patrol people these days it's a wonder we can keep on with the limited day-light hours' service we can provide."

"But of course, I was going to say that our coverage doesn't extend to everywhere in the country. Not yet. We only encompass some of the routes. Much of Wales has no coverage, and neither does the north. I mean, Newcastle does, but not the nearby hills. You can get to Edinburgh as well. There are a few boxes up there. I forget the names and places." Mr Wheelwright spoke with some regret.

"When this blasted war is over, it's to be hoped we can get on with the progress we started before the war. More coverage, a comprehensive road numbering system, that sort of thing. If our motorists are to enjoy the freedom of the open road, then they need an open road to drive upon."

Mason nodded along as he examined Mr Wheelwright's desk. It was mostly covered with some expensive paperweights, paper holders, and just two metal trays to the right of Mr Wheelwright. Like most managers, it seemed that Mr Wheelwright did as little as possible. No doubt, Bettie really knew what was happening here and directed her manager as she felt he needed to be.

"I'll ask Bettie to get you one of the keys. She might insist on you bringing the key back when you've finished with it. But don't worry about that. Is there a particular sentry box you need access to? I've heard whispers about some problems with box forty-two over at Mile Oak. Is this related, or is Patrolman Grant just making a big fuss, again." A look of exasperation crossed Mr Wheelwright's face as he spoke. It seemed Grant was known for his annoying nature.

"I have been to box forty-two, yes, but this is unrelated. Something that struck me while I was talking to Patrolman Grant. Hopefully, it won't amount to anything. But tell me, how many sentry boxes are close by, say, within thirty miles of here?"

"I wouldn't know just like that." Mr Wheelwright grimaced as he spoke, revealing a selection of teeth that were jagged and had gaps between them. No doubt that was why Mr Wheelwright grew the thick moustache over his lips.

"I know there's number three hundred and fourteen. Just follow Hagley Road to the west, and you'll come across it. Closer to Warwick, we have a few sentry boxes, and towards the east, as well. Again, Bettie will have those details to hand. She used to be one of the switchboard operators at Fanum House in London. I'm lucky to have her," but the half-smile Mr Wheelwright wore didn't quite ring true. Maybe he wasn't that pleased to be saddled with someone who knew his role better than he did.

"I'll escort you out, and we can find out along the way. As you know, we've not been here long, just over six months now, and I confess to not being an expert on the local area. With the petrol rationing, I'm trying not to spend too much time in the car, driving around." He spoke quickly, as though the argument was well-rehearsed. Mason nodded along with him.

"And just one final thing," Mason asked as Mr Wheelwright moved to push his chair back so he could stand. "Can you tell me, are all your patrol people accounted for?"

"What?" Mr Wheelwright asked, slumping back into his chair, his eyebrows furrowed.

"Do you know if everyone has been reporting for their shifts in the last, say, seven days? There's no one missing or anything like that?"

Mr Wheelwright shook his head, his forehead wrinkled in thought, lips pursed. He'd picked up the pen once more and was passing it between his fingers. Mason thought he probably spent quite a bit of time doing that.

"Not that I've been made aware of, no. Come on. We'll ask Bettie as well. Perhaps you should have arranged to speak with her, and not me, after all." Mr Wheelwright forced a bark of laughter, but it ended on a cough that had him fumbling for his chair once more. Mason looked around for something to drink, but it was O'Rourke who found the glass and splashed water into it from a waiting jug. Mr Wheelwright took the glass eagerly, taking careful sips while he recovered.

"Sometimes my chest plays up, apologies," he eventually gasped, making to stand again.

"Take your time," Mason all but ordered him. "Bettie needs to hear from you what information she's to provide." Mr Wheelwright nodded, closing his eyes as he focused on breathing evenly. Mason shared a look with O'Rourke. Mr Wheelwright didn't sound well, but it was impossible to know what ailed him. It could be anything from an injury sustained in the Great War to smoking too many cigarettes. There was undoubtedly an ashtray on the desk, although it was clear of any ash or discarded cigarettes. It could just be for show.

Mr Wheelwright settled back into his chair while Mason glanced out the window. Down below was a view of the yard where O'Rourke had left the Wolseley. Mason studied the assortment of motor bicycles and trucks down there. O'Rourke scribbled something in her notebook, the sound of the pencil moving over paper a reassurance that even though the mystery of the dead man seemed chaotic, there was order to be found in careful record keeping.

Eventually, Mr Wheelwright cleared his throat.

"Right, I feel better now. Come on. Let's see if Bettie can help you."

They walked once more to the large desk area, behind which a handful of people were busily typing or filling envelopes. Bettie didn't attempt to hide her curiosity. She watched them as they made their way from Mr Wheelwright's office to stand before her. Mason met her eyes and didn't flinch away from the stern look on her tight face. Perhaps it was caused by Mr Wheelwright's coughing, which must have been heard here, but he doubted it. Bettie was a fierce woman. It would account for why none of the other employees so much as looked up at the sound of footsteps.

"Ah, Bettie," Mr Wheelwright began, his voice just about recovered although he sounded a little hoarse.

"Can you assist Chief Inspector Mason with his queries, please? I'm afraid they're a bit more about the day to day business than I can answer." Mr Wheelwright offered this with a tight smile, and Bettie bowed her chin just a little. "He'll also need to borrow one of the sentry box keys. I've said it's perfectly acceptable. I do think the local police should have access to the boxes."

"Of course, Sir," she stated, no inflexion to her voice. "Now, what else can I help you with?" Again, the piercing eyes met Mason's.

"Can you tell me the numbers and locations of all your sentry boxes in, say, a fifteen-mile radius of this office? As I've been explaining to Mr Wheelwright, I'm aware of three of that number – Mile Oak, Moxhull and the one just down the road from here, three hundred and fourteen, I think, but I'm sure there must be many more."

This request caused Bettie's eyebrows to rise into her hairline. It was clear that she'd not been expecting such a question.

"Of course," she offered quickly, hands busy on the desk below her.

"Before the war, we'd have had a map on the wall, but these days, we keep the details under lock and key during the night, when they're not needed."

"So, you have no patrols working in the evenings?"

"No, none at all, and head office don't have anyone on the telephone exchange then, either. Of course, people should be at home during blackout times. If you're out and about and you break down, then members are welcome to take what aid they can from the sentry boxes, but there'll be no one available until the sun rises and the blackout ends."

Mason nodded, turning to O'Rourke to make sure she was writing all this down. She was, of course, and he flashed her a grateful smile.

"I'll just head back to my office," Mr Wheelwright wheezed dramatically. "If you need anything else, please do ask for me."

"My thanks for your assistance," Mason offered and then remembered. "And Bettie is to answer my questions about the patrol personnel as well, isn't she?"

"Yes, yes, Bettie, tell the Chief Inspector everything he needs to know." The words were cast over his shoulder, but Mason was watching Bettie. Her head had dipped behind the desk while searching for the information on the sentry boxes, but he saw her stiffen, all the same.

He doubted it was anything more than concern for Mr Wheelwright. But all the same, he couldn't help but be a little suspicious of her, although what she might have to hide, he didn't know.

"Ah, here we are," and Bettie produced a folded map. "It'll be easier if we look on the table. Come round here," and she moved to open up a part of the long wooden desk that allowed entry and exit.

Inside the hub of the office, there was more room than Mason expected.

Bettie noticed his appraisal.

"There should be at least double the number of people, if not triple. The war has had a terrible impact on subscriptions, and we're not currently allowed to answer any requests for route plans. Even for people who are members and have been for many years. These days it's better to have a copy of a map yourself than ask the Automobile Association." Mason could hear the disapproval of such a limitation in Bettie's voice.

But as she spoke, Bettie spread out a large map on the table before them. Mason noted it looked very similar to any normal road map, but on this one, he could see numbers inside small boxes, which he assumed represented the sentry boxes.

"So, fifteen miles," Bettie scrunched up her face. Mason was impressed that no one else in the office had paused their work to watch what was happening. The sharp clacking of typewriter keys rang out, as did the soft murmur of people working together on projects.

"There are quite a few of them, but out on the smaller roads, where it's much easier to get lost than when travelling into Birmingham itself. I think almost all roads lead into the centre, and if you do get lost, it's easier to follow the trams and buses than ask for directions," Bettie offered, her eyes remaining fixed on the map before her.

"So here, I assume, is one of the sentry boxes you've already discovered?" Bettie was pointing to number three hundred and fourteen.

"Yes, we went there on the way here," Mason confirmed.

"Yes, of course," Bettie mused. She was trailing her finger along the map, but Mason could easily see where the numbers were. Still, he stayed silent. He didn't think that Bettie would appreciate being told he could do it quickly enough himself.

"So, you've been to forty-two and three hundred and thirty-five. I would add numbers four hundred and fifty-one to that. It's on the A47, to the east of Coleshill, and number ninety-two, where the A458 and A449 meet, towards Stourbridge. At a place called Stewponey."

Mason was aware of O'Rourke scribbling in her notebook as he eyed the map before him.

"There is no order to the numbers," he mused absentmindedly.

"It drives me a bit batty," Bettie advised, conspiratorially with him, which surprised him.

He found a smile but continued to look at the map.

"As you say, there aren't many close to Birmingham itself, are there?"

"No, it's the way. They try and go for places where there's little or no information available. Around here, you could ask just about anyone, and they'd be able to help."

"Now, if you go say, up to thirty miles away, you can add S thirty-three, in Hampton on Arden. That's on the A45, number four hundred and thirty-four, Mappleborough crossroads, which is where the A435 meets the B4095, and six hundred and thirty-six to the north-west at Calley crossroads, where the A5 meets the A449 to your list."

Now Mason stared at her, his forehead furrowed.

"I don't know where the 'S' came from either. But it's there, so we have to use it, because even more confusingly, there is a sentry box number thirty-three in Yorkshire, on the A1. We used to have to be very careful when taking telephone calls from either of those sentry boxes not to direct our patrol personnel to the wrong one."

Mason pursed his lips. Ideally, he'd have liked to take the map away but appreciated that it probably wasn't going to be possible.

"Did you get all the roads?" he asked O'Rourke, aware it was confusing with so many road numbers and sentry box numbers flying around.

"Yes, thank you, Sir," O'Rourke answered quickly. She was also peering at the map, squinting as she did so.

"It is the intention, when this war is over, that no one need travel more than fifteen miles in any direction without being able to call for assistance," Bettie spoke with pride. Mason had to admit he was impressed.

"Thank you," he said once more as Bettie began to fold up the map. She clutched it tightly to her chest, and Mason snapped down on his request to borrow the map.

"Now, can you tell me, are any of your patrol people missing? Have they all reported for their duties, as they should?"

Bettie's eyed widened at the request, and Mason could tell that she was burning with curiosity, but equally, she seemed to know better than to ask, just as he refrained from asking for her map.

"I'll just check with my payroll clerk. He'll know—just a moment. You're lucky to have caught him. He'd been queueing at the bank for the weekly notes and coins for the best part of two hours. The poor man. He's quite exhausted by it all."

And Bettie walked through the organised chaos of her office until she rounded a corner, where she could be seen bending her head as she spoke with someone.

"There are not as many sentry boxes as I thought there would be," O'Rourke mused.

"No, not if we've already visited three of the five close ones. Still, we should probably see if they've been tampered with so that we'll know to dismiss the idea from our minds if nothing untoward has been seen."

"Chief Inspector Mason," Bettie was back, a triumphant gleam on her face. "I can tell you that everyone has attended for their duties, as they should. There are no discrepancies with the pay this week. Mr Jameson has calculated the wages for payment on Thursday already. Now, is that all?" She held out her hand to place one of the brass-coloured keys into it as she spoke.

Mason would have liked to ask many more questions, but for the time being, he had his Automobile Association key to show the pathologist, and he had his list of local sentry boxes, if not a map showing them all. There was little else for which he could linger.

"Yes, thank you for your assistance."

"Very well," and Bettie turned aside and dismissed them immediately.

Mason and O'Rourke walked towards the door and down the handful of steps, but neither spoke, too caught up in their thoughts.

CHAPTER 6

"Is Doctor Lucey available?" Mason asked when his knock on the mortuary door was answered by the older man they'd seen the day before.

The man eyed them, recognition sparking on his face and almost smiled.

"He is, yes, but he's in the middle of a case. Do you want to wait? It won't be more than twenty minutes?"

The astringent smell from inside the mortuary assaulted Mason's nose.

"Yes, that's probably for the best," he admitted. "But first," and he pulled the Automobile Association sentry box key from his pocket. "Ask Doctor Lucey if he thinks this might have left the mark on our unknown man's head."

The man did a double-take as he reached out to grip the key. His mouth fell open a little as he met Mason's eyes for confirmation.

"I know, but I'm curious, all the same."

"I'm sure Doctor Lucey will speak to you about it in a few minutes," the man acknowledged before closing the door and walking away.

"Right, let's wait outside," Mason stated.

"That's fine with me, but I'm going to see if I can find us a cup of tea from somewhere," O'Rourke offered quickly. "There must be a canteen on the floor above us. I saw some steps."

"I'll be outside," Mason confirmed, keen to be away from the sharp smell of bleach that seemed to permeate everything.

Outside, the day was moving on quickly, but it was still warm, and the sun was only just starting to descend towards the west. Mason's mind was absorbed with the identity of the dead man. If the key he'd borrowed from Bettie could be matched to the mark on the man's head, it didn't help at all with finding out who he was. If anything, it just made it even more mysterious.

While the sentry box tampering made it clear that someone was up to no good, it still made little sense. Yes, of course, he admitted it could be something to do with the enemy, perhaps with spies, but that didn't seem to fit, not with the recent news. Only that day, the local newspaper had run the headline, 'British Tanks racing into Holland.' No. Whatever the tampering was about, Mason didn't believe it was anything to do with the war effort. But the war efforts were perhaps making it easier for whatever was happening.

"Here you go, Sir," O'Rourke spoke from behind, offering him a white china cup with a murky substance contained inside it.

He looked from her to the cup, and she grimaced.

"The tea-lady assured me it was tea, but she wasn't prepared to tell me how often the leaves had been used. I would say for quite some time." All the same, O'Rourke drank with some relish.

"I put a spoonful of sugar in for you. No biscuits, so the sugar will have to do. At least," and now she looked worried. "I hope it was sugar."

Mason smirked, lifted his mug to his lips and took a tentative sip. It tasted better than it looked, and it was scoldingly hot.

"Thank you," he offered, but O'Rourke was looking at something over his shoulder.

Mason turned and met the perplexed expression of Doctor Lucey. He was holding the sentry box key in his hand and shaking his head from side to side.

"How on earth did you know it was an imprint of one of these keys?" Doctor Lucey sounded almost excited, and Mason found it preferrable to the disdainful tone the pathologist had used last time they'd spoken.

"By chance," Mason admitted. "But tell me, is it possible that's what it is?"

"Not possible, but definite. I'm sure it was the angular 'A's that allowed you to make the connection, and you're absolutely right." Doctor Lucey was shaking his head in wonder.

"I don't suppose it tells you any more about who he might have been?"

"Not at this time, no. And it doesn't explain the position he was in, either, does it?" Mason persisted.

"No, but I would think he was lying on the key, after he'd been killed, to make such a mark. When he was already dead, but perhaps, not for very long. The indentation is visible, clearly, but if he'd lain on it for a long period, it would have left a much deeper imprint on his forehead, and we would have been able to tell what it was right from the beginning."

Mason was nodding. He'd thought the same, but it was better if the pathologist confirmed the details for him.

"But of course, there are no doubt hundreds, if not thousands of these keys," Doctor Lucey continued.

"I've just been told they once had a membership of over half a million, so yes, many thousands of keys."

"So, some help, but not a great deal," Doctor Lucey continued, although his excitement hadn't dimmed.

"No, not really," Mason agreed.

"And of course," here, O'Rourke spoke up. "It doesn't mean there's not a connection with the aerodrome. If the army has access to the sentry boxes, then I don't see why the Royal Air Force wouldn't."

Mason fixed O'Rourke with his eyes.

"You make an excellent point," Mason admitted, sipping from his rapidly cooling tea.

"Thank you for confirming that fact for me," Mason held out his hand to take back the key.

"Not a problem. Now, if you could come back to me with more

than just a key, I'd appreciate it," Doctor Lucey offered, but there was no expected sting to his words as he turned aside.

Mason didn't watch him walk away, instead finishing his tea.

"I'll take them back," O'Rourke offered, "and find you at the Wolseley."

"Fine," Mason agreed, turning to walk back through the hospital. O'Rourke moved quickly in front of him, but he could feel his leg and back twinging and so slowed down, the key clasped in his hand.

Mason shook his head as he walked. He'd found an answer to only one part of the mystery, and he didn't know how he would find the rest of the solutions.

O'Rourke managed to arrive at the car before him and was already running the engine. He laboured to get into the seat, and she looked at him sympathetically.

"Have you got time to visit this other box, ninety-two? It seems silly to drive back to Erdington Police Station only to have to come back again tomorrow, but I do appreciate it's getting late, and we've had a long day already."

"Yes, that's not a problem, Sir," O'Rourke replied quickly. "But you'll have to give me directions. I don't know the west of Birmingham at all well."

"I think it'll be easy enough to find. Just take the A458 towards Stourbridge." Mason offered and then realised that it wasn't constructive. "I'll direct you. Just go back the way we came from the last sentry box," he quickly stated. "It's about ten miles each way from here. I know, it's stretching our rations, but all the same. Now we know there might be a military connection, I think we must check. And better us than asking the Automobile Association patrol personnel. We don't want any rumours starting up. Well, no more anyway."

O'Rourke kept alert as they drove. Mason noted the sentry box which had offered them nothing out of the ordinary on the right-hand side, and then they continued along the road. Around them, the expanse of the countryside grew for some time before it once more became urban, and then he noted the familiar sight of a sentry box on the side of the road at Stewponey.

It was quiet on the road and easy enough to park just beside the sentry box.

"There's no directions on this one, either, just as Grant and Mr Wheelwright stated."

"No, it's just there, with the word 'phone' written on the door," O'Rourke confirmed.

"Still, we should take a look, and it'll give me the perfect opportunity to have a look inside one of the boxes without being watched."

O'Rourke chuckled as she pulled the ladder from the back of the Wolseley.

"I didn't think you'd be able to stop yourself," she said, a hint of amusement in her voice.

"Well, I knew I wouldn't be able to," Mason agreed, the key already in his hand.

This sentry box was just as well-tended as the others they'd visited that day. The paint was fresh enough, the camouflage colour almost mingling with the black of the central part of the box. In time, Mason was sure the camouflage green would be replaced with the bright green he was so used to seeing.

"It works," he called to O'Rourke, surprised by the excitement in his voice as he slipped the key into the lock and turned it.

"Didn't you think it would?" she asked with amusement.

"Well, I suppose, I wasn't convinced that it would," Mason admitted.

"Here, help me with this." O'Rourke moved to position the ladder around the rear of the box, where it was overlooked by nothing other than a field ripe with wheat and waiting to be harvested. Mason paused for a moment, reminded of how simple such things as growing and harvesting food were. One day, he knew, the war would be over, and everything would be as it was. But that time hadn't come, not yet.

"Up you go," he stated to O'Rourke, and she scampered up the ladder while he kept his eyes level with the sentry box. It didn't take long for her disappointed words to reach him.

"Nothing here, either. It's the same as the other one, three hundred and fourteen. There's no sign of anything being changed."

"So, it's just number forty-two at Mile Oak and three hundred thirty-five at Moxhull, so far, that have been changed, both to the east of Birmingham," Mason mumbled to himself. He felt O'Rourke coming down the ladder and moved aside when she was in no danger of falling over.

He moved to the front of the sentry box and opened the door. The top half of the door came open, and he gazed at the equipment before him. There was the black telephone with the black and white dial and the number written on its centre. Lower down, when he unhitched the stable door, was a container that he kicked to ensure it contained some petrol. It did. But then his eyes caught on something else inside the sentry box, and he bent to pick it up and unfold it.

"I wouldn't expect to see this here," he said to O'Rourke, who'd come up behind him.

"What?" she asked and then gasped on seeing what he had in his hand.

"A map showing all the sentry boxes?" her eyes bulged with shock. "Just like the one Bettie was so protective about."

"All that secrecy at their regional command, and there's one, here, just like that." As he spoke, he folded the map carefully and then put it in his pocket.

"I'm not leaving it here," he confirmed. "Firstly, it'll be useful for us, but secondly, it shouldn't be here, I'm sure of it. The telephone and the petrol are just about acceptable, but not a map such as this. It shows all of England and Wales, just about, if not Scotland."

"At least we've got something new to look for now," O'Rourke announced quickly.

"You're right there. On the way back to Erdington, we'll check box three hundred and fourteen, and then tomorrow, we'll go back to forty-two, three hundred and thirty-five. And we'll visit four hundred and fifty-one, which we've not visited yet."

With that, Mason locked the door, being careful to ensure the stable door catch was in place, and then peered up and down the road. He didn't think a single motorcar or lorry had passed them. That was good.

"Are you still alright to drive?" Mason asked O'Rourke as she stifled a yawn making herself comfortable behind the steering wheel of the Wolseley.

"Yes, I'm fine," she assured him, but Mason was also yawning.

"It's been a long day. Shall we just return to Erdington?" he asked her.

"No, it's silly to do that. We'll drive past the sentry box at Beech Lanes anyway, and it'll be quick to jump out and check to see if there's a map there."

"I suppose it'll save us petrol in the long run." O'Rourke rolled her eyes at the words. It was such an oft-spoken phrase these days, but that didn't make it any less accurate.

In reverse, Mason watched the countryside morph into the houses, shops and schools as they neared the built-up area of Birmingham. This time, they parked up on the side of the road close to the sentry box. Wincing with the movement, Mason strode back to the sentry box, the key in his right hand.

O'Rourke was quick to catch him, and he knew he wasn't alone in holding his breath as he opened the top part of the door.

As before, he noted the black telephone, with the number written at its centre, this one read Bearwood 2359, but he was more interested in what else could be found inside the box.

But the sentry box seemed empty of even the items found at the previous box. There was a canister containing petrol, at least that was what it smelt of, but very little else. Mason turned aside, thinking there was nothing else to be seen, only for O'Rourke to cry with surprise.

"There, look, it's under the canister." And indeed it was. Mason opened the bottom half of the stable door and allowed O'Rourke to bend down and pick up the map. It smelt strongly of petrol and was much dirtier, but all the same, Mr Wheelwright and Bettie had made it clear that the regional command centres held all the maps. This map shouldn't be here, just as one shouldn't have been in the sentry box at Stewponey.

"We'll take it with us," Mason confirmed quickly, as O'Rourke held the map away from her body due to the strong smell.

"What is happening?" O'Rourke mused once back in the car with the sentry box locked up. Mason had no answer, not yet.

CHAPTER 7

WEDNESDAY 6TH SEPTEMBER 1944

"So, Roberts informs me that you've made some progress?" It sounded like a question but wasn't really.

"Well, we've realised it's a key from the Automobile Association imprinted on the dead man's head." Smythe nodded as he stood before Mason, a steaming cup of something that passed for tea in his hand.

"Yes, very strange, especially with all the problems we have with them about the speed traps. You would have thought that during the war, they'd just keep their mouths shut and get on with fixing motorcars and motorbikes for those who can still run them. None of this doing the police a disservice." Mason winced at the complaint in his superior's voice.

"It's the question of why the key that bedevils me," Mason interjected before Smythe could wax lyrical with his complaints about the Automobile Association once more.

"I'm sure you'll work it all out," Smythe offered a rare smile. Mason appreciated the confidence, even as he worried it was misplaced.

"But we still don't even know who the man was? I've asked at the aerodrome and the Automobile Association regional office, and neither place has any men missing from their rotas."

"O'Rourke tells me you have truly uncovered something strange with the Automobile Association sentry boxes," Smythe commented, making it clear he wasn't overly happy that there might be something amiss.

"Yes, we need to revisit two of the boxes from yesterday, and then there's another local one to check as well."

"Do you think it's worth all the petrol? Maybe they're just playing silly beggars," Smythe offered with a sniff. Smythe had waylaid Mason even before he could remove his outdoor coat. Now they stood talking in the centre of the office. O'Rourke was listening intently, as was Williams.

"I wouldn't waste the petrol, but if it's to do with signposts and maps, then I think it worthy of spending another day on it. And then, well, if there's nothing else to discover then, it'll be best to inform the regional office of the Automobile Association and the aerodrome of my concerns and leave it with them to resolve."

"It could be to do with military convoys," Smythe offered before turning aside.

"I would expect them to have their own maps and to know their way around," Mason retorted. "After all, the Automobile Association patrol personnel are working with them in local areas."

"Perhaps," Smythe mused. Mason shared his desire to dismiss the changing of the signs and the misplaced sentry box maps, but he couldn't help but think there was something more serious happening than stray maps in places they shouldn't be.

"Are you ready?" he asked O'Rourke, sparing a thought for Jones. He wasn't yet sitting at his desk. Perhaps, Mason hoped, he had the day off.

"Yes, just finishing my tea," O'Rourke called from behind a pile of folders on her desk.

"What's all that?" Mason thought to ask.

"Just routine reports that need filing. I told Williams I'd do it. I don't think he knows his alphabet at all well," she offered softly and with a furtive look. "I said I'd help him with it all and show him how to do it right. I don't want to be hunting through all our files for something that's been misfiled."

"You could just tell Smythe," Mason suggested. Williams was keen and good at his job. If he struggled with his letters and filing, then he could be given other tasks to do that better suited him. Certainly, he was good with the locals, and they all warmed to him when they came to report a problem. Mason mused that he muddled some of his numbers sometimes. It was just one of those things.

"No, I said I'd help him. If he still doesn't get the hang of it, then I'll let him speak to Smythe. We can't all be good at everything, after all."

O'Rourke's face was filled with determination, and Mason forbore to offer further advice. O'Rourke was keen to help the younger lad now that she'd been promoted. It was a good sign.

Outside, it was a bright day, the hint of heat in the cloudless sky. But there was the promise of autumn in the air. There wouldn't be many more days like this, and Mason resolved to enjoy it.

"So, are we going to Mile Oak first?"

"Yes, that makes sense, Mile Oak, Moxhull and then the new one."

"I've already loaded the ladder into the Wolseley," O'Rourke offered. "Williams helped me. He was quite curious about us needing a ladder for the second day in a row but didn't ask any further questions."

"I don't suppose you've had time to look at the fingerprints we took?"

"Not yet, no. We can do it when we get back this afternoon. That's another job that always ends up with me feeling dirty and dusty. But, the photographs have been developed so that we can check those as well."

"Good. Now, let's see if there's anything else out of the ordinary at these other sentry boxes, and let's hope we don't run into Patrolman Grant when we're at Mile Oak."

O'Rourke chuckled darkly at Mason's tone as she started the car and retraced their journey of the day before. As they travelled, Mason kept his eye on the surroundings. Overhead, the rumble of the aeroplanes filled the sky, but he barely looked, provided the engine sounded good, Mason was content that the aeroplanes would land or take-off without any mishap.

"Here we are," O'Rourke announced, pulling the Wolseley to the side of the road just before they reached the sentry box at Mile Oak once more. Mason quickly noticed that the signposts had been removed from their places above the roof of the sentry box.

"I've not seen Patrolman Grant, so let's have a quick look and escape before he comes on his patrol."

Mason moved with as much speed as he could, the sentry box key clasped in his hand once more. If he'd paid more attention yesterday, he wouldn't have needed to come back today, but then, yesterday, he'd not known for what he was looking.

The key fit easily into the lock and turned smoothly.

"It's well oiled," O'Rourke offered, hand above her eyes as she peered along the two roads at the crossroads, the A5 and the A453, no doubt keeping an eye out for Patrolman Grant or the two other patrolmen who might inform Grant that they'd returned to his sentry box.

"And the hinges don't creak either," Mason offered, thinking of the door at the police station, which had developed an annoying squeak of late.

"We need to get some oil on it," O'Rourke agreed, her thoughts mirroring his own. No one could enter or exit the building without everyone knowing. The sound could even be heard in the back room, which they'd used when solving the Middlewick Murders.

Mason peered inside the small sentry box, looking all around for a copy of the map they'd found at boxes three hundred and fourteen and ninety-two. He looked under the telephone, along the shelf it rested on, before bending to lift the petrol canister, surprised when it lifted so easily.

"This is empty," he muttered, thinking some poor motorist would be disappointed if they hoped to find petrol inside for their stopped car.

"But is there any sign of a map?" O'Rourke asked impatiently.

"No, not that I can see. You have a look. You found the last one."

But, there wasn't much in the sentry box other than the empty petrol container and the black telephone with the number written on it. Absentmindedly, Mason picked up the receiver and quickly heard the dull dial tone.

"So, this sentry box has the signs on it but no map," O'Rourke mused when she'd finished checking everything inside the sentry box. She'd even stepped inside and pulled the door closed behind her to see if there was anything hidden away in the gap between the hinges of the door and the wall.

"Perhaps we're just inventing a problem," Mason mused, moving to lock the door once more, keen to return to the Wolseley and get on to the next sentry box.

"We didn't concoct the changed signs," O'Rourke offered, the engine of the car already rumbling back to life.

"No, we didn't," Mason agreed. He had his notebook open before him but didn't know what to write in it.

After some thought, he noted that the petrol canister was empty and that there was no map to be found at Mile Oak sentry box forty-two. As they drove towards Moxhull, Mason caught sight of one of the patrol motorbikes coming towards them. For a moment, he thought to look away, but he didn't, instead looking at the figure beneath the steel cap he wore. Mason noticed that it wasn't Patrolman Grant on the motorbike. In fact, the man didn't even look at them, his moustached face looking instead at the road in front of him.

He had noticed the man saluting others in their cars. They, he assumed, must be members. He couldn't think it was particularly sensible to remove one hand from the handlebars to salute, but then, he wasn't making the rules that governed the actions of the patrol members, and as he well knew, the bigwigs making the rules didn't always make the best decisions.

O'Rourke was silent as she drove, but Mason knew it was because she was busy thinking. He was content with the silence. His thoughts were far from clear.

Again, O'Rourke brought the Wolseley to a careful stop beside the sentry box at Moxhull. Mason struggled to get out of the car, a stabbing pain running along his back.

"You alright, Sir?" O'Rourke asked as she waited impatiently for him.

"Just a bit slow today, thank you," he retorted through tight lips. Two days mostly sitting in the Wolseley weren't doing his back and leg much good.

"Here," and he handed her the Automobile Association key. "Go and get it opened up." O'Rourke almost scampered to the sentry box, but it gave Mason the time he needed to move more slowly, to give his leg the chance to decide to work.

Only then did he become aware of voices. He glanced up, first seeing O'Rourke, waiting by the sentry box, and then another man, more shouting at her than speaking.

"What's all this?" Mason asked, rushing as much as he could to her side.

"I've forgotten my key, and I need the Sergeant here to open the sentry box so I can get the emergency petrol. I know she has the key. I've seen it in her hands." The man was younger than Mason, probably by as much as a decade. His hair was neatly trimmed, a black moustache sitting above thin lips. He wore a shirt and smart trousers, but Mason noted his leather shoes had seen much better days. And there was no sign of a car anywhere close.

"Where's your car?" Mason asked him.

"It's not a car, but a motorbike. And it's a mile further along the road. I've walked all the way here because I remembered seeing the sentry box when I drove past it just before my bally motorbike stopped working."

"Are you a member?" Mason asked. He wasn't comfortable with the thought of handing out free petrol to anyone.

"What, of the Automobile Association? Of course, I am, or I wouldn't be here, would I?"

Mason looked to O'Rourke. He wasn't here to say who was and wasn't a member of the motoring organisation, and yet he was ill at ease with the man's peremptory tone, all the same.

"When did you realise you didn't have your key?" O'Rourke asked. A drop of sweat slowly slithered down the man's forehead as he huffed with annoyance.

"When I got here, of course. I wouldn't have walked all the way here if I'd known I didn't have the thing, would I?" His tone was becoming aggrieved. Mason wasn't sure what to do.

"We could offer you a lift to the nearest petrol station?" He suggested.

"Why would you do that when I can just take the petrol here and then come back and replace what I've taken?"

Now Mason felt his tension drain away.

"Is that how it works?"

"Yes, it's not as though the Automobile Association pay for everyone's petrol. We're allowed to use it but must use our petrol coupons to replace what we've taken. And we need to do it as soon as possible because it's very frustrating when you pull up and the petrol canister is already empty. Then we have to summon one of the patrol people, and they don't much like it for such a simple problem."

The more the man spoke, the more Mason realised he indeed was a member of the organisation.

"Open the door, O'Rourke. Let the man have his petrol, and then we can get on with our task." She nodded, eyes wide at the statement. Hastily, she slipped the key into the lock, and it clicked open, not quite as smoothly as at Mile Oak, but easily enough. She stepped back so that the stranded motorbike rider could take the petrol from inside the small building. It was no bigger than about two feet by two feet.

The man didn't thank them, instead leaning in quickly to snatch the gallon container from the floor. The metal canister sloshed with the fluid inside, and now he grinned.

"Thank God for that. Now, if you'll excuse me," and he turned to walk away. Mason watched him go, as did O'Rourke. Only when he'd turned the corner and could no longer see what they were doing did Mason peer inside the sentry box.

A faint smell of fresh wood shavings scented the air, and Mason stepped back, looking at the top of the sentry box.

"Anything?" he asked O'Rourke, who was carefully examining the interior of the sentry box.

"Yes," she cried, her hands busy over the surfaces as she stepped into the box and turned to face Mason, stretching upwards.

"Here we go," and once more, she pulled forth a folded map made of cloth and held tightly between two cardboard covers. "It was hidden, up here, over the door. And," she was running one hand over it again. "There are two little catches as though to hold it in place."

Mason took the map from her extended hand, noticing that it seemed well used. The cover wasn't dirty, but it was creased in places, and when he opened part of the map outwards, he could see what looked like oil stains on it. Again, it showed England and Wales, with the sentry boxes indicated as little squares on it.

"This is very strange," he mused. O'Rourke was nodding, her lips twisted in thought.

"Right, one more sentry box to visit, and then we'll try and make some sense of everything we know." O'Rourke stepped from the small building and turned to lock the door. As she did, she exclaimed.

"I didn't see this before." She pointed at the lock. Around it, there were pieces of cracked paint, and something had left a deep gouge in the door. Mason turned to look to where their stranded motorbike rider had gone, but of course, he was long out of sight.

"Do you think he did that?" O'Rourke asked.

"I've no idea. Was he here when we arrived?"

"Yes, but I don't know for how long."

"Well, it's worthy of note. It certainly looks to me as though someone has been trying to break into the sentry box. Come on, let's see if we can find our motorbike friend. He could be on the road we need to take to the next sentry box. I'd at least like to find out his name."

More quickly, O'Rourke brought the car to life once more and then pulled onto the A446. There was little traffic, so she slowly drove while Mason looked for the man or the motorbike.

"He can't have gone that far, not yet." O'Rourke worried.

"No, we've only been a few minutes," Mason agreed, and then O'Rourke was slowing the car.

"There's the motorbike," she commented, pointing towards the object left just below some trees, as far from the road as possible.

"But we didn't see the man?" Mason turned in his chair as though expecting him to appear from just behind them.

"Perhaps he walked along the fields?" O'Rourke offered. "We might not have seen him."

"Maybe," Mason offered, already opening the door to have a closer look at the motorbike. He didn't know a great deal about them. Certainly, he wouldn't know how to check if it was working or not. All the same, he fancied taking a glance.

The machine was entirely black, apart from small golden wording that proclaimed it a 'Triumph.' The registration number was proud on the front wheel, white letters on a black background. The seat looked well-worn while the handlebars extended a long way out to either side.

"They make these in Coventry," O'Rourke offered, her eyes gleaming.

"The factory escaped the bombing then?" Mason asked.

"No, it didn't, but this is a pre-war model anyway. It would have been expensive to buy."

By then, Mason was aware of footsteps coming from behind him and the laboured breathing of the man they'd met at the sentry box. He looked up, and a quizzical expression touched his face, his hairline showing a shimmer of sweat.

"What are you doing?" he asked, his tone far from friendly.

"We just wanted to ensure you'd made it back to your motorbike, that's all," Mason offered, trying to be pleasant.

"Oh, well, yes, but only just now. I had an altercation with the cows in that field," and he pointed back along the road some distance. "They didn't think I should be in their field, and I had to make a run for it and ended up going backwards instead of forwards." As he spoke, the man moved to his motorbike and began to pour the petrol into the petrol tank.

"Would you mind telling me your name?" Mason asked. "So that we can note it for our investigation."

"What are you investigating?" the man asked sharply, only to shrug his shoulders. "Yes, of course, you can. I'm Flight Lieutenant Bartholomew. You can find me at the Castle Bromwich aerodrome. I should have been there two hours ago, but best-laid plans and all." The man wiped an oily hand along his sweaty face, and Mason heard a soft sign erupt from O'Rourke. He knew better than to look at her just then.

"Thank you," Mason replied. "I hope you get there quickly now."

"I will, but of course, I'll have to have the petrol replaced here. It's going to take up the rest of the day, but it can't be helped."

Mason sensed O'Rourke's mouth open and knew precisely what she was about to offer. He cut her off quickly.

"We'll be on our way then. Now we know all is well." Mason finally looked at O'Rourke, and she nodded, even though she looked unhappy about it.

Back in the Wolseley, O'Rourke cast a lingering glance at the flight lieutenant.

"Pity he wasn't at the aerodrome when we visited," she muttered, and Mason laughed, the sound low and soft.

"I think it was probably a good thing he wasn't there. Now, come on, or we'll never make it back in time for lunch, and I'm hungry. We didn't get more than a sweet cup of tea yesterday."

With slightly too much force, O'Rourke returned the Wolseley to the road, and then they were off. Mason looked in the side mirrors, just to check the motorbike was moving again, and then settled back into his seat with his notebook before him.

Carefully he wrote down Flight Lieutenant Bartholomew's name and also the fact that someone might have broken into the sentry box. He didn't want to be held responsible for that by Bettie at the regional office.

CHAPTER 8

Sentry box number four hundred and fifty-one was in a place called Blythe, just one and a half miles east of Coleshill. It was easy to find, even with the camouflage paint masking the usually bright green stripes on the otherwise black box. The crossroads it watched over connected the larger road of the A47 with some country lanes, which promised to get a motorist lost very quickly. Mason didn't fancy trying any of them and noticed that there were no direction signs on this box either.

O'Rourke hadn't spoken on the journey here, even as Mason had offered directions. Now, as they again clambered out of the Wolseley, she was muttering under her breath.

"What's the matter?" Mason asked her, assuming it would be something to do with the flight lieutenant.

"Nothing," she shook her head and then looked at him and smiled. "I'd just have liked to ride that motorbike. I've never ridden a motorbike. I think it would be a fabulous experience."

Mason shuddered at the thought. "Not for me. I fall over easily enough just standing up without trying to stay perched on a motorbike as well, and one that's travelling quite fast."

"Ah, Sir, I'm sure you'd be good at it," but O'Rourke didn't sound that convinced.

"I don't think the police have any motorbikes. Maybe you should suggest it to Smythe." But O'Rourke looked horrified at the thought as Mason went to insert the key into the sentry box.

It opened easily enough and he glanced around, seeing everything he'd come to expect from the other sentry boxes they'd visited. He couldn't see any maps though, and the petrol canister was missing.

"You have a look," he offered O'Rourke. Quickly she looked around but shook her head.

"There's nothing here."

"No, there isn't." He confirmed, but it didn't sit right with him.

"Do you remember where the next closest sentry box is?" he asked O'Rourke, sure it would be written in her notebook.

"I'll find it, Sir. Ah yes, here it is S thirty-three. It's at Stonebridge on the road to Coventry."

"That's not far from here," Mason mused. "I think we should go there. Just to be sure that our strange collection of sentry boxes has come to an end."

"Come on, then," and O'Rourke hastened to return to the Wolseley. Mason quickly followed, and in less time than he'd thought, they arrived at the crossroads where the S numbered sentry box was located.

It was even more rural here, and he moved to the sentry box as quickly as he could, eager to be assured that this far from Birmingham, everything was at it should be.

"That's not right," he said after a few moments. He couldn't get the key into the lock.

"I thought all the locks were the same," Mason stated, perplexed, thinking of Patrolman Grant, Bettie and Mr Wheelwright telling him they were.

"Here, let me try. Maybe you need to get the key in at just the right angle or something like that. You know what the lock on the police station backroom is like, the wind has to be blowing in the right direction, and you have to be standing on one foot to get the bloody thing to open."

Mason was only too happy to hand over the key, but O'Rourke had no more luck than he did in trying to get the key to fit.

"It just doesn't fit," O'Rourke muttered unhappily. Mason was strolling around the sentry box. The paint on it was fresh enough, and yet it had the distinct feeling of neglect about it. There were no flowers, or wells and while the grass didn't reach up to his knees, it was far from what he'd come to expect from the pristine sentry boxes he'd visited over the last two days.

"Well, let's get the ladder out, just to be sure, but I think we'll have to let Bettie know that this sentry box is clearly not being used by their members. I wonder how long it's been like this?"

"Here, look after this," and O'Rourke placed the Automobile Association key into Mason's hand while she returned to the Wolseley for the ladder. Mason moved to the lock and bent low, gazing at it. Unlike at the last sentry box, there were no marks to show that someone had tried to break into the box or that the lock itself had been replaced. Well, nothing apart from the scent of paint, not fresh, but not old, either.

Mason shook his head. Maybe he was seeing problems where there weren't any, but it went against everything he'd been told to find this sentry box didn't allow anyone to open it with the standard key. After all, this was the fifth box in two days, and there'd been no problem opening the other four.

"Right, hold it for me," O'Rourke called to him. Although she was at the rear of the sentry box, there wasn't much room, and none of it was flat. Below them both, a field stretched away in the far distance. Mason eyes it, wondering if there were cows or sheep in it.

"Be careful," he cautioned O'Rourke as she placed the ladder and put one foot on the rung.

"I always am, Sir," she smirked before moving quickly along the short ladder. Mason wasn't sure it would reach, not with the slope.

"Alright," she called down to him. "I can just about see the top, and there's nothing here to show it's been changed in any way." Her voice reflected his frustration.

"Come down then, it's not very stable on this ladder," he called to her, and although for a few seconds he felt no change in the ladder, she did then start to move back down it.

He stepped away when she was almost level with him, only to lose his balance.

"Ah," the sound ripped from him as his left leg slid down the steep slope behind them. He'd already let go of the ladder, and even though he reached for it, arms flailing, he was too far away. He bent lower, trying to get at least a grip on some of the tufty grasses that grew there, but a handy looking dandelion proved to be no use as it ripped out of the mud, leaving him overbalancing all over again.

"Here, Sir, take my hand." Above him, O'Rourke was reaching towards him. He tried to grab her hand, only for a terrible stab of pain to wrench down his back.

"Sit down," she instructed, the words rich with command. He tumbled to his knees, gasping in pain as he did so, feeling the mud on the embankment seeping into his trousers. His wife wouldn't be pleased about that.

"Right, now you're steady," O'Rourke called to him, "reach up with one of your hands, and I'll pull you the rest of the way."

Breathing heavily, Mason tried to do as she said, but her fingertips were just out of reach.

"I'll stand up again," he gasped. "Be ready."

Mason thrust himself upwards and finally managed to grip O'Rourke's outstretched hand with a shriek of pain down his back. With her help, he succeeded in pulling himself upwards, feeling an utter fool, the pain bringing tears to his eyes.

"Sorry, Sir," O'Rourke called when he was once more level with the sentry box and the road.

"It's not your fault," he gasped. "I should have taken more care." Mason moved carefully, keen to return to the Wolseley. He didn't want to risk sitting down here, only to have to stand again.

"It is bally steep," O'Rourke commented, following him and bringing the ladder with her. "Do you think there used to be a river there or something?" she asked, curiosity aroused.

"Either that or they had to build the road higher to avoid one," he offered through gritted teeth. The pain was immense.

"Can you take some photographs," he asked her when he finally rested in the seat of the car. "Especially of the lock and the door."

"Yes, I'll put the ladder back and get on with it. Are you well? You look very pale?"

"My back," Mason offered ruefully. "I've hurt it this time. I have some medication to take, but it's back at the station."

"I'll be quick then, Sir, and then I'll get you back to Erdington."

O'Rourke was true to her word, and soon they were making their way back to Erdington Police Station. To distract himself from the pain shooting up his back, Mason talked throughout the journey.

"This is a proper little mystery. I only wish I knew what crime was being or had been committed."

"Are you going to let Bettie know about the locking mechanism?" O'Rourke asked.

"Yes, I want to know if it's been reported to them as well. It didn't look like a new fix, but equally, we can't be the first people to try and use it. So, to summarise the sentry boxes. We have maps that shouldn't be there, some have missing petrol, although we might already have an explanation for that, and then we have the box we can't access."

"You believe it's all connected?" O'Rourke pressed.

"I don't see how it can be, but equally, I don't like such coincidences."

"No, me neither. Ah look, the flight lieutenant's gone," O'Rourke interrupted herself to say as they passed the stretch of road once more where sentry box three hundred and thirty-five stood at the junction between the road they travelled along and the A4091 which would take drivers towards Tamworth.

"Yes, he'll have gone to Castle Bromwich Aerodrome, as he said," Mason grunted as he spoke. His back was so painful. Sitting, standing, lying; all of it hurt eventually. He might even have to go home and lie down for the rest of the afternoon, not that it tended to do him a great deal of good.

Back at Erdington Police Station, O'Rourke parked right outside the main entrance and leapt out of the car to assist him. He would have pushed her away, but he was grateful for her helping hand as he forced himself from his comfortable seat. His knees were stained black with mud, and his shoes needed a good clean, as did his hands.

"Get yourself inside. I'll get the ladder and the camera," O'Rourke trilled. Mason nodded, words beyond him for the time being. It seemed to take an age for him to return to his desk and his packet of painkillers that he kept for such eventualities.

Williams rushed to bring him a cup of pale tea and a mug of cold water, and only then did O'Rourke arrive, ladder under one arm, the camera bag slung over her shoulder. She looked remarkably cheerful, and Mason could admit he was jealous of her enthusiasm.

"Can you put this back for me?" she asked Williams. The lad made carrying the ladder look easy as he moved to take it to the store cupboard. Perhaps, Mason thought, they should have taken him with them. Maybe then he wouldn't have hurt his back and fallen over and gotten himself all dirty.

"I'll take these through," O'Rourke offered, and Mason didn't miss that she gave him an appraising glance.

"I'm fine. I'll drink my tea and take my medication, and then I'll be along."

She nodded, but Mason couldn't shake the thought that she might be about to tell his wife about the state into which he'd got himself.

"Ah, Mason, good, you're back," Smythe appeared before him and then stopped, fixing him with a firm look as well. "What have you been up to?" Smythe demanded, although not unkindly.

"A fall. I'll be fine. I just need a few minutes."

"A fall?" Smythe pushed him.

"I fell over, on a steep slope, behind one of the sentry boxes."

"Ah, right, well, as long as you're not feeling too bad." Mason appreciated that Smythe wanted to acknowledge the issue, even if he trusted Mason to know his mind.

"Now tell me, did you find anything out?"

"Yes, and also no, and none of it makes sense."

O'Rourke appeared then, snapping her lips shut as she held back whatever comment had been about to pour forth because Smythe was there.

"Anything to do with the dead man?"

"No, nothing, but we've found a sentry box that doesn't open with the universal key, and we've found some maps, which certainly shouldn't have been left lying around."

"Um," Smythe mused. Mason could tell what Smythe was thinking.

"So, what are you going to do next?"

"We need to contact the Automobile Association and tell them about the sentry box. Do you want to do that, O'Rourke? Make sure you ask for Bettie. And then we're going to see if our photographs and fingerprints from Mile Oak, Moxhull and the other boxes show anything, and if they don't, well, I don't see that we'll be able to do anything else. We can't spend our time driving around all the sentry boxes. There must be hundreds of them."

"Well, I've had Roberts here this morning. He had nothing to tell me, but he was curious about the key. He's going to return tomorrow morning. I told him you'd be available," Smythe confirmed. "And if there's nothing else, then you and Jones will need to press on with the counterfeit investigation. Williams took in another selection of coupons today from the local baker, Mr Jones, which he says are counterfeit because the local office won't pay out on them. He was fuming about it. Said he lost two pounds last week because of it. But then, he's always angry," Smythe mollified.

"Very good, Sir," Mason replied. He'd swallowed his aspirin and could already feel some easing in the pain that shot down his back. Now he needed to get back on his feet before he seized up on the chair. Old age was not his friend, and yet Mason didn't like to complain. He was lucky to have reached such a grand age, and he knew it. He might grumble about his injuries, but at least he'd lived through the Great War.

O'Rourke had taken herself to the front desk and was using the telephone, even as she joked with Williams about something. Mason could hear the low murmur of their conversation. Smythe had returned to his office, his wisdom imparted. Carefully, pleased there was no one looking, Mason heaved himself to his feet, grabbed his wrapped sandwiches from their place on the desk, and began to hobble towards the back office. Hopefully, O'Rourke would bring his tea with her when she followed him in, and it wouldn't be too cold.

In the back office, O'Rourke had placed the camera and the fingerprinting kit. He could also see that there was a small pile of photographs waiting for them to sort through. No doubt, Williams had had them developed that morning.

Mason picked them up, biting his sandwich as he did so, savouring the thin spread of butter and thicker strawberry jam. Hastily, he returned the photographs to the table and instead placed the top one to the side and looked through them one by one. Better that than risk getting them sticky.

They didn't show anything he didn't expect to see. If anything, in black and white, they were much less helpful than when he'd seen everything in the flesh, even the camouflage green reasonably bright. The sentry box stood proud before him, the neat and tidy garden strangely captured in greys and white. In the photographs that O'Rourke had taken on top of the sentry box, he could see the wood shavings from where the Mile Oak box had been adjusted. He could also determine where the adjustments had been made.

"Bettie wasn't there," O'Rourke commented as she slid his mug of tea on the table beside him. He'd finished his first strawberry jam sandwich by then. "I've left a message asking her to call me back. I didn't say it was urgent, but I didn't say it wasn't, either," she finished, looking at the photographs he was perusing.

"I'm not sure they're at all helpful," she commented.

"Me neither, but at least we have a record of what we found. You just don't know what we might need to look for in the images."

"I've asked Williams to run along to the photographers with today's films to be developed."

"And so we have the fingerprinting to look at."

"Yes, I need to look at yesterday's fingerprinting from the two sentry boxes and compare the results."

"It would be good if we were just trying to find one person," Mason mused.

Quickly, O'Rourke removed the white card from the file. Mason reached for it. In his mind, he remembered all the details of how to compare fingerprints, the identifying marks to look for, the arches, whorls, loops and tents, the need to count the ridges. It wasn't one of his greatest skills, but he argued with himself, he didn't need to find the sixteen points of similarity upon which the courts relied to make a conviction.

If the fingerprints were similar enough, he could ask Smythe to organise a visit from the regional fingerprints team or take them there himself. It wasn't far to go, and it would be good to have the results confirmed as soon as possible. At least it didn't mean a trip to London.

Only then could they begin determining who the actual person was. That would only be possible if the person had previously committed a crime and their fingerprints were on record. Mason wasn't at all convinced that they would be, but it would be helpful if they were.

Neither did he believe they'd retrieve the prints of only one person. And all the time, he couldn't help but think that if he knew what crime had been committed, beyond vandalism, then he might feel some more urgency for the task.

"Here we go," O'Rourke broke into his musings. "I've got some good prints from both of the signs from Mile Oak and Moxhull." She held out the white cards towards him, and he could see seven prints, all but one of them quite slim.

"I'm going to see if Constable Williams has returned," O'Rourke muttered.

Mason bent to examine the prints as she left the room. O'Rourke had a magnifying glass to hand, and he used it to bend over the prints. As always, he could detect nothing worthy of note in the prints, not until he took the time to concentrate and then to pick out the ridges and whorls which, he'd long been assured, were unique to every single person. No two people could have the same fingerprints. The knowledge astounded him even after all his years in the police force. Not for the first time, he considered how much more reliable fingerprints were than the old Bertillon system based on anthropometric identification.

A shiver of recognition rippled through him as he realised that there might be a match between the prints taken from Mile Oak and those at Moxhull. There were definitely similarities, but he'd wait to ask O'Rourke what she thought first. Only then did he appreciate that she'd been gone for a long time. Where was she?

As though summoning her, O'Rourke walked through the door, a perplexed expression on her face.

"What?"

"What have you found?" they asked one another at the same time.

"You first," Mason insisted.

"Bettie rang me back, and well, she was very concerned about the rogue sentry box on the way to Coventry that we couldn't open with the key, but it's something else she said that has perplexed me."

"What was that?"

"Well, she said, 'I know you were asking about missing patrol personnel, and there aren't any, but we are missing one of our road service outfits, an RSO as they call it; a motorbike and sidecar.'"

Immediately, Mason understood what she was thinking.

"There were tyre tracks close to where we found the body."

O'Rourke was nodding. "I know there were," she said.

"So, we need to find this missing motorbike and sidecar?"

"I think we do as well," O'Rourke confirmed.

"And I think, while we're at it, that we should ask Doctor Lucey if our unknown victim was the man to leave the fingerprints on our signs at Mile Oak and Moxhull."

"Have you found a match already?" O'Rourke still seemed dazed.

"I think so, yes. Look, what do you think?"

O'Rourke bent to look at where he was indicating.

"I think you're right," she beamed at him. "The two have a distinctive whorl pattern, don't they?" Mason nodded, pleased he wasn't seeing things that weren't there.

"We need to get these verified by the fingerprint experts in Birmingham."

"Yes, we do," O'Rourke agreed readily. "And what about the missing RSO?"

"Do they know how long it's been missing?" Mason thought to ask.

"Bettie said as long as two weeks, possibly not as long. They don't use all the motorbikes as often as they'd like to, not with the petrol rationing and their patrol numbers being so low. But, she said they did perform a full inventory when they moved there, six months ago, and they also did one only two weeks ago. It was the first one since they moved all the motorbikes and lorries to the new regional office."

"So, how does Bettie know it's missing?"

"Because they were going to use it. One of the Road Service Outfits they do use has developed a fault that will take some time to fix because there just aren't the spare parts. Rather than break a different machine to get a part, she ordered them to use a different motorbike. She says that's where she was, searching for it when I rang through, and it's not there."

"And where are they stored?"

"They have a large garage behind the building. It's kept locked all of the time. They have no need to go in there."

Mason felt his lips twist in thought. The missing motorbike, or RSO, could be very important.

"Right. We need to do a few things. Firstly, get these fingerprints to Doctor Lucey and also to the regional headquarters. Secondly, we need to know what the tyres look like on these motorbikes. There are photographs of where the body was found, so we should be able to compare them."

"So, we need to go into Birmingham again," O'Rourke asked.

"Yes, but I can't go like this," and Mason indicated his mud-encrusted knees. "We'll go in the morning. We'll set up appointments with Dr Lucey and Bettie, and we can take Roberts with us if he wants to come."

"And what should we do for the rest of the afternoon?"

"I think that's quite obvious. We need to see if there are fingerprints on the maps as well."

O'Rourke nodded, her lips twisted as she considered what he was thinking.

"Right. It looks like I'm going to get dirty fingers again," but there was no ire in her voice. Mason suppressed a grin, pleased to have forgotten about his aches and pains for a few minutes. It seemed that O'Rourke was just as intrigued as he was.

·   ·   ·

Mason wouldn't allow O'Rourke to drive him the short distance home. He thought it was better to use his bad leg and aching back rather than allow himself to wallow in self-pity. Yes, it was painful, but it could have been a great deal worse.

He had, however, forgotten about his wife's reaction to his dishevelled state as he hobbled along the path.

Annie's face appeared from where she must have been tending to the flowers in the front garden as he came through the gateway, the gate giving a funny high-pitched squeak, just as it always did.

"Well, you look as though you've been in a fight and lost," were her less than helpful words as she swept him with a gaze that went from his head to his feet. "And you're limping, the worst I've seen you for months. Wouldn't Smythe allow O'Rourke to drive you home? I never took him to be quite so mean."

"I told her I wanted to walk," Mason quickly stated. Sometimes Annie got it into her head that Smythe wasn't the most sympathetic of Superintendents. Mason was honest enough with himself to admit he shouldn't have been quite so stubborn. But stubbornness had ensured he endured far greater than this in his life. But, he was in a great deal of pain. The medication he'd taken had long since worn off. Soon, he'd be able to take some more.

"Well, I don't know how you expect me to get the mud out of your trouser knees. And your shoes? What have you been doing? Traipsing through farmers' fields? You really should have worn your boots," Mason shook his head while Annie watched him with her hands on her hips. She was wearing one of his outdoor jackets over her dress, and she had a sensible pair of ankle high boots on her feet. In her hand, she held the secateurs. No doubt, she'd been tending to the small amount of roses. He'd promised to begin digging the vegetable patch at the weekend. Annie's tending of the flowers was intended as a means of reminding him.

"Sam," and he didn't appreciate the tone she was using. He was not a small boy to be chastised in the front garden in such a way. "You need to start looking after yourself. You're not a young man anymore."

"I fell over." He thought to explain. "I wasn't in a farmer's field. I fell over on a steep slope while I was investigating something," he stated, walking past her to enter the house with as much dignity as he could muster. No matter how much it hurt, he walked straight, and tried not to limp. Of course, it didn't fool Annie.

"Well, if you think you're going in my house looking like that, then you're very much mistaken. Take your shoes off before you enter the house. Your socks will be cleaner than your shoes. And you can take your trousers off before you go in as well."

"Annie," he pleaded, meeting her eyes and seeing no sympathy in them. He realised how his son must feel when Annie mothered him as though he were a child, even though he'd fought in a war.

"I will not have my house left a mess because you fell over. But, I will help you run a bath. You look as though you could do with one." With that slight concession made, Mason forced himself up the steep front step, having kicked his shoes off his feet so that they landed outside with a dull thud. He wriggled his toes. His feet were damp but not muddy.

"I'll pick them up," Annie admonished him. "Get inside with you. The neighbours will be watching."

Mason knew they wouldn't be but hurried to do as she'd asked him, all the same. He shrugged out of his overcoat and left his hat on the hook beside his coat. Only then did Mason consider how to remove his trousers. He needed somewhere to sit down.

"I'll get you one of the kitchen stools," Annie announced, following him inside, his shoes held in her hands. "At the same time, I'll put these on some old newspaper. You're going to need to give them a good scrub and then a polish. Your good leather ones as well. These are for Court not falling down muddy slopes," Mason almost smiled as she muttered to herself. How, he thought, he was supposed to know he'd have been anywhere near a steep hill was beyond him.

In no time at all, Mason lowered himself into a hot bath, revelling in the warmth that travelled up his aching back. He appreciated it would be a struggle to extract himself from the bath in a few minutes, but for now, he could enjoy the sensation of being clean and free from pain. In the kitchen, he could hear Annie scrubbing his trousers with a vicious looking brush. He didn't think he'd seen it since their son had been a young boy, prone to coming home with dirty knees and dirty trousers, both.

He felt a moment of sympathy for his son's knees as he worked the mud from the creases in his hands and from down his short-cut nails. It was thick and black, not like the soil in the garden or on the allotment.

That set him to thinking. Just what was the locked sentry box being used for, and who was using it? Perhaps, by the time they arrived at the Automobile Association regional office tomorrow, Bettie might have an answer for him. Maybe it was just a mistake. Perhaps the lock had been broken, and the locksmith had fitted the incorrect one. But if that had been what had happened, surely Bettie would have known as soon as O'Rourke mentioned it to her.

He couldn't help thinking that it was a good way of hiding something in plain sight, but there was no guarantee that the lock wouldn't be broken and replaced when the Automobile Association became aware of it. It was a risk. Or was it? How many people were likely to be out driving these days, other than the army and other military vehicles? Mr Wheelwright had told him that Automobile Association membership was at an all-time low. Maybe it wasn't quite so much of a risk after all?

"So," Annie's voice sounded from the kitchen, raised so he could hear it over her vigorous scrubbing. "Where were you when you fell?"

"Stonebridge, on the way to Coventry."

Annie's face appeared at the door, her forehead furrowed, eyes alert. She could sense when he told her something interesting.

"And why were you over there? I thought you were working on the counterfeit ration coupons with Jones."

"I am, but I've also been looking into two other matters." Mason didn't like to be elusive with his wife, even if she was used to it after all these years.

"Is this anything to do with that dead man found at the aerodrome?" He gasped, and Annie pursed her lips, eyes flashing with triumph.

"There's always someone who will gossip, and of course, they do like to come and ask me what I know about such things."

Mason shook his head, dislodging water droplets from his wet hair as he did so.

"And do these 'gossips' have any idea who this mystery man might be?" For once, Mason thought it might be worth determining what these gossips knew about events of which they should have been ignorant.

"Well, there are thoughts it must be a German spy," Annie managed to make the statement without looking furious. "Equally, some think he might have been a British man up to no good, and killed by the Royal Air Force."

"Killed for what?" Mason asked, outraged that such terrible rumours were circulating.

"Now, no one said what they might have been doing, but I think they're implying they were working for the enemy, trying to undermine the war effort. I know it's all a lot of rot," Annie concluded. "The Birmingham Post is filled with details of how well the offensive is going now that the Allies can reclaim lost territories. Mind, if it is a spy, they might have been killed because they were no longer useful to the enemy or the British if he happened to be a double-agent." Mason's mouth dropped open in shock. Annie laughed at his reaction.

"The national newspapers are filled with such scandal."

"Well, yes, but here, in Erdington, or rather, at the Castle Bromwich aerodrome? I just can't believe it."

"It might be worth your while considering all possibilities if you want to find out who the poor man is. It would be better if he were buried with his identity and his family informed, whoever he happens to be."

"And are there any rumours as to whether this man is local or not?"

Again, Annie's forehead furrowed, and her eyes narrowed.

"No one knows the identity of the man, and I don't know of anyone missing in the local area. So no, we'll have to assume the poor man is from somewhere else. Surely, you should know these things?"

"I'm doing my best," Mason huffed, heaving himself out of the dirty water with some effort.

"I know you are, dear. And I've done my best with your shoes, and your trousers are hanging on the washing line. I suggest you wear your blue trousers tomorrow. I know you don't like them, but it's going to rain tonight, and I won't be able to get those dry in time, not when we're not going to be having a fire."

"My thanks," and he bent to place a kiss on her forehead, but she shooed him away.

"You're all wet. Now, get dressed, and then we can have dinner. I'm afraid it's not very exciting, and there's no custard, but I plan on going for a walk tomorrow, and might just find some blackberries. A bit of something sweet would be welcome."

CHAPTER 9

THURSDAY 7TH SEPTEMBER 1944

The following day, having donned his much-hated blue trousers and jacket, Mason walked to the police station with only a slight limp. His back felt much better, and he was wearing his black boots, on Annie's orders, just in case he ended up in a field again. Annie was having none of it that he'd not been near a field. In the end, he'd bent and laced up his boots and left before she could scold him further.

Constable Williams greeted his arrival with a cheery 'good morning' as he opened the door to a loud shriek of protest.

"Morning Sir," O'Rourke called to him, and Mason was almost smiling until he saw Jones' aggrieved expression.

"Sorry, Jones. I have to go to Birmingham again today. Hopefully tomorrow." Jones nodded, but he looked none too pleased. For a moment, Mason considered allowing O'Rourke to make the trips alone, but she wouldn't get quite the respect she deserved from Doctor Lucey. He might not even remember that she was from Erdington and had been asked to intervene by Roberts. No, he'd go with O'Rourke and help Jones when he had more time. The man was so contrary.

"Are you ready?" he asked O'Rourke. She had a large folder in front of her, no doubt filled with fingerprints and photographs. She was also carrying the camera bag.

"I don't want to leave anything. We might need to take photographs of the garage at the Automobile Association regional office or some such."

"No, that's a good idea. I'll get the fingerprint kit as well."

"I've already put it in the Wolseley," O'Rourke announced. "As you say, we need everything with us."

Mason grinned.

"Come on then. Let's see what today tells us."

O'Rourke had arranged appointments with Dr Lucey for 9.30 am and with Bettie for 11 am. Roberts was going to meet them at the mortuary. Roberts had agreed to take the fingerprinting details they had back to the main office in Birmingham. Mason tried to make himself comfortable in the Wolseley as they drove through the quiet streets. It wasn't that early, but people were tardy to be about their business now that the darkness of early morning was beginning to linger beyond the heady days of early summer.

His boots were heavy, and his trousers were too short, meaning a draft worried his ankles.

O'Rourke was cheerful at his side.

"If it's the same man, then what does it all mean?" she asked him.

"I wish I knew, but it might explain the imprint on his forehead."

"Um, yes, I'd forgotten about that. I wonder if he stole the motor-bike and sidecar as well, or rather, the RSO?" O'Rourke was enjoying using the term the Automobile Association used.

"We won't know that, not yet. Let's not get ahead of ourselves."

"Yes, of course, you're right, Sir. Sorry."

"Don't apologise, O'Rourke. I've been thinking the same thing. Annie was telling me there are some rumours about who the poor man is. Some say he's a German spy, others that he's a double-agent and has been killed by the British now that they're advancing into the occupied territories. Today's headline says that the Americans have crossed the Moselle."

"Really?" O'Rourke chuckled softly. "I didn't even think anyone knew about him. It's not been in the newspapers. They're more

concerned with the war effort, and in the local news, with the acci-
dental killing of that poor, young girl about which Doctor Lucey has
been testifying in court."

"It seems there's also been time to gossip about this dead man."

"I imagine someone from the Castle Bromwich aerodrome has been
chattering," O'Rourke couldn't keep the censure from her voice. She
was probably thinking of the woman who ran the canteen.

"Probably. Unless it's whoever found him, that's perhaps more
likely."

As they exited the car at the mortuary, Mason helped O'Rourke
collect all the fingerprinting details they had. O'Rourke had brought
along the photographs and the actual white cards which held the
fingerprints.

It was awkward going, but they made their way to the mortuary
where Roberts was waiting for them, a pained expression on his face.

"He's not ready for us yet." Roberts offered by way of an explanation. "It seems he's no good until he's had his morning cup of tea, and
today, he hasn't had one. Anyway, tell me what you've got?"

Mason explained what they'd discovered. Roberts looked
surprised.

"So, a missing motorbike, two vandalised sentry boxes, a locked
sentry box, misplaced maps and some fingerprints which, hopefully,
match our unknown victim?" It was almost a question, but not quite.

"I have to hand it to you, Mason. You do have a knack for getting to
the roots of some mighty strange cases. Ah, there you are, Doctor
Lucey," the door opened before them, and the man, with a semblance
of a smile, but no greeting, beckoned them inside.

"So, fingerprints?" Doctor Lucey eventually stated. "We've taken
some already. We did it when the body came to us. But, let's see what
you've got. I've already taken a fresh set this morning."

Rather than leading them into the mortuary, Doctor Lucey directed
them into an office that was large enough for all of them. At its centre
was a round table and on it were some fingerprint cards, a complete
set of them on white card.

Together, Mason and O'Rourke sorted through their files until they
found the fingerprint cards from the day before.

"Do you have a magnifying glass?" Roberts asked Doctor Lucey, and one materialised before him.

"I'm a bit of a dab hand at this sort of thing," Roberts offered, bending over carefully to examine the two sets of prints, the two from the different sentry boxes which seemed to be from the same person, and the complete set which Doctor Lucey had produced from the unidentified body.

For a long minute, there was only silence, while the three of them watched Roberts as he looked from one to another and then to another. When he stood, there was a triumphant smile on his face.

"They're a definite match. Absolutely. I can see thirteen markers that are the same, and I'm sure they'll be able to find another three when I take them to the fingerprint department. So, it looks as though we have some idea who this man might be, or at least, what he was up to before he was killed."

"Not that it helps a great deal," O'Rourke offered, unable to hide her enthusiasm.

"If we find that he was the one that stole the Automobile Association Road Service Outfit, then it'll be even more curious," Mason offered.

"Yes, there must be an explanation, somewhere. Did you happen to show the face of the man to the people at the Automobile Association regional office?"

"No, but they said no one was missing or had failed to report for their scheduled shifts. But I can ask today. That's where we're going next."

"It might be worth it, just to double-check," Roberts admitted.

"Then we'll do that, and at the same time, find out if this stolen motorbike might have been the one whose tracks were left in the soil close to the body."

"Yes, I have photographs of it for you. You can take them with you. I think the tyre tread is quite distinctive."

"Yes, it is," Mason stated, studying it carefully on the photograph that Roberts handed to him.

"Excellent, and now, if you'll excuse me, gentlemen and lady, I have another body waiting for me. A sad case, but nothing that you need to know about at this time." Doctor Lucey bowed to them and strode from the door, leaving the three of them looking from one to another.

"Half the mystery solved," Roberts clapped Mason on the shoulder. "I think I'll come with you and see what else we can find out."

Mason cracked a smile.

"Let's just hope we're not finding connections where there aren't any. But, at least a lost motorbike will give us something to look for, as opposed to nothing at all but a dead man with a strange mark on his forehead."

They arrived in a convoy to the Automobile Association regional office. This time, there was no problem with either car gaining admittance to the car park, and in fact, Bettie was waiting for them as Fergus allowed them quick entrance. Well, as fast as he could manage. Bettie was chatting to one of the mechanics from their previous visit, his forearms oil streaked, and she quickly stepped away when Mason and O'Rourke exited their cars.

"This is Chief Inspector Roberts," Mason introduced the other man quickly. "We've worked together in the past, and hopefully, between us, we'll be able to help with your lost motorbike."

Bettie watched them through narrowed eyes. Mason felt he was being appraised by the woman who stood with her arms wrapped around herself, a beige cardigan doing little to keep the wind off her.

"Is this something to do with the map and the locked sentry box, as well as the stolen RSO, motorbike and sidecar, if you will?" she asked. Mason wasn't at all surprised by the question.

"They might be connected, but we don't know, not yet. Oh, and sorry to ask, but do you know this man? Be warned, it's a photograph taken when he was already dead." Mason didn't show her the photograph until Bettie nodded and then swallowed to show it was acceptable to do so. For a few seconds, she examined the photo that Mason held and then shook her head, somewhat regretfully.

"I'm sorry, but I've never seen him before. Poor man," she added, wrapping her arms even tighter.

"Thank you," Mason offered. "I do appreciate it."

She gave him half a smile. "This is all very peculiar," she muttered. "All these years and nothing strange has happened when I've been employed by the Automobile Association, and then I move to Birmingham, and now all this has happened." She shook her head with unease. "I've sent one of the patrolmen and the other handyman employed here to check on the locked box. I've given them instructions to get the sentry box open and to fit a new lock. They'll also see what's being hidden inside it, but I have my suspicions."

Mason fixed her with a firm look. "Petrol?" they both said simultaneously, and when Bettie laughed, there was no joy to it.

"Where better to hide it than in plain sight," Roberts offered.

"I will, of course, inform you of what's found. Mr Wheelwright has also sent messages to Fanum House in London saying that all sentry boxes need to be checked for maps throughout the country. We can't leave such important documents lying around. He's fuming about the whole thing."

A moment of silence fell between them. Mason could appreciate that Mr Wheelwright was indeed unhappy.

"Now, what can you tell us about this RSO that's been stolen?" Mason quickly brought the conversation back to the here and now.

"Well, I was just talking to Gregory about it." Bettie had started to walk back towards the mechanic. He was bent over a motorcycle with an exposed engine. He looked up as he heard his name, and Mason sighted the older man, grey-haired, with intelligent-looking eyes and a squashed nose. He was thin and tall, his shoulders slightly hunched as though used to bending to speak with people. He seemed much more attentive now that Bettie was there to ensure he wasn't as rude as last time they'd met

"Alright," he said, in a thick local accent, eyebrows raised and suddenly finding himself speaking not only to Bettie but to three police officers as well. "It was there no more than two weeks ago," he sounded apologetic, as though he was to blame.

"It's not your fault, Gregory," Bettie offered. "I'm pleased you noticed as soon as you did."

Bettie turned to face Mason.

"I've ordered a full inventory, and three of my office staff are just now working their way through all the RSO's, lorries and vans. It shouldn't take them all day, but I'll let you know if there are any other," for a moment, she seemed to flounder for a word before deciding on "discrepancies."

"But, the vehicles are all kept in here," Bettie indicated a large building, almost more like a barn than anything else. "This door here is kept locked all of the time. The mechanics and Gregory included in that, work out of the sheds against the main building. It's only open today because I was waiting for you."

Roberts had walked away, keen to examine the locking mechanism, and O'Rourke had gone with him, having first bent to take photographs of the tyres on the motorbike Gregory was fixing. The doors were large, certainly wide enough for a lorry to be driven beneath. They were painted a dark green, just like the sentry boxes, and now stood wide open, the sunlight glinting on the motorbikes and lorries stored inside.

"How many padlocks do you use on the doors?" Mason asked. He could see all sorts of ways that the arrangement wasn't very secure, but equally, without petrol, it was unlikely anyone would get very far.

"It has three," Bettie announced. "The only other way to gain entrance is by a small side door that we could use if we wanted to, but for the time being, with all the equipment we're not using, it's all but blocked up. That's why the double doors are open."

Mason pulled his notebook from his pocket and wrote in it as Bettie spoke.

"It works like this," Gregory said slowly. "All the RSO's are turned over once a month, just to make sure the engines don't seize. It will be a problem with the brakes if we ever get to use them again, but I'd sooner replace the brakes than the engine. The vans aren't as easy because they're at the rear of the barn. They get run when we remember. It's not good to have the fumes in such a small space. We didn't think of that when we put them in there," he shrugged his slim shoulders, and Mason heard all sorts of frustrations in his bland statement.

It seemed that Gregory had been ignored and was making sure he wouldn't be blamed when none of the vans worked on being restarted.

"But when you check they're still running, you don't do it by number or anything?"

"No, we run down each line, there are five lines of them, and we just accept that they're all there. There's no reason for them not to be."

"And, if you don't mind me asking, what's the matter with the damaged motorbike that occasioned this discovery?"

"I'm just working on it now. It's not turning over. I'm going to assume it might have been run on low fuel. I probably need to get a lot of rubbish out of the petrol tank. Either that or some of the seals have gone."

Gregory indicated the motorbike which he'd been bent over.

"And where did it patrol?"

"Patrolman Archibald's route took him out the west side of Birmingham, covering Wolverhampton and Dudley." Bettie provided the answer.

"Did you ask him?" But Bettie cut off his words.

"If you'll come this way, Chief Inspector," her words were formal, and Gregory wasn't alone in being surprised.

"So, you've not shared the information with everyone?" Mason asked her.

"No, Mr Wheelwright thought it best not to cause any unnecessary concerns. I didn't speak to Archibald, no. But I can if you think it's necessary."

"It would be good to know if he knew anything about the maps. That's what I was thinking."

"Ah, yes. Well, when he returns the RSO, I'll ask him. It'll only be a day or two at the most."

Mason's gaze was drawn to Roberts and O'Rourke. The pair of them were working together to examine the doors and the locks. Roberts found the table where the padlocks were kept when not in use and held them up to the light, seeking out imperfections.

"Tell me, do all the motorbikes uses the same tyres?" Mason called to Gregory.

Gregory was startled at the question.

"Of course they do. We use Dunlop tyres here." Mason almost wished he hadn't asked, so firm was the statement from Gregory, but then Dunlop was a local manufacturer. Gregory was a proud Brummie.

"What do you think all this is about?" Bettie asked Mason, worry making her words sharp.

"I wish I knew, but I don't, not yet," Mason confirmed. "I don't even know if any of it's connected or if it's just a coincidence."

"But you're taking the matter very seriously," Bettie scolded him.

"I am, yes. There's a dead man and a missing motorbike. And, if we find that the sealed sentry box is also filled with petrol canisters, then we have to start to think that this is something that's long been planned."

Bettie nibbled on her lower lip, her consternation clear to see.

"Do you think we need to tighten up our security?" she asked. "We don't have anyone here in the evening, not when the service can only run during daylight hours. Or do you think I'm worrying too much?"

"For now, I would say to carry on as you are, but be alert. Ask Gregory to keep a keen eye on the motorbikes and lorries. He's the person that's most likely to know if anything's been meddled with."

"Of course, yes. I'll make sure that's done."

As she spoke, a younger woman walked out of the storage barn. She blinked rapidly in the bright light and then, sighting Bettie, walked briskly to her. She wore a thin coat over her demure dress and practical brown shoes. Mason thought her uniform was little different to O'Rourke's.

"Mrs Morton," the woman spoke respectfully. "I've concluded my inventory, and I can tell you that nothing is missing." She clutched a clip board to her front, no doubt to hold the papers flat against the gentle wind that blew.

"Thank you, Doris," Bettie offered her. "Now, get in the office and have a hot drink. You look chilled to the bone."

Doris bowed her head and all but ran inside the building. She didn't even startle on seeing the two Wolseley's blocking her way.

"She's a quick-witted girl," Bettie mused. "The other two will take much longer and call her all sorts of names, but she's always precise in her tasks."

By now, O'Rourke and Roberts had returned to their side.

"I can't see that the padlocks have been forced, or the doors," Roberts confirmed quickly. "Are there many keys to the padlocks?"

"We only keep one set in the office. The other is locked in the safe, and Mr Wheelwright is the only person that can access it."

"Hum," Roberts mused but offered nothing further. Mason looked at O'Rourke.

"I agree. There's nothing to see, and the padlocks will have so many fingerprints on them, I can't see we'll get anything worthwhile if we try to check for prints. I've taken some more photographs," and O'Rourke indicated the camera case she carried. "But, there's not a lot to see. I agree with Roberts."

Mason grunted. He hadn't been expecting any other outcome, and yet it was frustrating.

"What will you do now?" Bettie asked Mason, and he felt three sets of eyes on him.

"We'll search for the missing motorbike, the RSO," he announced with far more assurance than he felt.

CHAPTER 10

Once back at Erdington Police Station, O'Rourke was surprisingly quiet. Mason appreciated her restraint.

Mason sat at his desk, pleased to remove his uncomfortable jacket, and stared down at his notebook. Where, he thought, was he to find the missing motorbike or, rather, the RSO?

"I think they're a match," O'Rourke announced sometime later, sliding a photograph onto his desk. "This is taken from Castle Bromwich Aerodrome." Mason looked at the markings left by a wheel. The tread certainly looked as though it belonged to a Dunlop tyre. They did have a distinctive mark, crisscrossing across the tyre, no doubt for grip or some such.

"I think we're just getting more and more bewildered," Mason mused. "There are no answers to be found, only more parts of a puzzle, if these pieces are, indeed, connected." At that, Williams called through from the front office.

"Chief Inspector Mason, there's a telephone call for you. From the Automobile Association regional office." Sam lumbered to his feet and made his way to the black telephone that sat proudly on the front desk.

"Thank you," he offered Williams before picking up the receiver.

"Mason here," he spoke.

"Ah, Chief Inspector Mason, this is Mrs Morton, from the Automobile Association regional office."

"Good afternoon, Mrs Morton," Mason decided to be as formal as she was being.

"I wanted to let you know what was found at the locked sentry box, number S thirty-three. The lock has been fixed now and will open to any Automobile Association member's key. But inside, as we thought, there were petrol canisters. Thirteen of them and all but one of them were full." Mason could imagine Bettie's unhappy expression as she spoke.

"We've brought the petrol back to the regional office, so it can't be misused."

"Was there anything else strange?"

"Apart from the lock being changed?" Mason winced at the sharp tone. "No, just the petrol, I would say at least eleven gallons of it."

Mason whistled at the volume. He couldn't help but consider from where the person hoarding the petrol had been getting it. It was not an insubstantial amount, not with all the rationing, which had made private use almost entirely prohibited.

"Thank you for letting me know," Mason offered to break the heavy silence coming from the end of the telephone.

"And the rest of the vehicles are all accounted for," Bettie finished quickly. "I do hope you can tell me what's been happening sooner rather than later. I've had to send Mr Wheelwright home. His nerves aren't good at the best of times."

"I will do all I can," Mason promised, appreciating it was little and nothing.

"Thank you, Chief Inspector," and Bettie rang off. For a moment, Mason stood there, staring into space, his thoughts running wildly around his head. He just couldn't seem to find an edge to exploit in the bizarre cases he'd been handed in the last few days. There was nothing to peel aside, only more and more confusion the more they learned. It reminded him of the beginning of the Custard Corpses case. He didn't want this to remain unsolved for as long as young Robert McFarlane's murder. He didn't want this to become the case that defined his career, as Robert's murder had Chief Inspector Fullerton's.

"Oh, hello, it's you," Mason was startled as he focused and realised there was a man in front of him, and not just any man. It was the man whose motorbike had run out of petrol the day before.

"Hello," Mason replied, looking around for Constable Williams before realising he was off somewhere, probably making more tea or helping Smythe with something.

"Can I help you?" Mason asked.

"Well, yes, actually, you can. When I returned to the aerodrome, they told me about the dead man's body, and I realised it was all extraordinary. But I didn't think anything else of it, not until I found an Automobile Association branded motorbike hidden at the back of one of the store cupboards. Well, not in it, around the back of it. I wasn't sure who to tell about it and then thought I should just report it to the police who've been asking questions about the dead man."

"Of course, I don't know if it's related, but no one should be leaving motorbikes out in the open, with the war on. Even if it was actually hidden." Mason had remembered the man's name was Flight Lieutenant Bartholomew. He laughed and shrugged as Mason realised he was no longer alone.

O'Rourke had appeared, a smile on her flushed face, as she ensured her tight braids were carefully in place behind her ears. Mason gave no outward reaction but knew he'd tease her about it later. She'd quickly forgotten just how surly Bartholomew had been the first time they'd met.

"Have you touched the RSO, sorry, the motorbike?" Mason asked, shaking his head. Now he was insisting on calling it by the correct name, just as Bettie and Gregory had.

"No, I saw it. They're very distinctive, and I went into the office to contact the Automobile Association themselves. Well, to chastise them really for leaving something like that lying around. But the people in the office, well, the squadron leader, suggested I inform you first. There's been some unease about the dead man. A lot of people are on edge. I think it would help morale if his identity, and the reason for his murder, could be solved."

"Is the motorbike easy to access?"

"Yes, and also no. It's right at the back of some of the hangars. The hedges are a bit out of control, and it's riddled with brambles."

Mason knew what he wanted to ask next, but O'Rourke beat him to it.

"Can I ask why you were there?" Her words were softly spoken.

"Yes, we were having a game of football, and some damn fool kicked it right over the hangar. The damn fool was me, and so they sent me to retrieve it. Look," and he hitched up his blue shirt sleeve and revealed a thin line of cut skin. "Bloody brambles hooked me, and it was an effort to get out."

O'Rourke made consoling noises while Mason picked up the telephone. He wasn't at all surprised when Bettie answered on the second ring. She'd probably been standing next to it.

"Mrs Morton, it's Chief Inspector Mason here. It seems we might have found your missing motorbike, the RSO. Do you want to send someone to retrieve it while we take a look as well?"

"Already?" Bettie exclaimed, but Mason could hear her hands scrabbling around for something with which to write.

"Tell me where it is, and I'll get Gregory to come and get it. I'll arrange for him to get there as soon as he can."

Mason held his hand over the mouthpiece and turned to Flight Lieutenant Bartholomew.

"Where do you suggest we direct the recovery vehicle to come to?"

"If you tell them to stop on Chester Road, behind the aerodrome hangars, I think that's the closest we'll be able to get."

"What about the hedges and brambles?"

"Nothing to be done but to endure them," Bartholomew offered ruefully.

Mason uncovered the mouthpiece.

"Chester Road, opposite the Castle Bromwich Aerodrome hangars. I'll be looking out for him, and then he can explain everything to you on his return."

"Thank you," and before Mason could say anything else, Bettie had replaced the receiver once more.

"Did you come here on your motorbike?" Mason asked.

"I did, yes."

"So, we'll be able to follow you back then?"

"Yes, but I would recommend bringing a big coat or something to keep the brambles away from you." Bartholomew winced as he spoke, no doubt reminded of the pain from the deep scratch he'd shown them.

O'Rourke was still smiling, her grin wide.

"Will you get the Wolseley?" Mason prompted her when she lingered with a smirk on her lips.

"Oh yes, of course. And the camera and the fingerprint kit?" she asked, blinking rapidly, as though trying to remember what to do.

"Yes, all of those things, please, and I'll let Constable Williams know where we're going."

Mason walked away, but O'Rourke lingered.

"Now, O'Rourke," Mason muttered as he walked past her.

"Yes, yes, I'm doing it." Flight Lieutenant Bartholomew was once more inspecting his cut arm, seemingly unaware of the effect he was having on O'Rourke. Either that, or he was so used to it, he didn't think anything of it. Mason felt some sympathy for O'Rourke. All the men had been called up for duty or were too old or too young for her to have much fun in their company. And those who were her age had reasons for not being allowed into the army, navy and air force or had restricted occupations, which didn't make them the most exciting of all.

Hopefully, if the newspapers were to be believed, there was a chance of victory on the horizon, and then everyone would be able to return to living their lives as they usually would. Well, those who yet lived, at least.

Mason grabbed his long coat from the coat rack. He spared a thought for his trousers and hated jacket and was pleased he'd worn his boots for work, after all, even if it had been at Annie's urging.

In no time at all, he and O'Rourke were following Bartholomew towards the aerodrome.

"Who do you think hid the RSO, I mean the motorbike?" O'Rourke asked her eyes on the figure of the flight lieutenant and his motorbike in front. They were quickly beyond the small amount of built-up traffic in Erdington itself and following Chester Road past Pype Hayes Park on the way to their destination.

"It sounds as though they've tried to hide it. That's about all we can say. I don't think we'll know who did it, not for some time. Maybe we'll get a match on the fingerprints?" Mason filled his voice with hope but wasn't sure he quite succeeded in doing so.

O'Rourke remained quiet as he spoke. He considered what she was thinking, but he doubted it had anything to do with the dead man or the missing motorbike.

In no time at all, Flight Lieutenant Bartholomew pulled over to the side of the road. Mason could see the aeroplane hangars to the far side of the hedgerow. They were high, almost entirely obscuring the sun. The ground was, indeed, full of brambles and berries.

"I left this so I knew where to come to," Bartholomew called as he jumped from his motorbike, leaving it on the road and leaning to one side on the stand. Mason was already out of the car. He'd seen the deflated football as soon as the flight lieutenant had stopped. He hardly winced with the quick movement.

"I'll need to replace it," Bartholomew grumbled good-naturedly. "But at least it was to hand." Mason eyed the white football, the leather sides much distressed and now entirely flattened.

"It looks as though it's been punctured by a thousand thorns," Mason offered, not relishing the idea of going into the hedge, even with his big coat and boots on. He spared a thought for O'Rourke with her stockinged legs. He would have to try and keep her out of the undergrowth.

"It probably has," the flight lieutenant offered. He was bending down, peering between some of the bramble bushes.

"Look, you can just about see it," Bartholomew had donned some leather gloves, and Mason pulled his from coat pockets. O'Rourke was busy extracting the camera from the back of the Wolseley.

"It's very well hidden," Mason mused, bending as far as he could without upsetting his balance.

"It's very well hidden. I don't think it would ever have been found if not for the football. Maybe it wasn't such a bad thing that I kicked it so high in the air."

There was a low thrum of engine noises from the aerodrome and people speaking to one another, but it all felt a long way away, especially from this side of the undergrowth.

"I don't see how we'll extract it without walking from the other side of the aerodrome."

"Ah, yes, but see, a little way that way," and the flight lieutenant pointed back towards Erdington. "Is a footpath that only some of us know about. We should be able to squeeze through. At some point, I think it was a proper footpath, but it's been allowed to become overgrown, and now few people are aware it's here. But I do know about it."

Mason nodded, standing and squinting up at the hangars. They were painted a dull green, no doubt to blend into the surrounding countryside, but they were extremely high, the roofs made of corrugated iron.

"How did you even kick a ball so high?" Mason mused.

"I don't know," Bartholomew laughed, all good-natured now. "I can't see that I'll ever manage it again."

"Right, what's the plan?" O'Rourke asked, yet another dazzling smile of white teeth and pink gums for the flight lieutenant.

"We'll wait for Gregory to arrive. I think we should all go in together. But tell me, if you can, was it just the motorbike, or was there the sidecar as well?"

"The sidecar as well," Bartholomew confirmed quickly. "I don't know how they got it in there. However, thinking about it. The sidecar isn't connected to the motorbike. It's tipped on its side, facing one way, and the motorbike has just been dropped onto the ground, without using the stand." He shook his head, seemingly upset by the lack of care for the equipment.

"That makes more sense," Mason confirmed. By now, they'd made their way along the road, and Mason could just see the path about which the flight lieutenant was speaking. It was narrow but not thin enough to prevent a motorbike from passing. Mason could already see where the branches had been snapped and bent as someone had forced their way through.

"I take it this shortcut isn't used very often?"

"No, not when the hedges are like this. They should be cut down, but the farmers have better things to be doing, no doubt," the flight lieutenant mused.

"Thank you for bringing this to our attention," Mason half-smiled. "You can leave it with us now if you need to be back at your duties. If we discover anything, we'll telephone and let you know."

Bartholomew nodded sharply. "That's good. I do have somewhere I need to be." As he returned to his motorbike and started the engine, O'Rourke let out an audible sigh. Mason chuckled.

"Is it the motorbike or the man?"

"Both," she breathed and then startled. "Sorry, Sir. Sorry," but Mason grinned at her and shook his head at the same time.

"Don't apologise to me. War doesn't stop hearts from fluttering. If anything, it makes them worse. Now, I think we should go in with the camera, and then, once the motorbike and sidecar are retrieved, we can see if there might be any fingerprints on it."

"That sounds like a good idea," O'Rourke replied quickly, as the thrum of a lorry filled the air. Mason turned and caught sight of a camouflage-coloured lorry pulling up beside the Wolseley.

"Well, that was quick."

Gregory jumped down from the cab, his eyes on the hedge before them.

"You're going to tell me it's in there, aren't you?" He didn't sound happy about it as he pointed at the hedge. Neither did the man who accompanied him. He was almost bent double with age, his back so curved it looked painful. Mason thought he should probably have asked Bettie to send some of the younger men, but he'd not considered that before this moment.

"I'm sure that between us, we'll be able to retrieve the motorbike and the sidecar," Mason offered as cheerfully as possible.

"Just have to hope the brakes haven't seized," Gregory commented gravelly, his accent thick. He moved to the back of the van and pulled a wooden box towards him. Mason could see that it contained some spanners and other items that Gregory thought he might need.

"Come on then," O'Rourke said brightly, the camera bag against her left side. Mason led on, grimacing at the number of brambles and twisted roots he needed to avoid. Before he disappeared behind the undergrowth, Mason turned to run his eye along the hedgerow to where the deflated leather football still indicated the way. He fixed it in his mind, pulling his coat shut tightly and donning his leather gloves. He could hear the others taking similar precautions.

In no time, the shadow caused by the hangars turned everything into a strange grey haze. Mason made it through the slanting piece of the hedge and waited, catching his breath and shaking his booted foot around. It was tingling because the ground was so uneven, and it was hard to keep his balance. Perhaps, just like the Automobile Association men, he should have allowed someone younger the task. He didn't doubt that Constable Williams would be through the uneven ground quickly in his eagerness.

O'Rourke reared up before him, her eyes down, hat pulled as far down as it would go, for all her braided hair had hooked a short length of bramble and leaves.

"Here, let me get that for you." Mason pulled it away and immediately regretted the action when the hooks caught in his gloves.

"Damn stuff," he shook his hand, but the thorn refused to budge no matter how quickly he did so. Eventually it dropped to the ground. He stamped on it with some malice.

Behind O'Rourke, Mason spied Gregory and the other man making a racket as they stomped on the weeds and brambles that attempted to trip them all. It smelt dank, as though something had died there, although not recently. Mason hoped it was only some small creatures, perhaps knocked over by the passing cars and motorbikes, and nothing more sinister. He didn't need to find a second body.

"Not too much further now," Mason called, but even he could hear the hope in his voice. The grasses were long, reaching to his knees, so he had to lift his booted feet high just to move forward. But there was at least a bit more room between the back of the hangars and the hedgerow, so he didn't have to fight with the brambles while trying to stay upright.

Every so often, Mason glanced up, checking the white football was still indicating the way. Then, eventually, he caught the shape of the van and the Wolseley through the hedgerow and knew the motorbike and sidecar had to be close.

"There it is," O'Rourke called, her eyes picking out the dull green machine lying on the ground. Mason had almost stepped on it.

"It's here," Mason called to Gregory but received no response.

"Get the camera out," but O'Rourke was already doing so. She was moving around the motorbike, taking photographs of everything around it, while Mason hunted for the sidecar. It wasn't beside the motorbike but buried beneath more of the brambles, closer to the road. He imagined he knew why so much trouble had been taken to hide it.

He glanced to O'Rourke. She was bending over the wheels of the motorbike. Gregory had arrived as well. He and the older man were standing waiting for O'Rourke to finish with the camera.

"Where's the sidecar, then?" Gregory called, and Mason pointed.

"Bloody hell. We'll never get it out of there," Gregory complained, and Mason thought he might be right. It was very well concealed, almost impossible to see it for what it was.

"Let us know when you've finished," Gregory called to O'Rourke.

"Will do," she exclaimed cheerfully, but Mason was walking closer and closer to the abandoned sidecar. Here, and now, he'd finally realised the reason the dead man's body had been in such a bizarre position. Could it be so simple, he thought to himself? But already, he knew it was, even before he managed to pull aside enough of the brambles to peer inside the empty sidecar.

And there it was. At the bottom of the sidecar, underneath some branches and leaves, and something that might just be a home for one of the tiny creatures that must live amongst the hedgerow was an Automobile Association sentry box key. Mason reached for it and only just managed to stop himself from gripping it tightly.

"Well, that answers that," he mused, pointing towards the item so that O'Rourke could take photographs of it as well.

"So, the dead man was transported in the sidecar, and then whoever killed him abandoned the sidecar, here? Surely he must have been a local man to know where he could leave the motorbike and sidecar without fear of it being discovered. I mean, I didn't know the footpath was here, and I'm a police officer," O'Rourke commented.

"No, I don't think I knew about it either. So yes, this is where the body was, to start with, in the sidecar, and then the body was moved and abandoned at the bottom of the aerodrome, where the woodlands border the playing fields. I think it would have stayed hidden for longer here," Mason mused.

Behind them, Gregory and the other man had managed to get the abandoned motorbike upright and were tinkering with it. Mason could see that one of the wheels was entirely flat.

"Looks like this wheel hit something heavy and almost buckled it," Gregory was stating to his fellow mechanic.

"Aye. I imagine the man who did this fell heavily from his bike," he offered. He, too, spoke with a pronounced Brummie accent.

"It might even account for why the sidecar has come off," Gregory added.

"Take as many photographs as you can," Mason instructed O'Rourke, moving back to look at the deflated wheel on the motorbike. He felt a flutter of excitement. Were they about to solve the mystery of the dead man?

"The bike has hit something, perhaps a stone or a kerb, but if it were a kerb, they would have been travelling far too fast."

"What about an animal or a person?" Mason asked, out of curiosity, aware that Gregory looked shocked at the inclusion of a person in the question.

"Maybe, but I think it would be something less inclined to give. Those surfaces would bend. I mean, I might be wrong."

"So, a head-on collision?" Gregory nodded, his lips turned down.

"More than likely."

"Are you going to be able to move it?" Mason asked Gregory.

"Yes, but it's not going to be easy. And we'll have to push the sidecar out, as it's not attached to anything."

"We can help," O'Rourke offered, but Gregory shook his head.

"No, we're best to do it ourselves. You can leave it with us."

"Have you taken photographs of everything you need?" Mason asked O'Rourke, appreciating the firm refusal by Gregory.

"I have, yes, but I think we need to take fingerprints."

"I do as well. Here, we can do it between us. It's the sidecar I'm most curious about." Mason stated. He could feel that they were close to solving the mystery of the dead man and perhaps all the other strange occurrences as well. But he needed to be patient for just that little bit longer.

Quickly, he and O'Rourke unpacked the fingerprinting kit and began placing the fine dust over everything. As they worked their way around the outside of the sidecar, Mason felt his hopes dissipate. There were no fingerprints to be found anywhere on the edges of the sidecar, certainly where someone moving something in and out of the small space might have been forced to lean.

But then O'Rourke cried with triumph.

"There's two inside," and she pointed to the splotch of powder as she bent to extract the print from the surface using the special adhesive. Mason fumbled for one of the white cards to attach the stickiness, too, fingerprint as well. And then she repeated the action with the other print she'd found as well.

"Good," Mason grinned, buoyed by the finding, only for O'Rourke to drive the wind from his sails.

"I just hope it's not the dead man's prints." Mason twisted his lips at the thought. Would whoever had done this have known to wear gloves so they couldn't be detected that way? He certainly hoped not. But then, people did know about fingerprinting techniques. On this occasion, Mason would be grateful if their killer had been ignorant of that fact.

Once they'd taken the prints, Mason stood, stretching his back as he did so. Gregory and his fellow mechanic had managed to get the engine on the motorbike to rumble to life.

"Well done," Mason called to them.

"This is the easy bit," Gregory offered, his lips twisted in thought. "We'll get this onto the back of the lorry and then come back for the sidecar. Have you finished with it?" he asked.

"Yes, we've got everything we need, thank you."

"Not a problem. We'll get on with retrieving the RSO and you can get yourselves back to the police station." For a moment, Mason felt as though he was being told what to do, but then Gregory continued.

"You can get yourself a nice of cup and think about us, here, fighting with the brambles." There was no humour in his voice, and Mason didn't know how to respond.

"Good luck," O'Rourke called, responding for them both as she began the walk back to the gap in the hedgerow. Overhead, Mason could hear the rumble of an aeroplane and unconsciously ducked low. Gregory did the same and met Mason's eyes as they both straightened up.

"The damn things always make me duck," Mason offered.

"Well, you never know what might fall from them," Gregory confirmed and turned back to the motorbike. Mason hesitated but could think of nothing else to say, so hastened to catch O'Rourke who was already disappearing through the gap in the hedge.

"Good day," he called, but there was no response.

CHAPTER 11

Back at Erdington Police Station, Mason was impatient to see the fingerprints and have the photographs developed, but Smythe called him into his office immediately. Williams watched him with a sympathetic expression on his young face, but Mason noticed his cheeks were flushed bright pink, and he was making his way out, the squeaking front door attesting to it.

"Mason, take a seat," Smythe offered voice bluff and filled with good cheer. Mason knew that whatever Smythe was about to say wouldn't be good news.

"Now, I know that I pulled you off the counterfeit case, but I need you to jump back on it immediately. The dead man's identity isn't as concerning as the number of counterfeit ration coupons circulating the local shops. I've had the butcher, the baker, and Mr Wrenson from Kingsbury Road in here this morning. They've all realised they have counterfeit coupons, and it costs them dearly because the government won't settle the value of counterfeit coupons. They also said it was the business of the police to be fighting such crimes."

"Have they been keeping a record of who hands them the counterfeit coupons?"

"Sadly, no. They've only realised as they're not being paid for them when they come to redeem them. Mr McTavish at the butchers says he's lost nearly eleven pounds because of it. He's fuming and demanding that we do something about it. It doesn't help that everyone knows we're investigating both the counterfeiting and the dead man. Mr McTavish and Mr Wrenson both said the dead man didn't cost them any money."

"It sounds like you've had quite the visit," Mason tried to console.

"It's poor Constable Williams. He's never had to face someone quite so angry. I've sent him to patrol the park as a means of getting him away from here. I just hope no one assaults him while he's out there."

"I'll get back onto it," Mason confirmed. He was disappointed, but there was time before the photographs were developed. O'Rourke could check the fingerprints taken from the sidecar against those of the dead man.

"We've found the missing motorbike and sidecar for the Automobile Association, at least," Mason offered, moving to leave the small office.

"Good, and as soon as we've solved this counterfeiting scam, you can get back to it. It's shocking that people are so keen to rip off others, especially at this time. I don't like these spivs," Smythe finished, shocking Mason by using the slang term for such gangs.

Mason didn't respond but instead left the office to seek out Jones. Smythe seemed as upset about everything as Williams had been.

Jones was busy examining some counterfeit coupons, using a magnifying glass beneath a bright table lamp.

"How's it going?" Mason asked him. Jones grimaced, but his eyes also brightened.

"It's all well and good everyone complaining about these things, but if they took more care, they'd know they weren't legitimate coupons. Look, the ink is smeared on them, and it's not even the correct shade of orange. If the shopkeepers spoke to each other about it and shared information, it would be better than them coming in here and shouting at Constable Williams and Superintendent Smythe."

Mason nodded thoughtfully, glancing at the coupons as Jones

pointed out the discrepancy between a legitimate coupon and one of the forged ones.

"So, what have you discovered so far?"

"I keep thinking that I've made a breakthrough, and then I haven't. I've spoken to all the local printers, and they don't know of anyone ordering larger quantities of paper, or ink, than usual. So there's no help there. I would have suspected them of being involved, but Mr Pinshot is so straight-laced that I just can't see it."

Mason nodded. Mr Pinshot of the local printers was indeed a man who did everything correctly and in the correct order.

"So, do you know who's selling the counterfeit coupons?"

Again Jones shook his head.

"No one is talking about it. If I could find out who was buying them, I'm sure I could determine who's selling them."

"So, no particular day of the week that they're used, or anything like that?"

"No, but I think Mondays. According to the shopkeepers I've spoken to, Mondays are the busiest days. I think it would be easy to use counterfeit coupons then. No one has time to doubt the validity of the coupons when the queue is out of the door, and the money is flowing."

Usually, the shopkeepers were keener to get the money in the electronic shoot up to the cashier, alongside the coupon from the ration book, and only gave them a cursory glance. Mason knew this. The long queues of people waiting made it imperative that they were quick. When the shopkeepers knew most of their customers, they were less inclined to think them capable of using counterfeit coupons.

It should have fallen to the cashier, usually secreted upstairs with all the pounds, shillings, and half-pennies to double-check everything, to make sure the paper was of the correct quality, the colours the right shade, but that too brought problems and could slow everything down.

"Then we should watch on a Monday and make a list of everyone who visits the butcher or goes to Wrensons. We could work it out from there."

Jones sighed heavily.

"Everyone is already suspicious of me asking questions," Jones looked aggrieved.

"Ah, yes. I imagine it's not the easiest thing to do. Well, we'll think of something else then. For now, we should consider where the counterfeit coupons are coming from."

Jones nodded.

"I've been considering this for some time. I don't think it can be a local doing it because it would be difficult to hide something such as a printing press. If it were in someone's shed, then the neighbours would be nosy enough to ask what the noise was or why they needed the electricity So, someone must be bringing the counterfeit coupons to the area and then selling them on."

"It needs to be someone with access to transport then?" Mason asked, intrigued by Jones' idea.

"Yes, but I suppose they could come on the train. It depends how many of the counterfeit coupons they bring with them,"

"Perhaps, or they might need a motorcar or motorbike with a sidecar?" Jones quirked an eyebrow at Mason, and Mason shook his head.

"Sorry, I'm mixing my cases up," Mason smiled ruefully. "Wouldn't it just be neat and tidy if they were connected?"

"There has to be a lot of money to be made in counterfeiting the ration coupons. After all, people have to pay for them. And we all know the butcher is making extra money from his 'special' offers for those who can afford it."

"So, people have to be able to have enough money for the ration coupons, but it also has to be benefitting someone. Have we noticed anyone with more ready cash than normal? Anyone treating themselves to all these motorcars that others are selling on in the newspaper because they don't have access to petrol?"

At the words, Jones startled, and Mason glanced at him.

'What? Have you thought of someone?"

"I might have done, yes. I'll see what else I can find out, though, before I say more."

"Are you sure?" Mason checked.

"Yes. For now, Smythe wants me to put together a checklist for the shopkeepers, so they know how to tell if a ration coupon is counterfeit."

"Whenever I walk along the high street, the shops are filled with people, and there are long queues as well. I can see why they say they don't have time to check."

"That's what I've been told to do. Smythe says we can only do so much, and so they have to help themselves."

"What are you going to tell them then?"

"First things, first, all the coupons are on rougher paper."

"Rougher paper?" Mason quizzed him.

"Yes, the ration books are already not on the highest quality paper, but the counterfeit coupons are on even thinner paper. See?" And Jones offered two coupons, the orange dots on the one much brighter than on the other. Mason took them and ran his finger over the thickness of the paper.

"You're right. It's entirely different."

"I think the problem is that these counterfeits are being used too close together. If the people doing this were being a little more clever about it, then they'd be being used all over England, and not just here, and then they might just slip past the eye of the government officials just as they do the shopkeepers."

Mason nodded. It was clear that Jones had put a great deal of thought into what was happening.

"I hear you found a quantity of petrol in one of the sentry boxes. I imagine that's the sort of thing these counterfeiters would be interested in accumulating, or at least the people they sell the coupons on to."

"Yes, I think they would be. It's hard, not having access to petrol for all those who own a motorcar or motorbike."

"But if they're taking it from someone else, it's hardly right." Jones sounded outraged.

"I agree with that, but I'm not sure the petrol has been collected through counterfeiting or if it's just been stolen from the sentry boxes. They should all have a small amount of fuel stored inside them so that any waylaid motorist can drive to the closest petrol station and get more."

From the front office, Mason could hear the telephone ringing. He listened to it three times before remembering that Constable Williams had been sent out by Smythe.

"I'll get it," he grumbled and strode as fast as he could to the shrill device, wincing as pain spiked along his back.

"Erdington Police Station," he answered.

"Ah, Chief Inspector," Mason recognised Bettie's voice straight away. "I'm just calling because I wanted to let you know that I've asked head office, and although some of their records have been destroyed in the bombing, it looks as though sentry box S thirty-three hasn't been used for over two years. I was shocked, I tell you, but the person I spoke to said it's quite common these days. No one is travelling a great deal. Some of the remotest sentry boxes haven't been used since 1940."

Mason gasped at her words.

"Two years?"

"Yes, I know. So, it's possible the key hasn't worked for all that time, or that whoever changed the lock realised they could get away with it because no one was making use of it."

"That's certainly a long time," Mason mused. Still, even if the petrol had been there since 1942, petrol had been rationed even then.

"Thank you for the information," he offered.

"Not a problem. I thought it important to share everything with you. Gregory isn't back yet."

"No, he told O'Rourke and me to leave him to it. He said it was going to be a difficult job. The front wheel on the motorbike was entirely flat, and the sidecar separated from the motorbike and quite entangled in the undergrowth. I don't know if it had been ripped off or simply removed. And the hedge is thick and filled with brambles."

"It sounds terrible," Bettie replied quickly. "I'll keep my eye out for them."

"Did head office mention the numbers of any of the other boxes that haven't been used?" Mason asked out of mild curiosity.

"They mentioned they were in Kent and to the south of London. I imagine people are staying away from the coasts in fear of more bombing, and also to the far north, well, as far north as our sentry boxes currently go."

"So nothing up this way then?"

"No, she didn't say that. Why is it important? I can always telephone again."

"No, that's not a problem. I think it's enough for me to think about knowing the sentry box has been standing there for two years without being used. Thank you."

"Very good, Chief Inspector. Do let me know if you need anything else."

As he replaced the receiver, Mason reached for his notebook to add another line of his scrawl. The realisation that the sentry box hadn't been used for over two years was making him think that whatever had brought about the death of the unidentified man might have been going on for much longer than he'd previously considered.

But before he could pursue the thought, the squeaky door heralded the arrival of someone else. He looked up, hoping it would be Constable Williams, back from his patrol in the park, only to clamp eyes on Patrolman Grant.

"Ah, just the man I was looking for," Grant stated. Mason hoped he kept his frustration from his face.

"What can I help you with?"

"It's a bit curious, to be honest, but I believe that Patrolman Montgomery has disappeared."

Mason felt his forehead furrow at the news and only just managed to stop his jaw from dropping open.

He fixed Grant with a firm look.

"Come with me, and tell me everything you know."

Mason listened as Grant shared his story in fits and starts, sitting in front of his desk. It was an increasingly peculiar tale.

"Montgomery and I always go to the Lad in the Lane on a Wednesday. I might think he's a funny fellow, but, well, at the moment, sharing half a pint with anyone is something to look forward to, and of course, beer hasn't been rationed by the government. They don't think it would be good for morale, and I'm inclined to agree with them."

Mason nodded, encouraging Patrolman Grant to continue.

"Last week, he met me there, as usual. This week, there was no sign of him. I waited a good half hour and then made my way to his house.

He lives on Edgware Road. When I got there, the door was locked, all the blackout blinds were up, and there was no response to my door knock."

"I was just assuming he'd forgotten or been waylaid somewhere when the neighbour popped her head out the door and told me she's not seen him for two days; so since you came to the sentry box on Tuesday because I asked you to come. She also said that before that, he'd been acting a bit strange, almost as though he didn't remember where he lived or what he needed to do every day."

"Why haven't you seen him for two days?"

"He's been on leave, just as I was the week before. We are allowed some holiday." Mason grunted softly at Grant's outraged tone. That at least meant that Bettie had been truthful when she'd said that everyone had been turning up for their shifts.

"And the neighbour hasn't seen him since?"

"Not so much as a peek of him. She said it wasn't like him at all. He and her husband were quite friendly, but suddenly, it was as if he didn't know who he was."

Mason was writing in his notebook as Grant carried on talking. O'Rourke had joined them, hovering behind Mason's shoulder as Grant sat opposite him, on the far side of Mason's desk.

"And did you speak to him two days ago?"

"No. I'm sure you saw him drive off before I could speak to him. Not actually that unusual for him. I waved to him, and I saw his RSO."

Mason could feel the pieces of the puzzle starting to connect, but still, he didn't want to say too much. Not yet.

"Do you have a photograph of Patrolman Montgomery?" Mason asked.

"I don't think so, no." Grant's forehead was furrowed in thought.

"I'll go to the house if you give me the address," Mason stated. "There might be one there."

"Really? I didn't think you'd be interested in this, not when the police were so slow to respond to my concerns about the signs. Still, I felt I should come anyway." Patrolman Grant's tone was martyred.

"No, you've done the right thing," Mason tried half a smile, determined not to respond to the comment about the sentry box road signs.

He was torn as to whether he wanted the suspicions about Montgomery to be confirmed or not.

"Then, I'll let you get on," Grant stated quickly. "I wish I'd come sooner now, but I've been at work all day."

"Not to worry. We'll get to the bottom of this," Mason reassured the other man, eager to be on his way to Montgomery's house.

Grant made to stand but then paused. "Do you think it's connected with the road signs?"

"I don't know, but I'll certainly do my best to find out," Mason confirmed. Grant looked unhappy but walked away. As soon as they heard the squeak of the door being opened and closed, O'Rourke and he sprang to action.

"Do you think the dead man is Montgomery?" she asked, reaching for her hat and coat.

"I do, and I think the killer has been pretending to be Montgomery."

"But why?" O'Rourke almost whined with excitement.

"I don't know that, but I think we're getting there now."

Jones looked up from his desk. His eyes were hard and unflinching.

"Smythe wants the counterfeiting problem resolved," he reminded Mason, although his words weren't quite as fletched with anger as Mason was expecting.

"Yes, he does, but we have a missing man, and what's more, he might be our dead man."

"Let's hope he is, and then we can concentrate on more important matters," and Jones' head ducked behind the pile of paperwork once more.

Mason paused and then shook his head. This was more important. A man had been killed, and as of yet, they didn't even know his identity.

CHAPTER 12

Patrolman Montgomery lived on Edgware Road, close to the recreation ground of Stockland Green. As O'Rourke parked the Wolseley, Mason could hear the delighted screams and shrieks of small children playing in the park. He spared a thought for them, enjoying the last of the warm summer days. Soon enough, everyone would be huddled around their fires, trying to keep warm with the meagre fuel supply that rationing allowed people.

He wasn't looking forward to another cold and, no doubt, damp winter. It always made his back and leg act up, and that made him miserable. He just hoped the allotment and garden offered up some delicious vegetables to add some taste to the ubiquitous stews he'd be eating during the cold weather, when it was pot luck whether he actually got a bite of beef or pork. Cooking a stew kept the kitchen warm, even if the taste wasn't always the best.

"Number twenty-three," O'Rourke read from her notebook as they exited the car together.

"It's this one," Mason was already walking up the short pathway that led to the front door. The house was constructed of red brick, as almost all the homes in Erdington were. It was a reasonably new build, the small garden just starting to become overgrown and the roses needing to be trimmed back. As Patrolman Grant had said when reporting Mr Montgomery's disappearance, the curtains were all drawn. The front window jutted out slightly into the main garden, and below it, some small, bright flowers were visible amongst the strangling weeds.

It looked to Mason as though the house might have been falling into slight disrepair even before Patrolman Montgomery disappeared.

Mason knocked on the wooden door, painted black and with the number twenty-three in slight relief against the black paint. It was chipped in places. It could do with being repainted. The front step had some encrusted mud on it as well.

"There's no one in," a female voice called to him almost immediately, as though answering the door knock, even though the sound didn't come from inside. "Are you the police?" she queried. Mason turned to meet the eyes of the voice he heard. It was the neighbour, standing close to the small hedge that separated the two properties.

"Yes, I'm Chief Inspector Mason, and this is Sergeant O'Rourke." Mason thought O'Rourke's uniform spoke enough for who they were, and where they were from.

"Well, as I said, there's no one in. I've not seen Mr Montgomery for two days now." Worry edged the words.

"And who are you?" Mason asked. It was better to get her name straight away.

"Daventry, Glenda Daventry," she offered. She was a slight woman; long hair pulled back from a thin face in a severe bun. She wore a brightly coloured apron of yellow over her dress which was a sedate grey colour. Mason put her age at somewhere in her mid to late forties.

"Have you known Mr Montgomery for long?" Mason queried.

"I'd say, yes. Poor chuck. His wife, God rest her soul, was my best friend. He's not been the same since she died. I try and do my best, but he doesn't like me to interfere, and the last few times I saw him, he didn't even acknowledge me. He's becoming more and more surly with the passage of time. I don't think he'll ever recover from her death. Poor thing. I do pity him."

"And when was the last time you saw him?" Mason prompted.

"Saturday, no wait, Monday. I spoke to him on Saturday afternoon, but not on Monday. That was when he pretended not to know who I was. I sent Mr Daventry round in the evening with a bit of blackberry crumble, and he got the same response. Mr Montgomery didn't even open the back door, just sent poor Dickie on his way, shouting through the door that he just wanted to be left alone. I was offended, but my Dickie was pleased to get a double portion of pudding, although he thought Cyril, Mr Montgomery, sounded a bit strange." Mason nodded, and he could hear O'Rourke writing down everything Mrs Daventry was telling them.

"I don't suppose you have a spare key for the house, do you? We'd like to take a look around inside."

"Yes, I do. Hang on a minute, though. I'll have to go and find it. Sandra, Mrs Montgomery, gave it to me years ago. I'm sure it'll still fit the lock."

"There's no rush," Mason offered, watching her flee into the house.

"Go and try the back door and check the coal store," Mason turned to O'Rourke. She was already halfway around the corner of the abandoned house anyway. She disappeared, and Mason moved back to gaze at the upper storey of number twenty-three. The curtains were tightly shut there as well. At least, he thought, whoever it was who was impersonating Mr Montgomery had been thoughtful enough to ensure adherence to the blackout order.

"Here you go, chuckie," Mrs Daventry appeared, holding a thin brass key. "It's for the back door, not the front one."

"Thank you. I'll bring it back to you when we've been inside."

"What do you think's happened to Mr Montgomery?" A slither of worry had entered her voice. "I mean, you wouldn't be here would you unless you thought something was amiss."

"I don't know anything for sure right now, but once I do, I'll let you know," Mason tried to reassure. He felt Mrs Daventry's eyes on him as he walked around the corner of the house. He was pleased to round the corner where she couldn't see him.

He looked at the thin spread of grass that lay to the far side of the pathway, the waist-high stone wall that separated the house from the neighbours on that side, but he didn't see anything out of the ordinary and then he found O'Rourke. She had her head in the coal shed opposite the back door. The door of an underground bunker was also open, and Mason could smell the combined scent of mud and hope from it.

"Have you found anything?" Mason asked her, although he was sure she would have said.

"No," O'Rourke reared out of the coal shed, wiping a smudge of grey coal from her black cheek, and shook her head.

"No. But he has a good quantity of coal for the coming winter, and the bunker looks comfortable enough. There's some canned food in there, but not much else of note."

"I've got the key from the neighbour. Let's go inside."

O'Rourke nodded eagerly, pulling the coal shed door shut firmly before running her hands down her coat.

"Urgh, this stuff is so dirty," she complained, coughing as well.

Mason turned to the back door. It too was painted black, the bottom of the door much scarred, as though someone routinely kicked their boots against it. He gave it a sharp tap and waited a few moments for someone to answer, although he knew it wouldn't happen. The house was already giving off the air of something abandoned.

When there was no answer, Mason inserted the key and went to open it, but it didn't budge. Now he realised why the bottom of the door was so scuffed. The bottom was stuck tight, only the top giving.

"Give it a kick for me," Mason asked O'Rourke. He didn't want to risk his back.

Quickly, they swapped places, and the door eventually gave under the third of O'Rourke's increasingly rough kicks.

Mason peered inside, O'Rourke standing to one side to allow him to see first.

"Hello," Mason called. "It's the police," he followed on. "Hello," but there was nothing but the echo of an empty house.

"Come on, but be careful." Mason pulled his flashlight from his pocket and shone it into a kitchen that might once have been neat and tidy but wasn't anymore. It wasn't dirty. There were just a lot of things in there. Clothes hung haphazard on a clothes horse, magazines and newspapers were piled on the floor, perhaps waiting to start a fire in the front room, and the Birmingham Post was lying open on the table. Mason checked the date and realised it was the paper from Saturday.

He turned the single sheet over using one tip of his finger, and read the familiar headline, 'Allies tanks capture Verdun." The rationing of items had even spread to the Birmingham Post which was restricted to four pages of tight script.

The house didn't smell unpleasant, nothing above the scent of coal and the general aroma of long-ago cooked food. Carefully, Mason walked to a dresser in the sitting room and shone his torch over the ornaments on display there, preferring not to open the front curtains. There was a piece of grey rock and a few pretty coloureds shells, and then he saw what he needed—a photograph in a silver-edged frame.

He reached out, picked it up and shone his torch over the photograph it contained. A man and a woman, in typical 1920s clothes, the woman's dress low on her hips, standing together, almost smiling, on their wedding day. Mason squinted at the face of the man, pulling the photograph closer to his nose, but it was unmistakable. Mr Montgomery was the man lying cold and unclaimed in the mortuary even if he seemed much younger in the picture he held.

"Why," and O'Rourke voiced Mason's thoughts, as she viewed his find, "did Bettie at the regional office not recognise him when you showed her the photograph? It's a good likeness, even for a corpse."

Mason shook his head.

"I have no idea."

"Do you think she's involved in some way?" O'Rourke demanded.

"Again, I just don't know. But I'd like to discover the answer. First, we need to see if this imposter left anything behind that might enable us to identify who they are. I'm going to assume it's a man, but it might not be. And then we can inform Doctor Lucey that we know who his dead man is in the mortuary."

"Should we take some fingerprints so that we can confirm it?"

"I think we can leave that to Doctor Lucey. We'll take the newspaper from the table, and also a glass or something with us. For now, can you get the camera, and we'll take more photographs."

"I'll get it now," O'Rourke confirmed, turning to leave.

"If Mrs Daventry accosts you, tell her we know nothing yet, but that we'll need to keep the key for the time being."

"Sir," and O'Rourke walked away, leaving Mason standing in the middle of the dead man's sitting room, wondering what had brought about such a strange turn of events. Why was Mr Montgomery dead since Saturday night, and yet someone had taken his patrol duties on Tuesday when Patrolman Grant called the police at Erdington to report the mixed-up road signs at Mile Oak?

By the time O'Rourke returned, Mason had walked through many of the rooms in the house. He'd not seen anything that particularly concerned him. It was the home of a man who lived alone, a man who'd once been married, evident in the small touches such as dirty lace doilies and little knick-knacks gathering dust on long-forgotten shelves. And then the reality of what he was now, with dirty shirts and shoes scattered throughout the house. Plates and mugs as well, although they were at least free from food.

The house smelled but only of being locked up tight during the warm days and nights of the summer months.

It was not an unpleasant house, far from it. Mason wondered who would live there next because Mr Montgomery had no children. That was clear because there were no rooms filled with children's toys. Neither were there any photographs of babies becoming young children and then becoming adults, such as someone would find in his own home if they were ever to come looking.

The sound of the camera alerted Mason to the fact that O'Rourke had returned. She was in the kitchen, or at least, it sounded as though she was while he was upstairs.

Here, in the bedroom, he'd found some disarray. The bedding was thrown back, the blankets trailing onto the floor, and there was a glass of water with a dead fly in it. It also looked as though someone had struggled to find the right clothes to wear because there was a pile of discarded Automobile Association uniform shirts and trousers flung over the back of the chair next to the dressing table. There was no sign of the smart jacket that Patrolman Grant had been wearing.

Mason noted that all of Mrs Montgomery's clothes were still in the wardrobe. He swallowed his sadness for the man. Hadn't he endured enough without having been murdered as well?

Mason poked into the two other rooms, but they held little furniture. One must have been a spare bedroom, perhaps for the hoped-for child that never materialised, while the other had been used as a storage room. It contained boxes and tins of food. It seemed that Mr and Mrs Montgomery had anticipated the shortages of the war years and had stocked up before rationing made it impossible to do so.

Randomly, he picked up a tin of soup, noted the use by date was still good and thought of the people the food could help once the house was no longer a crime scene. He heard O'Rourke on the stairs.

"Anything?" he popped his head out of the door.

"Nothing that seems unusual, no. Cor, the bedroom's a bit of a mess," she commented on looking inside.

"It is, yes. I imagine our killer was a larger man than Mr Montgomery, and he needed to find some clothes that fit him. Or, a smaller man, and he struggled to find something he could walk in without fear of his trousers falling down by his ankles."

"I still don't understand why anyone would impersonate Mr Montgomery."

"Me neither, but I'm sure we will, in good time. At least we know who our victim was now."

"I'm almost relieved he was a widower. I wouldn't have liked to inform his wife of what happened to him."

Mason grunted softly. "If he'd been married still, he would have been reported missing more quickly. Then we would at least have known who he was." O'Rourke nodded in agreement, her eyes never leaving the mess of the bedroom.

"Right, finish up in here, and I'll go and see if Mrs Daventry can tell us if Mr Montgomery had parents who still lived or a brother or sister."

"I'll lock up on the way out," O'Rourke confirmed. "I haven't spoken to her yet, but she's hovering behind the net curtains in the sitting room."

Mason grimaced at the news and made his way slowly down the very steep stairs with care. At the bottom of the stairs, he paused to examine the front door. It had the key in the lock, as though whoever had been here hadn't used the door at all. Then he went to the side door, beneath the stairs, and again noted the key was inside the locking mechanism. It seemed that only the backdoor had been used. That wasn't unusual. He often forgot they even had a side door in his house. Two doors were more than enough in any home.

Outside, he squinted into the bright daylight and made his way to Mrs Daventry's front door. He was unsurprised when she opened it before he'd even knocked.

"Mrs Daventry, I'm afraid we'll have to hold on to the key for a bit longer. I hope you don't mind. We'll get it back to you as soon as we can. Now, can you tell me if Mr Montgomery's parents still live or if he has brothers or sisters?"

Immediately, Mrs Daventry shook her head, her eyes fearful.

"What's happened to him?" she breathed.

"I can't confirm anything just yet, apologies."

She nodded, even as a tear leaked from her eye. Mason wouldn't be surprised if she'd belatedly made the connection that Mr Montgomery might well be the man found in the woodlands close to the aerodrome. But she didn't ask, and he didn't offer the information.

"He had no one, but his wife has a sister. She lives in Liverpool, though. I do have the address if you need it."

"That would be most helpful, thank you," and once more, Mrs Daventry scurried away to find the information. Mason waited patiently, enjoying the time to think. Why had Bettie lied about knowing who the dead man was? The photograph of the dead man had been a good likeness, based on the wedding photograph he'd seen. He didn't like to think that Bettie was somehow involved, but it was certainly something he needed to consider.

He'd shared a great deal of information with her, probably too much. If it were found that she was somehow involved in the murder of the dead man, he'd have to admit what he'd done. Not that he had a problem doing so, but all the same, he chastised himself for making such a simple mistake of trusting someone too quickly who might be implicated in the crime he was investigating.

"Here you are. I've written down all the details for you," Mrs Daventry startled Mason with her words, and he smiled as he took the small piece of paper with crabbed but neat writing on it.

"My thanks," he offered.

"Is everything alright with the house?" Mrs Daventry turned to eye her neighbour's house with unease.

"Everything with the house is fine. There's no sign of Mr Montgomery inside, so it shouldn't be anything for you to worry about." Mason noticed that her hands were twisting one inside the other, the knuckles showing white, and he thought to reassure her.

"I don't see that there's anything that could have been done by yourself. Mr Grant reported Mr Montgomery missing, and you've provided me with a key. Now, I'll hurry to bring you back some answers as to what's happened, but you should just go about your normal day to day affairs. There's nothing else you can do." Mason admitted it sounded far from reassuring, but Mrs Daventry smiled all the same.

"Thank you, Chief Inspector."

CHAPTER 13

"Where now," O'Rourke met him at the Wolseley, the camera over one shoulder, the newspaper and glass both in brown paper bags.

"Doctor Lucey," Mason announced firmly. "But first, I better let Smythe know what we're doing, and we can leave the photographs you've taken for development."

O'Rourke brought the car back to life without argument, having stowed the items on the back seats, and they made the short journey back to the police station. It really didn't take more than a few minutes.

"Just leave it here. We'll only be a minute or two," Mason instructed O'Rourke, as she pulled up close to the police station on Sutton New Road. Together they walked inside, O'Rourke carrying the camera once more. Smythe pounced on Mason as soon as the door squeaked to announce their arrival. Mason was used to his superintendent waiting for him.

"Mason, a word with you, please." There was no warmth in Smythe's words, and Mason arched an eyebrow at O'Rourke as he followed the other man into his office.

"I told you the counterfeiting took precedence," Smythe began as soon as the door was closed behind Mason. His cheeks were flushed red, his fury evident to see, as he peered at Mason. Not for the first time, Mason considered just how poor Smyth's eyesight was.

"I know who the dead man is," Mason countered immediately. A slow smile spread on Smythe's face, his flushed cheeks highlighting the scar of his old war wound on the left side, his useless eye seeming to sparkle with the knowledge as Mason explained everything he'd discovered while away from his desk.

"But why?" Smythe asked, just like O'Rourke, his forehead furrowed in thought.

"We'll have to discover that as soon as we can. What do you think I should do about Bettie at the Automobile Association regional office?"

"I think you should arrest her," was Smythe's immediate response. "No. No, don't do that," he quickly changed his mind, shaking his head. "Go and ask the questions and see if you think she knew who Mr Montgomery was. Perhaps they never met?"

"That's what I'd been thinking," Mason confirmed. "Can I leave you with the address of the sister-in-law which Mrs Daventry gave to me? As soon as we confirm who Mr Montgomery is, we'll need someone to visit her and explain what's happened. She might know of other relatives that'll need to be informed."

"Yes, I'll ensure it's done. Now. Go on, get on with you. I'll help Jones with the counterfeiting while you're gone. It'll be a feather in my cap if we can solve this case as well. Well done, Mason," and with that, Mason was dismissed by a gleeful, smiling Smythe, very different from the man who'd met him on arrival at the police station. Quickly, he returned to the Wolseley. He walked passed Williams on the way. The lad looked pale but smiled brightly enough on seeing Mason.

"People are strange, Williams, never forget that," Mason offered him, thinking that the words really couldn't be more apt.

Doctor Lucey greeted them at the door to the mortuary. He was dressed in a dark suit, bowler hat in hand and seemed to be in a rush.

"Sorry to disturb you, Doctor Lucey. But I think we've found the identity of the dead man."

"What? Or rather how?" Doctor Lucey asked, already turning around, and beckoning them into his office, his tone far from brusque.

"So, you know who the man is?" Doctor Lucey hastily summoned his assistant.

"Can you check for prints on these items," and O'Rourke handed over the two brown paper bags carefully. "Hopefully, they'll match those of our dead man."

"Certainly," the older man said, caught up in the palpable sense of excitement.

"It won't take us a moment, and we'll be able to tell if it's the same man," Doctor Lucey informed Mason and O'Rourke. As he spoke, Doctor Lucey pulled a file on to his desk, and Mason could see a diagram of a body on the sheet of paper. There was also a page showing the fingerprints taken from it. They showed as black splodges on a white background.

"I'm not an expert, of course. We'll have to have them double-checked, but we should be able to pick out some of the details." Mason could see a lamp that overhung the desk. He was sure it would contain a particularly bright bulb for close work.

"But," and Doctor Lucey fixed Mason with a stern eye. "I take it that it brings you no closer to knowing why the man was killed."

"No, not yet. But he worked for the Automobile Association, so it does explain some of the other findings, the key for a start. I'm sure all the patrol personnel must have one."

"Yes, but why was he bent double?"

"Ah, now I think he must have been folded into the sidecar of one of the patrol motorbikes, or the RSO's as the Automobile Association call them. We've found one that was abandoned close to Castle Bromwich aerodrome amid some hellish bramble bushes. There was a key in the bottom of the sidecar and no equipment. That's where the patrolmen keep their tools, usually."

"Do you have the key? Just to confirm?"

Mason nodded, and O'Rourke handed over the retrieved key and the brown paper bag it had been placed within. Doctor Lucey shook it onto his desk and bent to examine it, having turned on the fiercely bright lamp.

There was silence for a minute or two as Doctor Lucey moved it around using two pencils so as not to mark it with his fingers.

"Yes, this is the one. It's got a rough cut on one side, and it's left a deep cleft on the forehead. It certainly fits better than the original key you showed me." Doctor Lucey peered at Mason as he flicked the bright light off once more.

"What's it all about?"

"I'm going to have to assume that Mr Montgomery saw something he wasn't supposed to and was murdered because of it. Why the murderer then pretended to be him, I have no idea."

Behind them, the door opened, and Doctor Lucey's assistant walked in and handed over a white card with one fingerprint on it.

"It's the best I could do," the older man offered wryly. "Do you think it's enough?"

Once more, Doctor Lucey turned on his bright light and looked from the card to the fingerprints he had on record for the dead man. There was silence. Mason hardly dared breathe. And then Doctor Lucey nodded.

"It's him alright. This fingerprint matches the one for his index finger. If this print belongs to Mr Montgomery, and I think we have to assume it does, then it's the same man. Now, we just need a family member to identify the body." Doctor Lucey spoke with satisfaction, but Mason was already shaking his head.

"That might not be very easy. It seems that Mr Montgomery had no family. The neighbour only knows of his sister-in-law, and she lives in Liverpool."

Doctor Lucey looked crestfallen at the news.

"Well, at least we know who he is, even if official identification is yet to take place. Now we can move him on from the mortuary in quick time. If you'll excuse me, I was on my way to Court, and I'll be somewhat late now."

Mason and O'Rourke followed Doctor Lucey from the mortuary. The pathologist walked too briskly for Mason, and in no time at all, they'd lost sight of him through the maze of corridors that ran beneath the hospital.

"So, we know who he is," O'Rourke offered quietly and with some satisfaction.

"Yes, and now we just need to know why he was killed. Let's hope the answer to that doesn't lie with Bettie, or my judgement has become impaired of late." Mason sighed heavily. He wasn't looking forwards to the following interview he needed to conduct.

At the Automobile Association regional office, Bettie eyed Mason with surprise.

"Do you have an appointment?" she asked, even though it was apparent they didn't.

"No, but we need to speak to you and Mr Wheelwright, please," Mason spoke firmly. He didn't want Bettie to think of a reason why they couldn't. Fergus had allowed him into the car park without any fuss. Mason might have preferred an argument to the calm acceptance.

"Very well, come this way, and I'll inform Mr Wheelwright that you're here." She walked briskly, and Mason tried to decide whether she was more nervous than usual. But she didn't appear to be. He was perplexed by her combative attitude to him and O'Rourke. It didn't seem to be anything that Mason had done. Perhaps Bettie was just having a bad day.

"Good morning," Mr Wheelwright chirped to them when they were seated in his office. "Is this about the lost RSO? I'm pleased you managed to find it. I don't think we'd have ever thought to look at Castle Bromwich Aerodrome." Mr Wheelwright seemed entirely restored to his normal self, considering Bettie had said she'd had to send him home earlier. Perhaps he'd made a quick recovery.

"We've also determined the identity of the dead man," Mason offered. "And that's why we're here." He'd have liked to watch Bettie's face at the news, but she was stood beside him and not in front.

"Why's that then?" Mr Wheelwright asked.

"It seems he was one of your patrolmen, and yet when I brought his image here, neither of you knew who he was."

"What?' Now Mr Wheelwright's face glowered, and he eyed Bettie aghast. Again, Mason couldn't see Bettie's face. He did notice she was standing exceedingly still.

"I understood all of our men and women were accounted for in the last week." Mr Wheelwright directed that to Bettie.

"They are, yes." Mason finally managed to glance at Bettie, and she seemed as confused as the rest of them, her forehead wrinkled in thought, her arms hanging limply to either side of her.

"I did show you the photograph of him," and now O'Rourke extracted the photograph of the dead man's face from the brown file she carried with her.

"I've never seen him," Mr Wheelwright exclaimed. "But then, I don't know all the men and women by name. There are too many of them, and we're a recent establishment."

"And you?" This Mason directed at Bettie.

"I've never seen that man before," she said softly, the words wrenched from her. She spoke them, but unwillingly. That much was evident.

"This is Mr Montgomery, who lived in Erdington and worked on the route that included Mile Oak."

"With Mr Grant?" Bettie demanded, forehead still furrowed, eyes widening.

"Yes."

"Well, I never met him either. Now, let me think about it for a moment. There was a reason for it." A heavy silence filled the small office, Mr Wheelwright positively glaring at Bettie as though this was all her fault.

Mason waited. He didn't want to accuse Bettie of anything, not yet.

"Ah, that's it," Bettie exclaimed eventually. "His RSO was so new that there was an agreement that he need not come here and could keep his equipment at home. We prefer it if the RSOs are regularly serviced and kept here overnight, but with it being so new, I thought it acceptable to allow the little arrangement. After all, it meant Mr Montgomery had more petrol for his patrols."

"So, in six months, Mr Montgomery never once came here?"

"Now. I did speak to him on the telephone on a few occasions. He called me via one of the sentry boxes, and then head office put the call through to me. I thought it was most unusual, but Mr Grant explained he'd been widowed and wasn't quite the chatty man he'd once been. I did ask you about it?" Now Bettie fixed her stare on Mr Wheelwright. He reared back as though under attack and then nodded slowly, just the once.

"You're right. I vaguely remember. You asked if it was acceptable in light of the tragedy, and we decided we could allow it to happen for a few months, but no longer. I take it, those few months were extended?"

"Yes, it's all been such a flurry of activity. I can hardly believe we've been in the building for over six months." Bettie didn't laugh at the end of the sentence, although Mason was half expecting it.

"So no one here would have met him?"

"No, just the men he worked with; Mr Grant and the other patrolman. What was his name? Ah, yes, Mr Richardson. He regularly brought his RSO in for a service. He's a very gregarious fellow. He likes to chat with Gregory. I often have to send him on his way, or they'd spend all day gossiping like two old women." Bettie's hands remained still at her side, but Mason could tell from her tone that she disapproved of Gregory being tardy with his duties.

"I understand that Mr Montgomery had no immediate family?"

"I'll have to get his personnel file," Bettie announced.

"O'Rourke, will you go with Mrs Morton, please?" Mason instructed as Bettie made to leave.

"Of course, Sir," and O'Rourke hurried to catch up. Mason was inclined to believe Bettie, but it was only right to be cautious.

"You can't think that Bettie had anything to do with this?" Mr Wheelwright demanded, leaning forward over the desk. He was the most animated that Mason had seen him to date.

"I think it better to show some caution," Mason countered. "Wouldn't Mr Montgomery have come to collect his weekly pay packet? It all seems a little strange?"

"We have some different arrangements at the moment. We have to do all we can to ensure we don't use too much petrol. And we can't have the patrol members having to use the buses or trams to get here all of the time. They work six days a week, ensuring breakdowns and other problems don't unduly inconvenience our members. Before the regional office was here, we had someone drive around handing out pay packets. It was the only way to do it."

Mr Wheelwright was becoming agitated, and Mason sighed inaudibly.

"So, who was this person that delivered the pay packets?"

"Oh, I don't know that. Bettie would know." It wasn't the answer that Mason wanted. But by then, Bettie, with O'Rourke trailing her, had returned to the office. Bettie clutched a brown folder to her chest, but Mason could see her hands shaking slightly.

"I have it here that Mr Montgomery has his wife listed as his next of kin. The details have then been crossed through, and a Mrs Phillips from Liverpool has been added. Poor man," she finished with a wobble to her voice. Mason was surprised that the usually stoic Bettie was so upset.

"Thank you," Mason offered. "We'll ensure that she's informed of his death."

"We need to do something, a collection of some such, to pay for his funeral," Bettie continued, her comments directed to Mr Wheelwright.

"Yes, we will, but first, I think we need to know more of why he was killed. If it was an unsavoury business, then we don't want to draw attention to what happened." The harsh words fell flatly in the room, and Mason almost winced as Mr Wheelwright 'the company man' made the statement.

"We'll be going," Mason was already standing. "Before we do, can we look at the file you have for Mr Montgomery? We might find other details on there that are pertinent to the case."

"Yes, of course," Mr Wheelwright swept his right hand towards Bettie, and she hesitantly handed over the folder to O'Rourke.

"There's a desk in the office you can use," Bettie continued, standing as well. She remained unsettled by this turn of events.

"Perhaps you can have one of the secretaries make you a cup of tea, Mrs Morton," Mr Wheelwright commented, having noticed her discomfort. However, it was clear he disapproved, showing it by addressing her formally. To date, he'd always called her Bettie.

"An upsetting day," Mr Wheelwright continued, but Mason was already closing the door on him. Bettie staggered in front of him, and

O'Rourke leapt to offer her a shoulder, and together the pair made it to an arrangement of four chairs around a low table. Mason nodded to O'Rourke to acknowledge such quick assistance, and then she strode to the open office to demand a cup of tea for Bettie.

Mason sat in front of Bettie, watching her face. Her breathing was too fast, and her eyes frantic. Away from Mr Wheelwright, it seemed that Bettie had more to add to the puzzle.

"In your own time," Mason said when she opened and closed her mouth a few times.

"Yes, yes, of course," Bettie agreed, her hand fluttering on her lap.

"Mr Grant and I, well," and Mason sucked in a shocked breath. This was not what he was expecting to hear. "We had a personal relationship, and I confess, I may have allowed things I might not have normally allowed. I believe Mr Wheelwright suspects, but we've never spoken of it. I'm a war widow. Nineteen thirty-nine my poor Jim met his end. Mr Grant and I struck up a conversation because we're both quite pedantic about things, and well, it went on from there, I'm afraid."

Mason held his tongue, curious to see if she'd offer any further information. O'Rourke was slowly making her way back, holding a tray with three mugs on it. Mason doubted it would taste very tea-like, but he was thirsty. It had been an extremely long day.

"So you never met Mr Montgomery, then?"

"No, Mr Grant said he was 'a funny old fish', those were his words, and didn't want to have to come to collect his wage packet or anything like that. When his RSO developed a problem, it was Mr Grant who brought it here for repair. I shouldn't have allowed that to happen."

"Well, I don't think that's a criminal offence," Mason tried to console. Bettie had two tears falling down her cheeks now.

"No, but if I'd only met the man, then I'd have known who he was when you asked me the first time around."

"Yes, but it's only delayed us by a few days," Mason wasn't sure what to say. Luckily, O'Rourke placed a steaming mug of tea between Bettie's hands. Bettie took it and went to raise it to her lips without thought.

"Careful, it's hot," O'Rourke cautioned her. Bettie pulled the mug away from her lips like an obedient child.

"Do you think Mr Grant is somehow involved in his murder?" The words were spoken through very tight lips. Mason again startled. He hadn't considered that option. Not yet.

"Why would you think that?"

"I. I don't know," and Bettie began to cry in earnest. Mason looked to O'Rourke with a grimace. O'Rourke rolled her eyes at his discomfort and placed her arms around Bettie, holding her close.

"Is there someone we can get for you?" O'Rourke asked, but Bettie shook her head.

"No, no," she gasped, trying to control herself.

Mason looked from one woman to the other, knowing he should say something but unsure what would help. Instead, to the soft gasps of Bettie, as she tried to control herself, Mason pulled Mr Montgomery's file onto his lap and began to flick through it. He heard O'Rourke's huff of indignation but chose to ignore it.

He doubted there was anything to find inside the file, but at least it gave him something to do while Bettie composed herself.

The thought of Bettie and Mr Grant as lovers was quite shocking, but only because he couldn't imagine two people more unalike. But, what did he know? It wasn't as though the idea of them together offended him, not at all. It was just, of all the things Bettie could have said to him, that was, without doubt, the most surprising. She could have confessed to murdering Mr Montgomery, and he would have been less flabbergasted.

Opening the folder, he found a printed form filled in with rounded handwriting. Here, he discovered that Mr Montgomery's first names were Cyril Wilfred. Somehow, the name didn't fit with the image he had of the man. He'd been forty-four years old at the time of his death. He'd been born in Erdington, and he'd worked for the Automobile Association for fifteen years, although there was a gap when he'd enlisted in the army. The next sheet was a list of his pay packets for the year, showing that he earned three pounds and fifteen shillings a week in his role as a patrolman. That amount hadn't changed since before the war, as Mason scanned back through the sheets of paper and found details of his pay for the entire fifteen years of his service.

It seemed then that Cyril Montgomery was a local boy who had no doubt known the routes he'd patrolled well. Mason couldn't remember having ever met him before, but then, Erdington wasn't a small place, and if he'd never had cause to reach out to the police, there was no reason for Mason to have known who he was.

A soft whimper, and Mason glanced at Bettie, who'd finally stopped crying and was now sipping carefully at her hot tea. Mason reached for his mug and swallowed the slightly unappetising mixture. At least it was warm.

"What will happen now?" Bettie asked, eventually.

"We still need to find out why this happened," Mason acknowledged. "Knowing who our poor victim was is only part of the puzzle."

"Yes. And his family?"

"They'll be informed."

"If you could let them know that there are his wages to collect, thank you," Bettie gulped, and Mason nodded.

"Will you be alright if we leave now?"

"Yes, I'll get back to work," Bettie nodded, no doubt trying to convince herself.

"Here, you can keep this. It doesn't contain a great deal."

"No, it doesn't," Bettie admitted.

"But, I did notice that Cyril had never become a sergeant, only ever a patrolman."

"From what Mr Grant, Alfred, told me, Cyril never wanted to be a sergeant. He was content to work with Alfred. They got on well, in their own way."

"Didn't he have to be promoted?"

"Only if he wanted to be, and he never asked for it."

"And, if I remember correctly, he was in the army, and they released him on compassionate grounds when his wife was killed?"

"Yes, there was talk of the patrol personnel becoming members of the army. It didn't come to anything, but it remained a possibility for many months, and I think that Mr Montgomery would have welcome that. I'm not sure he enjoyed being at home, alone."

"Thank you," Mason stood, feeling a twinge in his back. It had been a long day.

"Before you leave, you might want to ask Gregory about the retrieved RSO. I know he's been working on it all day."

"Thank you. I'll do just that." And Mason carried his mug back to the office and muttered his thanks to the older man who leapt to take it from him. As he and O'Rourke walked outside, he turned back to see Bettie squaring her shoulders and knocking on Mr Wheelwright's door. Mason couldn't imagine it was going to be an easy conversation for either of them.

Gregory was waiting for them when they stepped outside the doors. Mason was still considering just what Bettie had said to him. He was still surprised. He couldn't deny it.

"I think I need to show you something," Gregory spoke without preamble, already walking away from them, making it clear they were to trail him.

Mason shared a glance with O'Rourke and followed the overall-wearing mechanic to the enormous barn inside which all the moth-balled vehicles were being stored.

"What have you found?" Mason asked of Gregory.

"Not a great deal, but then, when we went to clean the sidecar down, something struck me as a bit strange. It looks to me as though the sidecar was driven into something as well as the motorbike itself." Gregory was pointing at something on the sidecar, but Mason struggled to see what it was, even when he bent down even closer to examine it. He could only just tell that there was a slight dent at the front of the sidecar, showing as a shadow against the camouflage green.

"What is it?" He asked, making way for O'Rourke to try and determine what it was while Gregory watched them.

"It looks like ink or paint to me," O'Rourke stated quickly, her eyes squinted to get a good look at it.

"I think we probably need to photograph this," Mason commented. O'Rourke was already on her way back to the Wolseley before he'd finished his sentence.

Gregory watched Mason carefully.

"You've got a bizarre crime here, haven't you?" he stated conversationally.

"Yes. Tell me, did you manage to extract the sidecar and the motorbike, alright?"

"Yes, it took us a long time. It was nearly dark, but we managed to make it back here before the blackout came into effect. I was a bit worried at one point. Those brambles were vicious," and Gregory held out his oil-stained hand to show Mason a deep cut there.

"You need to keep that clean," Mason said quickly.

"Aye, I know. I've been wearing gloves most of the day."

"And you still think the wheel hit something heavy?" Mason asked as O'Rourke returned and began taking photographs of the retrieved sidecar and motorbike before focusing on the area of possible printed text.

"Yes, and I can tell you that they kept going long beyond the time they should have done. Whoever was driving should have stopped long before the wheel got into such a state." Gregory continued thoughtfully.

Mason was trying to think of what the wheel might have hit and why it might have been driven long beyond the endurance of the tire.

"So, they wouldn't have been able to drag the motorbike very far then, once the wheel was completely deflated?" Mason asked, just to be sure.

"No, not at all. It would have been difficult to steer. They went to a lot of trouble to hide what had happened."

In his mind, Mason was starting to piece together a timeline of events. It seemed clear to him that the body of Cyril Montgomery had been forced into the empty sidecar and driven to the spot where his cold, dead body had been abandoned. It didn't explain how the culprit found another RSO, and neither did it explain why they'd then pretended to be Cyril Montgomery, but he thought the answer might be becoming more evident.

"Thank you for showing me the markings," Mason said to Gregory.

"Is it alright if I clean them off now?" Gregory asked.

"Yes, if they'll come off," Mason confirmed.

"Well, if they don't, I'll just paint over them. It's not as though this motorbike is going anywhere in a rush. I've been told to put it back in service but then make sure no one uses it anytime soon. I'll be putting it back where it was when it was stolen."

With that, Mason and O'Rourke made their way back to the Wolseley, having thanked Gregory for his sharp eyes.

"Now where?"

"Erdington Police Station," Mason instructed. "I'm curious to see if they've managed to make contact with Cyril's sister-in-law."

He settled back in the car to watch the traffic around them. He knew who the dead man was, but there were still too many questions to satisfy him. Certainly, there was no end in sight, not yet.

CHAPTER 14

"Mason, a word please," Smythe called before Mason could so much as plant himself in his chair. The squeaky front door must have given him away, Mason thought wryly. Jones was out of the office. There was a space where he usually sat. Constable Williams was watching the front counter with a morose expression. Only O'Rourke had a smile on her face.

"Sir," Mason addressed Smythe on entering the small office. His superintendent didn't look pleased. Sam wondered what had happened now. He was expecting to see some satisfaction in Smythe's bearing for having solved the case of the unidentified dead man.

"I've made contact with Liverpool Police Station, and they have a strange story to tell me. They know exactly who our victim's sister-in-law is because she too has been found dead in the last four days."

Mason shook his head, entirely perplexed by the news.

"But, they have an idea why. It seems that our sister-in-law was involved with a counterfeiting scheme being run from a local farm in the countryside surrounding Liverpool. She was the one who was selling the counterfeit coupons in certain areas of Liverpool. She was notorious for it, but the police couldn't find the proof whenever they took her in for questioning. She kept her supplies somewhere and they never managed to find out where it was, even though they had been watching her."

"They needed to find her with the actual counterfeit goods, or they couldn't charge her with the crime of supplying counterfeit goods. It didn't matter how many people said it was her, and to be honest, it was only the shopkeepers who said it was her. The people she was selling to were quite content with the arrangement."

"So, what, we think Cyril, sorry, Mr Montgomery was involved as well?"

But Smythe was already shaking his head. "No. I don't think that. But I'm led to believe by my counterpart there that he tried to help the police find the proof. It seems the two, Cyril and his sister-in-law, hadn't been getting on for quite some time. He was happy to implicate her even if others wouldn't."

"What, she was selling in Erdington as well?" Mason gasped. It outraged him that someone could come to the place where he lived and sell to people he considered to be his friends and neighbours.

"Yes, well no. The counterfeits were being sold here as well, but not by the sister-in-law. There's no doubting the same operation at the Liverpool farm accounts for our problem. Mr Montgomery had an idea how the counterfeit coupons were being moved to Erdington and who was doing it. I think it wouldn't be too much of a stretch to assume he was murdered by one of the counterfeiting spivs when he went after that proof for the Liverpool police."

Mason exhaled slowly.

"So both are connected. As Cyril worked for the Automobile Association and had access to their sentry boxes, I'm going to assume there were drop-offs in the local area. Now wait," and Mason almost shouted the words as he darted from his chair and snatched the counterfeit ration book from Jones' deserted desk. He'd not moved so quickly for years.

There were only a few of the counterfeit ration books because it was harder to counterfeit the ration books with their serial number and local office stamp on them than just print the coupons themselves. Those coupons could then be inserted inside an existing ration book by whoever purchased them from the spivs.

"Right under our noses," Mason announced, presenting it to Smythe triumphantly, holding the book so close to his nose that Smythe reared backwards. Smythe had no idea what Mason was showing him, his forehead furrowed in consternation.

"What? What are you saying? I don't understand"

"The numbers they're using on the counterfeit ration book. How didn't I see this before? Look, the serial number is a combination of the sentry box numbers for the local area. See?" And Mason pointed at the small brown covered booklet where the stamp showed in the bottom right hand corner, the food office stamp for Erdington on the left. The serial number read EJ9242335, above which there was the surname and address of the person who the book had belonged to before being confiscated, even though it had been a fake name and address.

"What?" Smythe asked again, looking from Mason to the ration book, his expression still perplexed.

"Stewponey is sentry box number ninety-two, Mile Oak is sentry box number forty-two, and Moxhull is sentry box number three hundred and thirty-five."

"Bloody hell, Mason, you've cracked it?" Smythe beamed at him as he spoke, abruptly understanding what Mason had seen on the brown cover.

"Well, I sort of have. We still need to find our murderer and catch the spivs at it," Mason conceded, the thrill of discovery draining from him as quickly as it had arrived.

"We need Roberts and his team. This is too big for us to solve alone." Smythe was already on his feet, heading for the telephone on the front desk, his mind made up. Simultaneously, Mason moved back to the small pile of counterfeit ration books on Jones' desk they'd been given by the local shopkeepers, alongside the actual forged coupons. Now he picked them up, and then he pulled his notebook from his pocket and called O'Rourke to his side. She hadn't heard what he'd been saying to Smythe, although she could sense that something had changed. Mason could tell in the narrowing of her eyes as she watched him.

"Do we still have one of the maps showing all the sentry box locations that we took from sentry boxes ninety-two and three hundred and fourteen, or did we return them to Bettie?" he demanded to know.

"Yes, Sir, we do still have one," O'Rourke had lapsed into her role as subordinate and was already reaching for something from her locked drawers.

"Get it for me, and in fact, bring it into the back room. I'll bring the counterfeit ration books and forged coupons with me."

"Are the two cases related?" O'Rourke demanded to know, even as the front door squeaked and Jones appeared, looking flustered. His gaze swept between the two of them, but he didn't speak. Smythe could be heard informing Roberts over the telephone of what they'd discovered, his speaking voice far from quiet. Jones' mouth slowly dropped open in shock and wordlessly he moved to follow them into the back room. O'Rourke had listened as well, and her lips were bent in satisfaction. She looked even more pleased than when they'd first arrived.

O'Rourke fumbled the map but quickly had it open on the table before them where the photographs they'd taken were piled up. The entirety of England and Wales was spread before them. Scotland wasn't on the map.

"I need to know the sentry box numbers, say around Liverpool," Mason explained as he peered at the map.

Jones' eyes narrowed, and he looked from Mason to the map. Mason assumed that Jones had been following up on the lead he'd devised for the counterfeiting case. It seemed he'd had no success, and now it was irrelevant anyway.

"Look at the numbers," Mason instructed Jones, thrusting the counterfeit book at him, before pointing down at the map. His finger circled the three sentry boxes they'd visited close to Birmingham, the one at Stewponey, Mile Oak and Moxhull, even as O'Rourke began to call out numbers to Mason.

"There's another of those strange 'S' numbers," O'Rourke muttered. "S twenty-seven. Three hundred and twenty. Four hundred and ninety-five. Five hundred and eleven."

Mason wrote them down in his notebook, having handed the ration book to Jones, and picked up the few other complete books they had. It wasn't very often that people could use ration books issued other than by the local government office. On rare occasions, it did happen. In this instance, the counterfeit had been confiscated by Wrensons on realising what it was. The name on the book had been false, and Mr Wrenson hadn't been able to determine who the person was, their face covered by a scarf on a chilly morning. Mason remembered the story well. Mr Wrenson had come to the police station, in person, to report the crime. He'd been furious.

"Ah-ha," Mason all but exploded with triumph. Jones was slowly starting to understand the connection that Mason had made, while O'Rourke looked at Mason, her eyes bright with excitement.

"This one is for the Liverpool region," Mason exclaimed with triumph, once more pointing at the serial number. "See, the three numbers from the local sentry boxes. They're using the sentry box numbers as ration book numbers, and then they're using the sentry boxes themselves to transport the boxes or envelopes of the counterfeit coupons around the country. I'd lay money on it. That's why spare sentry keys are being left in the bottom of sidecars. It's a bloody brilliant idea," Mason continued. He was shaking his head, appreciating just how clever it all was.

"That's why there are maps in places there shouldn't be?" O'Rourke stated quickly, understanding precisely what Mason was saying.

"Yes, so that the men and women delivering the counterfeits know where to go. Maybe they send someone different every time. I don't know. But that must be why there are random maps in the sentry boxes. And that's why there's a missing motorbike and sidecar from the regional office. The gang of spivs want people to think they're real patrolmen or women when they visit the sentry boxes. That'll be what the adjustments are for on the roofs. Somewhere to store their supplies. I just know it is," Mason spoke with conviction the more he thought about it. "You've just got to hope that they're not prevailed upon to help fix someone's broken motorcar."

"And that's why they're storing petrol as well. They need it to get around and ensure the counterfeits get to where they should be. It might even have been someone who knew Mr Montgomery well that thought of taking the RSO."

Jones shook his head, mouth opening and closing, as though he didn't know what to say. His eyes moved quickly from the ration book he held, to the map, and then back again. He opened his mouth as though to speak, and then snapped it shut again.

At that moment, Smythe appeared in the doorway, glowing with triumph.

"You've done it, haven't you?" he directed at Mason.

"Yes, Sir, yes, now all we need to do is catch them at it."

"And for that, we need Roberts and his gang. He's coming as soon as he can. I think he'd be here already if it weren't bloody rush hour," Smythe crowed.

"And I imagine Cyril's sister got the idea because she had access to Cyril's sentry box key, and to his RSO if she wanted it. Poor Cyril. He must have been examining the sentry boxes and watching the spivs at it, and then they killed him." Mason mumbled. And then looked to Smythe. "Why didn't the bloody Liverpool lot tell us what was going on?"

"I didn't ask, not yet. It'll be a question that does need answering, though. If not for them, Cyril might still be alive."

"He just very well might, yes," Mason conceded, slumping into a chair that O'Rourke had pulled out for him.

"We'll wait for Roberts. Then we'll determine a way to discover who's involved in this, and we'll find Cyril's killer. We can put an end to angry shopkeepers, and people can sleep more easily in their beds. Well, even more easily now, what with the Allies starting to win this bloody war."

Smythe beamed, and Mason did the same, the fear of a new failure leaving him as everything became clear. This wasn't going to be a case to haunt him, like that of the Middlewick murders, and he was absolutely thrilled about it.

Roberts watched intently as Mason explained everything he and O'Rourke had pulled together about the two seemingly unrelated cases of the unidentified dead man and the strange going-ons at the sentry boxes, as first discovered by Patrolman Grant.

Roberts had been standing when Mason began his story, but now he was sitting, a mug of pale tea pushed into his lifeless hand by Constable Williams, as he looked and listened to everything that Mason had to say. He'd come with two of his sergeants, and they listened in silence. Smythe listened as well, a huge smirk of delight on his face. Even Jones had half a smile on his face, and every so often he shook his head and muttered, "Well I never."

"So, how do we catch them at it?" Roberts asked when Mason had finished. It was a good question. Mason had been thinking about.

"Well, I have a theory about that as well," Mason offered.

"Then tell us what it is?"

"Jones, you've been telling me that the counterfeit coupons seem to be used on a Monday? I think they bring the coupons, and the booklets, in on a Saturday night and distribute them on a Sunday, when the shops are all shut and most people are attending church. Then they're ready for use on a Monday. What we need to do, is have eyes on the sentry boxes on Saturday night."

"Which sentry box?" Roberts demanded.

"All of the local ones. We know it's not S thirty-three because it's been locked up for two years. I would suggest it's the sentry boxes to the west, but I might be wrong. It would make sense to me if they used the A449 to get to Stewponey."

"Or, they could use the A51 to get to Mile Oak?" Smythe offered, looking up from the map that still lay on the table before them.

"Right, so we need people in place to watch from before sunset to sunrise. Smythe's right, they could come to any one of the sentry boxes close to us. It'll be a long night but worth it if we apprehend them. Someone must bring the counterfeits in and then there must be distributors as well, assigned to the sentry boxes. I'll need steady people for the task." Roberts eyed his sergeants as he spoke. The two men sat a little taller.

"Yes, I think we'll find the man who pretended to be Mr Montgomery and the man who killed him. Then we can find out the answers to everything that happened on that fateful night, last Saturday," Mason confirmed. His confidence in the solution was growing the more he considered it. Nothing else made sense.

O'Rourke spoke into the sudden silence that fell as Mason made his pronouncement.

"Would it be wise to ask the local police in Liverpool to visit S twenty-seven? Or perhaps to ask Bettie about it because it would be interesting to see if it's also being used as a petrol store, just as S thirty-three is?"

Mason turned fierce eyes on O'Rourke, grinning at the same time.

"That's brilliant, O'Rourke. Of course, that would make perfect sense. Go and ring Bettie. We'll wait for the answer."

"I think it might be a bit late, right now?" Jones offered, looking at his wrist watch. Mason startled, realising the lights had been turned on in the backroom and the black-out blinds drawn. He didn't even know what time it was until he glanced at the clock. It was 8.45 pm.

"Goodness me, we need to get home before the black-out comes into effect. Isn't it 9 pm tonight?"

"9.12pm, sir," Williams offered. Mason hadn't realised the lad was still at work.

"Yes, we'll meet back here in the morning," Smythe took control of the situation. "We have all of tomorrow to plan what will happen on Saturday, and then we can solve both cases." Satisfaction radiated from Smythe, and Mason didn't mind. He was feeling just as pleased.

CHAPTER 15
SATURDAY 9TH SEPTEMBER 1944

Despite Smythe's objections, Mason and O'Rourke insisted on taking the overnight watch on sentry box number ninety-two at Stewponey. Mason was convinced that would be the drop off box. O'Rourke shared his resolve. They did make the concession of allowing Roberts to accompany them.

The other sentry boxes all had a crew of three of Roberts officers waiting to pounce on whoever turned up. There'd been a great deal of discussion about what they were likely to see. Would it be men and women working under darkness, or would they be bold enough to simply drive up to the sentry box, open the door, leave the counterfeit coupons and books and then drive off, ready for the person who would collect them?

Mason thought this most likely. Smythe believed that the counterfeiters wouldn't be so bold. Especially now there was a dead man. They must, he believed, think that some caution would be needed.

"I've never been on a night-time investigation before," O'Rourke said quietly. The two of them had a clear view of the sentry box from their location behind it, whereas Roberts kept watch from the other side of the road. The Wolseley was parked over a mile away, down a side track that led to a farm. The farmer had been more than willing for them to park there.

Mason hadn't wanted to be dropped off at the sentry box first, but he admitted it had been a good idea. If not, he might still be walking to their hiding place.

Bettie and Mr Wheelwright had arranged for two people to remain on duty at Fanum House so that any of the police stationed at the sentry boxes could call for assistance, if needed, during the night when the recovery service was typically closed. Smythe was on duty in Erdington. Roberts' superior was doing the same from their main office in Birmingham. Still, Mason was concerned that something could go seriously wrong.

He was also worried that he might be wrong about the exchanges taking place on a Saturday night, but no one else had any better ideas. Better to try something than nothing, Smythe and Roberts had agreed.

"It's not very exciting," Mason offered. "At least it's not cold and wet. We should stay quite warm in our thick coats and boots."

Annie had dressed Mason for the occasion. She'd tutted and complained about him malingering in a field once more, but she was as keen for Mason to solve the two cases as Smythe was.

"Perhaps," O'Rourke admitted, but her voice, although she whispered, rippled with excitement.

They waited in silence. Quickly, full dark fell, the sound of any motor vehicles dying away to silence, and then the sounds of the night took over. Wings flapped overhead, an owl hooted, and O'Rourke gasped in fright.

"It's nothing to worry about," Mason reassured her. His eyes had quickly adjusted to the gloom, and he could easily make out the angular shape of the sentry box against the blackness of the sky. Now they just needed something else to happen.

It wasn't possible for the telephones in the sentry boxes to ring. The exchange was entirely one way, but a police car would be dispatched to inform them if the counterfeiting spivs had been discovered at one of the other sentry boxes.

The moon appeared from behind a bank of clouds, illuminating the darkness far more effectively than a handheld torch, and still, nothing happened.

Mason offered O'Rourke a flask of tepid tea, and she eagerly drank it and ate the sandwiches that Annie had made for them as well, and still, nothing happened.

Mason stifled a yawn. None of them had been on duty that day. Smythe, Jones and Williams had taken on all the responsibilities for a Saturday, and he and O'Rourke should have been at home, sleeping and preparing for their night of staying awake. But Mason had found it difficult to sleep beyond his usual waking time, and now he regretted it. Perhaps, as O'Rourke had done, he should have stayed up as late as possible last night so he could have at least slept-in today.

Only then O'Rourke yawned, and Mason knew it hadn't necessarily helped her.

"What's that?" Mason pointed, his attention caught by something flashing in the darkness. Only then did he hear the rumble of an engine as well. His heart sank. It seemed he'd been wrong in his assumption, only it wasn't a Wolseley that pulled up before the sentry box, but rather a motorbike.

The engine's sound died away, filling the air with silence once more, and a figure jumped from the seat and bent to fiddle with something attached to the back of the bike.

"This is it?" O'Rourke breathed rather than spoke, and Mason nodded. He wished he could see Roberts, but no doubt, the other man was paying careful attention.

Something small flashed in the man's hand, and Mason heard the sound of a key being turned, and a door opened. O'Rourke reached out and gripped his forearm. But they didn't move from their concealment, not yet. They needed to catch both counterfeiters, the one who brought the papers and the other who collected them.

Mason watched as the man took something from his saddlebags and placed it inside the sentry box. From such a distance, it was possible to watch the figure pause to listen before once more turning the key in the door and moving to mount up on his motorbike.

Only, when the figure returned to the motorbike, he was no longer alone. Roberts was there. Mason watched the two figures wrestle one another, almost quietly, before one of them tumbled to the ground.

"Is it Roberts?" O'Rourke demanded to know.

"No, it isn't. The counterfeiter came off the worse there." Quickly, Roberts moved the prone figure, handcuffs glinting in the moonlight, before removing the motorbike as well. In no time at all, it was as if nothing had happened.

And still, they waited.

Mason was expecting to hear the rumble of another engine, but the noise never came. Instead, on the still air, he listened to the sound of someone breathing heavily and the unmistakable sound of a bicycle clunking as it changed gear.

"This is it," Mason said softly. O'Rourke was almost asleep. She was startled to wakefulness and peered at the figure.

"Now we go for this person as soon as they've opened the sentry box." Roberts would have his hands full with the counterfeiter. They needed to collect whoever it was that distributed the coupons.

O'Rourke was quicker to move than Mason. He cursed his bad back but set off after her. He kept his eyes on the bicycle. Once more, a slither of light flashed in the darkness, and Mason knew it was the key for the sentry box.

The sound of a lock being opened filled the air, and the figure leant inside to retrieve whatever had been left for them. By then, O'Rourke was level with the sentry box.

Mason wasn't far behind, but he would have preferred to be much closer.

"You're under arrest," O'Rourke's words were so loud, Mason almost winced.

A shriek of outrage greeted the statement, and Mason heard something heavy being lifted. He knew what it was and staggered ever more quickly forwards. The damn brute was going to try and hit O'Rourke with the petrol canister.

Wishing he could move faster, Mason aimed, not for the sentry box but instead for the bicycle. He thrust it away from him, into the road. The sound of a fight reached his ears.

"No, I'm not," a male voice shrieked.

"Yes, you are," Mason added his authority, but still, he could see O'Rourke fighting with the other figure. O'Rourke had one handcuff on the man, but he tried to punch her, even as he fought free from the handcuff. If O'Rourke wasn't careful, the man would escape with just one hand in the cuff, and then he'd be able to do whatever he could to remove the handcuff.

The petrol canister hit the ground with a metallic shriek, but Mason could hear O'Rourke fighting onwards, her cries of outrage rippling through the almost silent night air.

Finally, he reared up before the man. O'Rourke had managed to slip the other handcuff over her wrist as a means of keeping hold of the counterfeiter. She was attempting to force him to the ground, even while he pulled at her arm. Mason winced, waiting for the pop of her shoulder, only for Roberts to erupt from the night in front of him.

Moving with the ease of a fighter, Roberts took a running jump at the man and punched him forcefully in the face. Now Mason heard the crack of bone, and the man went limp. Just in time, Mason managed to get an arm to the man to ease his fall to the ground.

Only then did he turn to look at O'Rourke and Roberts.

O'Rourke's hair was wild, half of her braids ripped free, a dirty smear running along her face, and her uniform was in disarray. Roberts was rubbing his left hand with his right, groaning as he did so, and the man they'd come to arrest, well, he was lying on the ground, twisted onto his side, one arm snaking along the damp grass to O'Rourke's hand.

Quickly, Mason clapped his handcuffs on the man.

"Give me your key. You don't need to be tied to him," Mason urged O'Rourke, and she fumbled in her pocket for the key and handed it over silently. Her breath hitched, and Mason knew she was just concentrating on stilling her rapidly beating heart. She snatched back her arm once Mason had released her from the unknown man.

"Nasty piece of work," Roberts spoke into the silence.

"Yes, but who is he?" Mason demanded to know. Into the gloom, Roberts flicked on his bright torchlight, and all three of them peered down at the pale face illuminated by the beam of the torch.

'No idea," O'Rourke admitted.

"Me neither," Mason confirmed. Roberts didn't speak but rather slowly shook his head.

"I don't know the man either," he eventually admitted, even as he moved towards the sentry box to make the important telephone call that would let everyone know they'd caught their men.

Mason turned his torch on now, looking at the scene before them.

The bicycle was still in the middle of the road, a bag on the rear of it having come open so that pieces of paper fluttered in the gentle breeze. Mason stooped to pick one up, unsurprised to feel the roughness of the counterfeited ration coupons.

"He's definitely our man," Mason confirmed, bending to pick up more and more of the pages before they could blow away. Hastily, he righted the bicycle and returned the coupons to the saddlebag. Only then his hand closed on something cold, and his heart stilled.

The man had a gun. They were lucky he hadn't used it.

With the telephone call made, Roberts marched along the road to the parked Wolseley, and the dim glow of headlights quickly returned their way. The man was slowly stirring, his eyelids fluttering, even as Mason helped O'Rourke to her feet.

"Are you hurt?" he demanded from her.

"Just a few bruises," she tried to laugh it off, but Mason could tell she was shaken. He'd not expected such a violent response either, and now that he had the man's gun in his coat pocket, he felt easier. This could all have gone terribly wrong.

"Can you walk?" Mason called to the nameless man.

"Yes," the sullen response, the word too thick because of the swelling nose and cut lip.

"Then get in the police car," Mason stood close, his hand on the handcuffs behind the man's back as he walked him to the car.

"You've made a terrible mistake," the man said, hooded eyes meeting Mason's beneath the dull light of the moon.

"I don't think so," Mason replied. "I don't think we have. Not at all."

And Roberts and O'Rourke lifted the prone body of the first man and sat him in the Wolseley as well. That left them with a problem because all five of them couldn't fit in the car.

"I'll take the motorbike back," Roberts quickly offered. "I'm used to driving one," he added, moving to roll the machine onto the road.

"The bicycle will have to stay here, but we'll take the bag with the counterfeit coupons in," Mason added.

"I'll stay close behind," Roberts assured Mason as the motorbike roared to life. The prone man groaned while the man who'd arrived on the bicycle tried to get as far away from him as possible. Mason was looking forward to questioning both of the men.

The ride back to Erdington police station was uneventful. Mason didn't question their prisoners, and neither did the prisoners say anything incriminating. The man who'd fought O'Rourke did ask for the blood to be cleared away from his nose and lips so that he could breathe more easily.

Only when they were inside the police station, the squeaky door announcing their presence did Mason get a good look at the men they'd apprehended. The first man was more alert now, his grey eyes filled with malice, while the second man merely looked terrified. Mason wondered who'd done what in the organisation.

Looking officious at the front desk, Smythe glared at the first man and spoke in clipped tones.

"Name."

"Benjamin Yeoman."

"Address."

"The Farm, Liverpool."

Mason eyed the man carefully, trying to decide if it had been him who'd been pretending to be Cyril Montgomery, but he didn't believe it was. He was a much larger man with a thick beard. Mason was sure it must be the other man.

"Do you understand what you've been arrested for?" Smythe asked, his voice cold. Benjamin didn't flinch, and neither did he answer.

"Counterfeiting of ration books, distributing counterfeit goods, profiting from counterfeit goods."

When there was still no reply, Roberts spoke. "I found this on him," Roberts showed another gun, and Mason almost shuddered. Both men had been armed. All of them could have been killed.

Roberts took Benjamin away to one of the two interview rooms, one of his officers accompanying him, while Mason stood with the second man. Mason was sure this was the imposter.

"Name."

"Walter Easterman."

"Address."

"167 King Street, Liverpool."

"Do you understand what you've been arrested for?" Smythe demanded as he had of Benjamin. Walter reacting by shaking his head. His eyes were fearful, although he seemed less terrified now Benjamin had been led away. O'Rourke held her place in front of the squeaking door so that he couldn't dash for freedom.

"Counterfeiting of ration books, distributing counterfeit goods, profiting from counterfeit goods." Smythe repeated the same charges and didn't mention the murder of Cyril or his sister. That would come soon enough, Mason was sure of it, when they'd decided who had been responsible for those crimes.

In the light, Mason finally got a good look at Walter.

He wasn't an attractive man, with a coarse moustache, his eyes set deeply into an elongated face. His lips were bloodied, his nose as well. He wore black clothes, and they smelt of damp. He certainly didn't look to be profiting from the sale of counterfeit goods.

Walter faced Smythe without an expression on his face. Mason detected a stubbornness in his shoulders that meant it wouldn't be easy to get him to admit to the killing of Cyril or Cyril's sister-in-law. Not that they needed him to confess. Hopefully, they'd match his or Benjamin's fingerprints to those found on the sidecar.

"You're making a mistake," Walter offered instead, furtive eyes seeking out Mason. It was as though he wanted to say more but was unsure.

"Take him through to the interview room," Smythe said, his tone implacable. Mason had a feeling that Smythe would be asking the questions. He wasn't sure that was such a good idea, but neither did Mason know if he wanted to be doing the talking. Whenever he looked at Walter, he felt a spark of fury and outrage. It might make it difficult for him to maintain the detachment needed for a good cross-examination.

Mason walked into the main room of the police station, encouraging Walter to walk behind him, and then turned sharply right. The interview rooms were at the far end of the office area. They weren't appealing rooms, but Mason had seen far worse in his time.

Jones was already waiting in the interview room. Mason hadn't expected that but shared a raised eyebrow with him. They'd caught the men. Now they just needed to hear the whole story from both of them and piece it all together.

With more care than Mason expected, Jones had Walter sit in the chair and then released his hands from the handcuffs so that his hands were in front of him. They needed to be there so that they could take his fingerprints.

Quickly, Jones completed the procedure and handed Mason the two white cards showing both sets of fingerprints from his left and right hand, and Mason left the interview room. Jones remained to glower at Walter.

"Here we go," Mason said, as Roberts appeared with the fingerprints from Benjamin as well. They lay the white cards on the table in the back room. O'Rourke was already there with the print from the sidecar and a magnifying glass. Her hair remained dishevelled, and Mason could see a tear in her police jacket on her shoulder, revealing her blouse beneath it. Smythe was watching her slightly aghast, and yet he said nothing. Mason thought they could all do with something hot to drink, and as though conjuring him, Williams walked into the room.

Mason hadn't realised he was even there.

"Right. Is one of them our man?" Smythe asked of O'Rourke. She pulled a bright lamp closer and bent over the two fingerprints scrutinising them.

Mason breathed slowly, not appreciating until that moment just how badly he wanted Walter or Benjamin to be the man they'd been searching for, the murderer.

O'Rourke took her time. Looking from one print to another and then focused on only one. Now time slowed, and from the interview room, he could hear a low murmur of conversation as Williams took hot tea to the prisoners and the men watching them.

"I would say they match," O'Rourke sat back and fixed Mason with her warm eyes as she pointed to the fingerprints that belonged to Walter.

"I can see at least eleven matches. I'm sure Roberts would find more, and the experts, even more."

"So, he's the killer?" Smythe demanded clarity.

"His fingerprint is on the sidecar," O'Rourke was quick to rectify.

"So, he's probably our killer?" Smythe continued.

"Yes. He was there. He doesn't work for the Automobile Association, so his fingerprints shouldn't have been on any sidecar."

"Right. We need a confession from him," Smythe announced gruffly.

"But we can charge him with counterfeiting anyway, and Benjamin," Mason confirmed.

"Yes, but we want Walter for the murder of Cyril as well. And I imagine that Benjamin might have been responsible for the killing of Cyril's sister-in-law." Smythe's eyes glowered with fury. "I'm not content with stopping the counterfeiting, not now. We need a confession, and we need the names of the rest of those who are also involved."

"I don't think they'll tell us," but at that moment, Williams reappeared. His young face was flushed.

"The first prisoner wants to confess, Walter," he announced. "He wants to make a full confession of his part in the counterfeiting scam. He also says his sister has been murdered, and he needs to be protected from the mastermind behind it all and Benjamin." Mason felt his eyes widen at the news.

"You do it, Mason. And O'Rourke, do you want to face our prisoner?" O'Rourke nodded.

"Absolutely, sir, but first, I need to change my jacket." She stood and walked away, forgetting about the fingerprints and her tea. Mason admired her determined stance.

"We'll be listening as well," Smythe confirmed. "We'll take notes, and you and O'Rourke can just do the talking. And then we'll interview Benjamin."

As soon as O'Rourke returned, Mason made his way to the interview room. Walter was slumped in his chair, all defiance gone from his face. Jones was discussing the day's headlines as though he and Walter were friends in a local pub. Mason recognised the tactic. It was always easier if the criminal thought the police were their ally. Mason was impressed that Jones had thought to soften up the prisoner.

"Mr Easterman, I believe you want to make a full confession," Mason began, sitting in one of the uncomfortable steel chairs in the small room.

"Yes, I do. I'll tell you everything I know about the counterfeiting operation, but you have to keep me away from Ben next door. He's mental."

"Very well," and O'Rourke took her place as well. Walter looked to O'Rourke.

"Sorry, miss, sorry, Sergeant. I should have come without the fight." The words appeared heartfelt as he eyed O'Rourke's injuries.

O'Rourke merely nodded, but she held her chin high.

"So, tell us about the counterfeiting scheme," Mason prompted Walter. Walter cleared his throat and then reached for his tea. He tried to hold it to his mouth, but his handcuffed hands made it difficult even though he bent as low as he could.

"Here, I'll release one hand for you," Mason stated, leaning over the table to do just that. Walter flexed his wrist as soon as it was free. He took a sip of the hot tea, wincing at the heat on his cut lip, and then swallowed half the mug.

"I wasn't in it from the beginning," Walter began. "But my sister was. Brenda. She was desperate for money, always wanted more than she could have. She was the one that had the idea about using the sentry boxes. Too clever for her own good, she was." Walter paused. A tear trickled down his filthy cheeks, and he sniffed. He hadn't come away unscathed from his fight with O'Rourke. Already, his left eye was purpling, to match his bloody nose and lip. O'Rourke handed him a piece of tissue, which he used and then scrunched into his handcuffed hand.

"She knew all about the sentry boxes because of Cyril. I don't think he realised why she was quizzing him so much about them. I think he was just pleased they finally had something to talk about together. My sister disapproved of Addie marrying Cyril. Thought he was too boring, but Addie didn't want a hectic life. She was happy to get away from Liverpool and live in Erdington. She liked all the open space."

He paused, for a moment, his recollections of the past taking him away from the police station.

"Anyway, the counterfeit coupons are printed up in Liverpool, out in some farm buildings. I know the address. Then the problem was distributing the coupons and the few ration books they decided to counterfeit as well. They were pushing their luck with the dodgy stamps they used. They never quite looked like the real thing from the government offices."

"Anyway, they needed to be moved in a way that no one could track them. My sister received a bonus for that idea about the sentry boxes. They use them all over the country, not just here and in Liverpool. So few people had cars on the road that it was easy to leave packets inside them. She got hold of the key from Cyril and a map and had copies of the keys made. The next part was more difficult, finding people to act as a distributor in the local areas, but people are desperate. Some don't even realise it's a crime. They think they're just helping out their friends and neighbours who are desperate for stuff they can't get hold of."

"It was all going well in Erdington until the Automobile Association people opened their regional office in Birmingham. It became more difficult then. Not there were more patrols or anything like that, but it felt as though there were. It felt as though more people were watching. That's how I got involved. One of the local distributors got cold feet, said he couldn't take the risk because the police were aware of the counterfeit coupons. My sister told 'em that I'd take over the task without even asking. I didn't want to, but well, I was desperate as well. No money for the likes of me." As he spoke, Walter pointed to his chest.

"Enlarged heart," he stated when Mason shook his head. "They won't let me join up, and everyone thinks I'm worse than scum because of it. If I had no arm, or limped or showed some sign of injury, other than puffing sometimes, people might give me a job, but no. Not for the man who seems hale. It's not as though you can look at people and know they're got a dodgy heart."

"Anyway, she got me into it, and I started coming down here with the counterfeit coupons and distributing them to all the sentry boxes. I don't need to be able to run far to find one of 'em." He paused again and drank more of his tea.

"Only then old Cyril got suspicious of me and what I was doing around here. He saw me at that box near Mile Oak when I was scouting it out in the daylight. He recognised me, of course, he did, even though we only met at the wedding all those years ago, and tried to become all pally with me. Poor sod was lonely. And then he started to ask me questions about how I could afford to live, and I'm not a very good liar," Walter shrugged as though that accounted for everything.

"Last Saturday night, I went out, as I normally do, to pick up my supplies and then distribute them to the other sentry boxes, but I could tell someone was following me. I knew it was Cyril. To be honest, I thought it would be easy to lose him in the darkness. He wasn't exactly quiet with his RSO. That's what they call 'em, the motorbike and side-car. Not sure if you know that," Walter looked at Mason. Mason nodded to show that he was aware of the title.

"But it was a big night for me. They'd decided to double the usual number of coupons for distribution. I think they fear the chance to make money will be gone soon, what with the advances being made by the Allies. I was struggling on my bicycle. It was taking me too long to get everywhere, and I knew that Cyril was close. I'd made my drop at sentry box number three hundred and fourteen. I was on my way to numbers forty-two and three hundred and thirty-five when the chain came off my bike, and I fell off the bloody thing."

"There were coupons all over the road from where I'd fallen, and the bag had come open. I rushed to collect them together, but I could hear Cyril and his RSO coming closer and closer all the time. Damn fool. He should have left it well alone." Walter's words were fletched with remorse. "If he'd just stayed at home, but no, he was looking for some excitement in his life or some such. There were rumours he'd been messing with the sentry boxes." Walter glanced down at his hands. Another tear leaked from his eye. Mason wasn't sure he'd ever met a murderer so sorrowful for his actions.

"He came around the corner too fast, and he didn't see my bike in the road or me. At the last moment, he tried to veer aside, but it was too late. I watched it in slow motion. All of it. And when he went over the handlebars of his motorbike and landed in the hedgerow, I thought he'd be fine apart from a few scratches, but he wasn't. He just lay there, not moving even when I called to him and slapped his face."

O'Rourke gasped at the story. Mason's forehead furrowed. This wasn't what he'd been expecting.

"I didn't know what to do. He was clearly dead. I checked his pulse. I held my ear close to his mouth, but there was nothing. Poor sod."

Silence filled the room. Mason didn't want to break it, even though he had so many more questions. Eventually, Walter began to speak once more.

"I didn't know what to do with him. I couldn't just leave him there, but what could I do with him? Then I saw the sidecar, and I had an idea. The motorbike was still in one piece, although the front tyre looked a bit flat. I did the only thing I could think to do. I emptied all of his tools out of the sidecar, stuffed him in the sidecar, and took him to the woodlands at the bottom of the aerodrome. I'll never forget the feel of his body as I forced it into position. I hoped it would give me some time, before his death was discovered, to complete the rest of the task the counterfeiters had set me. They'd threatened my sister if I didn't do what they wanted me to do with all the coupons. They'd promised me the same if I failed them. Him next door, he's the one they sent to make sure I did what I should."

"I moved Cyril and got him out of the sidecar with some effort. It took most of the night, and the branches were a right bugger. Then, I hid his RSO somewhere else, behind the hangars at the aerodrome. The two had come apart by then, and I was scratched all over. Only then could I make my way to the regional office. I thought if I pretended to be Cyril, no one would know he was missing, and without the suspicion, I could get the coupons to the sentry boxes this week. But the neighbours were nosy buggers, and I had to leave before I was ready. So, this Saturday, I was going to deliver a double portion. I was also trying to avoid that Ben. He's a nasty piece of work."

Once more, silence fell in the room.

"So you didn't murder Cyril then?" Mason asked, just to be sure.

"No, he had a terrible accident. But I take full responsibility. He wouldn't have been there if it weren't for me."

"You could have just left him?" O'Rourke suggested.

"I couldn't. I didn't want the police looking too closely at the sentry boxes. He'd been playing silly buggers with the roofs of the boxes. I had to undo everything he'd done. Make sure the big-wigs knew it wasn't my fault, or I'd face their wrath even more, and that Ben, well, he's not a nice bloke. I've been trying to get hold of my sister all week. I think they've already done something nasty to her."

"And now?" Mason pressed. Walter fixed him with a watery smile.

"It don't matter now, does it? You know all about 'em and what they've been up to. You've arrested me, and if I'm here, then they can't get hold of me. And with Ben next door, he's done for as well."

Mason nodded. There was a great deal of truth to Walter's words.

"So, you feel safer locked up here than you do on the outside?" O'Rourke's words were filled with confusion.

"Yes, miss. I certainly do. I should never have got involved in the counterfeiting scam. Neither should my sister."

"So, did you steal another RSO from the regional office?" Mason asked.

"Yes, I had to, to be able to pretend to be Cyril. I'm pretty handy with mechanical things. He tried to encourage me to join the Automobile Association when I was younger, but they didn't want me."

"Do you know the names of everyone else involved in the scam, other than Ben next door?"

"I do, yes. I'm not supposed to, but everyone slips up and tells you their name in the end."

"And you say they distribute throughout England?"

"Yeah, not as easy in Scotland, and they've tried in Wales as well.

But here and the south is their preferred locations. People in the cities ain't so used to fending for themselves as those in the countryside."

"Thank you for answering our questions," Mason said, standing. And then he paused. He had the answers he wanted, and yet it still felt unresolved.

"What was the gun for?"

Walter looked sullen at the question.

"It was old Cyril's. I thought it best to have some protection in case the spivs came after me. I wouldn't have used it on you. You just frightened me. I thought it was old Ben and his gang of wrong 'uns."

"We'll speak to Liverpool. Tell them everything you know."

"And make sure they all get arrested—all of 'em. I'll spill everything I know. It'll please me to see 'em punished for murdering my sister. That's both of 'em gone now. Just me left and no one else." Walter's words trailed off, and his shoulders began to shake as O'Rourke and Mason left the interview room, making way for Jones to enter and watch their prisoner.

Quickly, they walked through to the backroom, where Smythe and Roberts were busy talking.

"Did you hear all that?" Mason asked them.

"Yes, we did. And it's not a pleasant story to hear, but it seems he didn't kill Cyril. We'll see if Doctor Lucey can confirm that."

"It explains why Cyril's chest was bruised."

"It does, yes. But what do we do with Walter and Ben now? If this gang are after Walter, he's probably not as safe as he thinks he is in police custody, even with Ben in the next room."

"We'll move both of them to Birmingham right away. Once there, it won't be easy for anyone to get at Walter or Ben. There's more room to keep them apart rather than here." It was Roberts who spoke. Mason decided he knew more about such large scale crimes than he did. Mason was happy to allow Roberts to make such decisions.

"What did Ben have to say?"

"Nothing. He won't speak. Not even to ask for his solicitor."

"If we're going to move them, we should do it first thing in the morning," Smythe confirmed, nodding. Mason appreciated Smythe was uneasy.

"I've arranged for three police vans to arrive at first light. We'll remain here until then."

"Three?" Mason asked Roberts, perplexed.

"Yes, a crime of this scale needs some deception, or we might lose Walter. We know his sister was murdered. If those above him get word of his arrest, they'll be sure to want to silence him. There was probably someone waiting for Ben to return, and when he doesn't, well, they'll know to suspect something's amiss."

Mason nodded, but the blood suddenly ran cold in his veins. Just what were they involved in?

CHAPTER 16

The night dragged while they waited. O'Rourke stifled a yawn and kept everyone supplied with warm drinks because it gave her something to do, washing the mugs and then refilling them. Walter slept, head on his arms where they rested on the table. Mason had to force himself not to pace from one end of the police station to the other. Benjamin snored loudly, head flung back on the small chair, appreciating he wasn't about the be released anytime soon. One of Roberts two sergeants kept a firm eye on him, as the door remained closed so that he couldn't get to Walter.

Roberts was alert, his eyes trained on the outside, the door to the police station locked tight, no lights spilling onto the street to show that there was anyone inside, thanks to the blackout blinds, and still, Mason couldn't shake the feeling that it was all too little, and too late. They'd known the case was a big one, that was why they'd brought Roberts into it. But, Mason admitted, he'd not realised quite how large the counterfeit operation could be. He regretted that now he had Walter in custody in front of him.

Smythe wasn't his usual cheerful self, where he sat in his office, furiously filling in paperwork that could have been done on any other day. Williams was kept busy with his filing, O'Rourke, in an attempt to stay awake, deciding it was time to show him how the system worked in between making cups of tea and washing the mugs. Mason almost wished he'd thought of the distraction. Williams and O'Rourke spoke quietly to one another, and every so often, soft chuckles could be heard from the pair of them.

Eventually, the grey light of dawn began to appear around the edges of the blackout blinds, and Roberts grimaced at Mason, where they sat facing each other in the main office, Mason having given in to his need to pace, only to return to his seat when his back and leg started to ache.

"It won't be long," Roberts reassured, assuming that was why Mason was uneasy and yet Mason didn't find the words at all calming.

Walter woke, asked to use the bathroom and then drank yet more tea provided by O'Rourke. They were all yawning. None of them were used to working through the night, not even Walter. Benjamin continued to snore. Mason had the thought that Benjamin could have slept through an air raid siren, so unconcerned was he at being arrested.

Roberts beckoned Mason into Smythe's office, and spoke to them with assurance.

"When the first police van arrives, we'll decide as to whether Walter gets into that one or not. All three of the vans will park close to one another, blocking the view of the front door entirely."

Smythe nodded, his eyes wide and alert.

"We've done this sort of thing before," Roberts stated flatly. "Sometimes it works. Sometimes it doesn't." Mason almost wished Roberts hadn't offered such a caution.

"You'll lead on this," Smythe confirmed with Roberts. "We'll do whatever you instruct us to do."

"Thank you, Sir," Roberts nodded, and moved away to confer with the second of his two sergeants.

"Walter," Smythe walked through to speak to their counterfeiter. Before he'd slept, Walter had written as much as he knew about the counterfeiting spivs. He'd spared no detail that he knew. Mason now had three long sheets of information; names, dates, addresses. It would ensure no one got away with their part in the rouse. "I want to thank you for your assistance. We'll make great use of your information," Smythe spoke with a confidence than Mason was missing.

"I would say it was my pleasure," the man offered half a smile on his lips. "But it probably means my death no matter what happens now. Still, at least you have all the evidence to string the rest of 'em up with, especially that Ben." Smythe reached over and shook Walter's hand. Mason watched with keen eyes. He wasn't used to seeing Smythe quite so subdued.

"It's time to go," Roberts announced from the main office. "Get the front door open, Mason, and then stay out of the way. My men are waiting for us. They've done extractions like this before." Benjamin was awake by now. He was blinking blearily. It seemed he didn't know what was afoot, even when he was dragged to his feet by Roberts' man.

Hastily, Mason moved to the front door, the brass key for the lock in his hand. He gazed at it. So much of this had come down to keys. It surprised him all over again.

Outside, Mason could see three police vans, when he lifted the blackout blinds. The dark blue colour almost allowed them to blend into the shadowy surroundings. If the engines had only been quieter, they would have been impossible to spot.

Mason met the eyes of the driver of the first van, bent forward to watch what was happening inside the police station. He saw the man offer a hand of greeting. There was another man to the far side of him, who jumped down from the cabin of the lorry. He could see the other two vans behind the first one.

Mason quickly stepped aside, the door shrieking as he pulled it inwards. A stray gust of wind rushed into the police station.

Roberts was behind him, Walter beside him. Walter was handcuffed to Roberts by one hand.

Roberts nodded towards Mason as the other figure from the van appeared in the doorway.

"It's all clear, Sir. Come on. Let's get him in the first van."

The chill of the early morning swirled into the front office, and Mason shivered as Roberts led Walter outside, Roberts head swivelling as he tried to look everywhere at once. Smythe was standing in front of

Williams, Jones and O'Rourke, the four of them all showing signs of worry and fear in their stances, as they stayed behind the front counter where people usually came to report lost purses and mislaid pets. Mason almost wished he could join them, but he wanted to ensure Walter made it into the police van in one piece. And then Benjamin was led outside as well, by Roberts' two sergeants.

Once outside, Roberts moved swiftly towards the rear of the first van with Walter. The door was flung open already, and the second van was as close as it was possible to be, without making it impossible to close the door. The open door ensured no one could see what was happening from Sutton New Road. The third van also blocked much of the view from Osborne Road.

Mason watched intently as Walter placed one foot on the step of the van and then bent to place the second. Behind him, Benjamin was just stooping to do the same in the second van. Mason stepped outside the front door to watch. He didn't like this. Something felt wrong, although Roberts and his men all seemed competent enough at what they were doing.

And that was when a loud bang rang through the air. And not just one. Mason ducked as low as he could. He watched in horror as Walter tumbled to the ground, taking Roberts with him so that Roberts lay on top of the other man. The smell of gunpowder was thick in the air, and Mason shook his head, trying to clear his ears from the loud shots, as he heard a bellow of outrage from Roberts man as well.

"Stay inside," Roberts roared just as Mason was about to rush to help Walter. "Get inside," Roberts urged him, meeting his gaze as he did so.

Mason did as he was told, with the aid of O'Rourke who helped him to his feet. Roberts was on his knees, turning Walter to get a look at him, but Mason could already tell Walter was dead. There was no chance that he still lived. His body was too still.

A shot from somewhere close. Mason shuddered. They hadn't been careful enough with moving Walter. They hadn't been careful enough when they'd arrested him and Benjamin. It was clear that someone else had been watching what they were doing. Mason cursed their bad luck.

Hastily, Roberts released the handcuffs and closed Walter's eyes. There was no need to stay shackled together. Walter wasn't going anywhere anymore.

"Sir, my one's dead as well," the other sergeant shouted, the words ringing as loudly as the gunshot.

"Sir," a respectful voice called to Roberts from the gloom, startling Mason, because he hadn't appreciated there had been more than the six police officers driving the three vans. "We've got him."

Mason didn't understand what was happening. He watched as Roberts walked away, his eyes turning time and time again towards Walter. Mason felt the same. The poor sod. Just as dead as his sister.

"You need to see this," Roberts shocked Mason when he once more appeared before him. Mason kept blinking, as though not believing what he saw.

"What?" Mason asked Roberts, unsure what the other man needed him to see. He couldn't keep all of his thoughts together. They kept jumbling together. He just couldn't reconcile that Walter was dead.

"We got the killer," Roberts informed Mason quietly. "The assassin sent to kill poor Walter and Benjamin to make sure they didn't spill all they knew. We've got him."

"How?" Mason demanded to know. He'd been concerned that something would happen to Walter and Benjamin, but he'd thought it more likely that the two men would attempt to escape, or that someone would try and help them escape. Mason hadn't considered that they'd be killed to prevent them from talking.

"As I said, we've done this before. We know how these criminal gangs work. Now, come and see. I'm curious to see if you recognise him."

Mason meekly followed Roberts, unsure where to look. This place, so familiar to him throughout his life, didn't feel it anymore. He eyed the lifeless body of Benjamin as he allowed Roberts to lead him to the side of the police station, just to the corner with Sutton New Road. Turning back, Mason realised it would have allowed the assassin to see when Walter and Benjamin were led from the police station, despite the precautions that Roberts and his team had taken.

"Here, do you know this person?"

Mason bent down, Roberts torch illuminating a face he did know. Not well, but one he'd encountered in recent days.

"It's Mr Foreshaw," Mason gasped, remembering the man they'd met by the Moxhull sentry box. He focused on the spread of blood on his dark suit from close to where his heart once beat.

"This Mr Foreshaw, I think we'll find, is the brains behind the entire operation in the Erdington area." Mason nodded, unable to speak as Roberts continued.

"A bloody nasty business," Roberts offered. "Very nasty indeed."

Mason couldn't disagree with him.

He turned to meet O'Rourke's eyes. Ignoring the advice of Roberts, she'd left the police station.

"That's the man from the sentry box?" she spoke in confusion.

"Mr Foreshaw," Mason supplied.

"He had a Morris Minor," she continued. "And he told us about the key needed to open the sentry box."

"He did, yes," Mason confirmed. In fact, now he thought about it, Mr Foreshaw had been particularly helpful to them. But, in asking his questions, had Mason made Mr Foreshaw suspicious? Had Mr Foreshaw realised what had happened long before Mason had even made the connection between the dead man and the counterfeiting.

"And it seems," Roberts announced. "That he was a skilled marksman, assassin and a counterfeiter, to boot."

O'Rourke met Mason's eyes. She looked shaken by Roberts words, and the very visible sign of the assassin. He couldn't say that he felt any better than she did.

CHAPTER 17
THE FOLLOWING WEEK

Mason stood to the back of the small collection of mourners in the churchyard at St Barnabas. It had been a doleful service, but then, they were burying two men that day—an unusual occurrence in Erdington, even during the war.

O'Rourke stood to his left, Smythe to his right. Jones was behind him. Williams as well. Two of Roberts' men were ensuring the police station ran in their absence. With everything that had happened, they'd all wanted to pay their respects when Cyril Montgomery was buried beside his wife. And when Walter was buried to the other side of her. It hadn't been possible to reunite the three siblings. Walter and Addie's sister had already been interred in Liverpool before Walter's unfortunate death. For a few days, Mason had thought that Walter might be buried in Liverpool, but in the end, it had been easier to arrange the funeral for Erdington. Once more, the petrol rationing had come into play.

It had been five days since the events outside Erdington Police Station had taken place, and Mason remained shocked by what had transpired. Roberts had been stoic about it all. As too had Smythe, but Mason found it difficult to comprehend just what they'd been investigating. Bad enough to have to be faced with the body of a man who couldn't be identified, but the counterfeiting scam had gone much further than that. It had been far more violent than Mason could possibly have imagined.

The police in Liverpool had uncovered a massive operation when they'd attended the farm that Walter had named in his handwritten confession, in the hours before his death. There'd been not one but two printing presses, running day and night, the pile of counterfeit coupons waiting to be distributed standing almost from floor to ceiling, piles of paper waiting to be converted into the coupons, and even supplies of the special orange ink which would have lasted them for at least another year.

When the officers in Liverpool had tallied up the number of coupons waiting for distribution, they'd determined there had been over a million of them. The number staggered Mason.

The Liverpool police had made at least ten arrests, and even now, police officers up and down the country were arresting others who'd been implicated in the crime. Mr Foreshaw was the man in charge of the Midlands area, but he'd not been alone. Two others had performed a similar role in London and the southern counties. There had been more gunshots fired between the criminal spivs and the police, but luckily, no one had been killed, other than in Erdington.

While news of what had happened hadn't yet spread to the newspapers, Mason knew it would do as soon as the court cases began to be heard. There'd been enough of a reaction to the three dead men, Benjamin and Walter, as well as Mr Foreshaw. The Birmingham Post had run the same story on Tuesday and Wednesday, just to make sure everyone knew what had happened.

It hadn't taken the newspaper report long to piece together all the information which made sense of what had happened with the unidentified dead man, and the counterfeiting scam.

Mason and O'Rourke had managed to put more of the details into chronological order. On seeing his brother-in-law in Erdington, Cyril Montgomery had become suspicious of his intentions in the local area. It seemed he'd quickly reconciled the counterfeiting case with Walter's appearance. Maybe, O'Rourke had posed, he'd long held suspicions about his sister-in-law, but grief for his dead wife had driven all such considerations from his mind.

Cyril had then approached the police in Liverpool, not in Erdington because he'd known the Erdington police were a long way from solving the counterfeiting scandal. Mason also imagined it was because Cyril didn't like the thought of implicating his friends and neighbours in the scam. It would have been easier for Cyril if people far away from him had been prosecuted for their crimes.

The Liverpool police had half-listened to what Cyril had to say to them when he'd telephoned them. Mason couldn't help thinking that if Cyril had come directly to him or Jones, they would have taken the matter far more seriously, and that Cyril would still be alive.

Cyril's activities, visiting the sentry boxes after dark, finding the secret hidden compartment in the roofs, which was how the spivs planned to distribute the counterfeit coupons in the future because they were worried that their night-time activities might soon come under greater scrutiny, had aroused the suspicion of Mr Foreshaw. Those suspicions had only been further heightened when he'd found the police at the sentry box close to Moxhull when he'd pretended to have a broken down Morris Minor.

It was a pity that Mason had been so concerned to stay away from Patrolman Grant but hadn't thought to be quite so careful elsewhere, away from sentry box forty-two. He held himself responsible for that. Mr Foreshaw had been attempting to track down Walter after that fateful meeting, and that was why Walter had been forced to leave Cyril's home. If not for that, it was just possible that the Saturday handover would have gone smoothly, and Walter might have been able to make good his escape having discovered the supply of petrol at sentry box S thirty-three which would ensure he'd not need to worry about petrol coupons while he fled north with what money he had.

Mason looked up now and noticed Bettie standing with Patrolman Grant, both with heads bowed as they watched the coffin of Cyril being lowered into the ground. Patrolman Grant's face was grief-stricken as he clutched Bettie's hand tightly. Both of them looked sunken with sorrow. Bettie's eyes were red-rimmed, as though she'd not been able to stop crying throughout the service, while Grant had his eyes half-closed, as though trying not to watch what was happening.

Next, Mason met the eyes of Mr and Mrs Daventry. The couple sagging with their grief. It had only been a few years since they'd laid Cyril's wife in the same graveyard. Such sorrow for their friends must be difficult to bear.

Mr Foreshaw had been quick to realise that the police were close to uncovering how the counterfeit coupons and the few ration books were being distributed. He'd been watching the police station carefully on Saturday night, just waiting to see if they truly knew enough to convict Walter for the counterfeiting. It seemed that he'd acted quickly to put a stop to both Walter and Benjamin spilling all they knew. Mason was pleased Mr Foreshaw had been too late to do that.

Finally, the vicar mumbled his final words, and with Cyril interred, it was time for Walter to be buried as well. There hadn't been much of an argument about burying Walter next to his sister and brother in law. It seemed only fitting that they all be reunited in death.

Beside him, Smythe cleared his throat as soil was thrown down onto the second coffin. The name plate on the coffin briefly flashed beneath the sullen sky, before disappearing.

"A nasty business," Smythe offered, already turning aside. Above their heads, the sun was hidden behind clouds that promised rain, and there was a bitter chill in the air. Mason was pleased he'd worn his long winter coat, and his boots. The grass in the graveyard was damp. His good shoes would have been sodden by now.

"And to think, it was people we know using the counterfeit coupons? Thinking nothing of stealing from our shopkeepers and one another," Smythe continued. This had left a bad taste in the mouth of all of them. Bad enough that the shopkeepers had been denied payment for accepting counterfeit goods, but to know it was Mrs Fortune at number thirty-nine who was in on it was hard to understand.

Smythe had made it clear that everyone would be charged for their part in the offence. Mason knew that there would be some furious people in and around Erdington for much of the winter. Perhaps, if a victory were declared soon, people would forget what had happened.

Perhaps. But for the next few weeks, they would be busy with their charge sheets.

"At least it's all solved now," Roberts offered as they entered the welcome warmth of the police station, the door miraculously silent as they entered. Someone had finally gotten round to oiling the squeaking door. Mason imagined it would have been Williams. He was a good lad, practical by nature.

"Yes," Mason agreed. But he wasn't sure how pleased he truly felt. He didn't feel the same sense of satisfaction as with the Middlewick murders. That case had plagued him for decades, this one had been solved in just under a week, and while it had been vexing, the solutions had been close at hand.

"Come on, Sir," O'Rourke tried to cheer him. "At least you won't need to climb any ladders anytime soon or fall down hills," and Mason admitted, that did cheer him, but still he didn't smile, not until Williams presented him with a brown wrapped parcel.

"What's that?" he demanded to know.

"No idea, Sir. It was dropped through the letterbox while we were out, but it has your name on it."

Mason quickly untied the string, and opened the brown wrapping wide, and then he met O'Rourke's eye and offered her a smirk.

"It seems," he stated, as he reached for the shining badge, the two A's joined together by one long line crossing the A's, "that I've been made a member of the Automobile Association." O'Rourke quirked an eyebrow at him, while Smythe's forehead furrowed.

"Well, you can't put that on the Wolseley. What would people say if the patrolmen and women saluted you to tell you that there was a speed trap ahead?"

Mason chuckled.

"What indeed?"

THANK YOU

Thank you for reading the Automobile Assassination. If you've enjoyed it do please consider leaving a review. Thank you.

AUTHOR NOTES

Sometimes a little bit of research reveals all sorts of delicious details. The main idea for this book must once again fall at the feet of my Dad, who asked me to watch an old film on TV one day, a documentary about the Automobile Association sidecars, the RSO's, being made in Birmingham in the 1950s. I think, at Small Heath. They looked fantastic, and I just had to work out how to include them in my next 1940s mystery.

But from there, it all became even more exciting as I read up on some aspects of the early Automobile Association and discovered the Automobile Association sentry boxes (somehow, we only know about the police telephone boxes thanks to Dr Who), as well as more details about how the organisation used to function.

Unfortunately, I was unable to find the specific details of any route the patrol motorbikes might have ridden in Birmingham at this time, but I was able to find *A History of the Automobile Association* from 1980, which covered the first seventy-five years of their history and contained some wonderful images of the sentry boxes, uniforms, vehicles they used, and also the badges.

I have changed a few minor details – during the war years, most of the patrolmen had a pedal cycle, not a motorbike – thanks to petrol rationing. I thought it was stretching it a bit to have my poor patrol officers cycling upwards of thirty miles a day.

The list of known Automobile Association sentry boxes I have made use of when placing them on roads is also from the 1960s, and so these might not have been there in 1944. Certainly, when I was trying to place the sentry boxes, I discovered a few on the list that couldn't have been there in 1944 as the roads didn't exist. I also came to appreciate how much the roads might well have changed in the intervening years – not just the Spaghetti Junction – but the implementation of the motorway system and the renumbering of the A roads.

It is true that the Automobile Association patrol members used to salute their members if there was a speed trap ahead, resulting in a legal case being brought against them. It is also true that members had a key to access these sentry boxes. After the war, these keys became interchangeable with the boxes used by the Royal Automobile Club (the RAC) as well, and during the war, unofficial use of the sentry boxes by the army did occur. At one point, it seemed as though the patrolmen who hadn't enlisted would come under the army's command, but in the end, this didn't happen. The Automobile Association was pleased about this as they didn't like the idea of their patrolmen being employed directly by another organisation.

Sadly, only a few of the Automobile Association sentry boxes remain in their original positions. If you're lucky enough to have one close to you, you might not even realise. Indeed, I've driven past the one close to me and never noticed it before because trees hide it. There are also a few at museums, and you can, it seems, buy one from eBay for £5000.00. Yes, I am tempted.

It does not seem as though women could be patrol officers in the Automobile Association at this time, but I've chosen to suggest that there could be female patrol personnel. For those who are curious, women weren't allowed to wear trousers if they were police officers until the 1970s when they were introduced as part of the winter uniform.

Dr Lucey, the pathologist, was a real person, taken from a newspaper archive for the Birmingham Post, but I have simply used his name and haven't researched who he was etc. Sometimes, I don't think it's necessary to cover every avenue of research available to me.

While I am aware that there was an Automobile Association building in Birmingham from 1944 onwards, the building's location I have used has been taken from a photo image from the 1960s. I'm unsure if the building was in the same location.

Research – as always, I'm surprised where research takes me. For this book, I researched the history of fingerprinting, which is much longer than you might think (and which mentions that the first fax was sent from Europe to the US in the 1920s), but I also caught up on some rather interesting means of determining if a person was a criminal or not, and how to tell one person apart from another. The Victorians had some strange ideas.

Counterfeiting of ration books was a huge problem during the Second World War. One syndicate seems to have managed to get away with nearly three million pounds (in today's money).

I have used the National Newspaper Archive to look at the head-lines from the Birmingham Post for 1944. It also lists black out times.

I do hope you've enjoyed this new foray into the 1940s. I hope that The Automobile Assassinations has taught you, as well as me, some-thing about the 1940s that you perhaps didn't know or provided a little bit of nostalgia for those old enough, or nearly so, to remember.

I am once more indebted to my father for answering all my strange questions about the period, for explaining 'old money' to me, and for the little details that make this book come alive, such as the 'payment' system in place in the local greengrocers, where there was one teller who received all the money via a wired system and then returned change in the same way. I would have loved to see that.

I would also like to thank my beta reader, CS, for pointing out that there weren't fridges in mortuaries in the 1940s, as there weren't in the 1970s. Thank you.

MEET THE AUTHOR

I'm an author of fantasy (viking age/dragon themed) and historical fiction (Early English, Vikings and the British Isles as a whole before the Norman Conquest, as well as two 20th century mysteries), born in the old Mercian kingdom at some point since AD1066. I write A LOT. You've been warned!

Find me at mjporterauthor.com and @coloursofunison on twitter. I have a newsletter, which can be joined via my website.

BOOKS BY M J PORTER (IN CHRONOLOGICAL ORDER, NOT PUBLISHING ORDER)

20th Century Mysteries

The Erdington Mysteries

The Custard Corpses – a delicious 1940s mystery (audiobook now available)

The Automobile Assassinations (sequel to The Custard Corpses)

Cragside, a 1930s murder mystery

Stories of Mercia and Saxon England

Gods and Kings Series (seventh century Britain)

Pagan Warrior

Pagan King

Warrior King

The Eagle of Mercia

Son of Mercia

Wolf of Mercia

Warrior of Mercia

Enemy of Mercia

Protector of Mercia

The Ninth Century

The Last King

The Last Warrior

The Last Horse

The Last Enemy

The Last Sword

The Last Shield

The Last Seven

The Earl of Mercia

The English Earl

The Earl's King

Viking King

The English King

The King's Brother

Lady Estrid (a novel of eleventh-century Denmark)

Fantasy

<u>The Dragon of Unison</u>

Hidden Dragon

Dragon Gone

Dragon Alone

Dragon Ally

Dragon Lost

Dragon Bond

<u>As JE Porter</u>

The Innkeeper

Printed in Great Britain
by Amazon